SOLOMON'S VINEYARD

THE DIARY OF AN ACCIDENTAL VIGNERON

VOLUME II

ROGER DIXON
& SOPHIE WOOLLVEN

authorHOUSE®

AuthorHouse™ UK
1663 Liberty Drive
Bloomington, IN 47403 USA
www.authorhouse.co.uk
Phone: 0800.197.4150

Published by AuthorHouse 01/13/2017

ISBN: 978-1-5462-8740-7 (sc)
ISBN: 978-1-5462-8763-6 (e)

This is the continuation of Volume I under the same title. In here you'll read the part four and last part of the entire book – Solomon's Vineyard, The Diary of an Accidental Vigneron

PART FOUR

'Les Hirondelles'

CHAPTER ONE

It was not long after Lisa was born that Chrissie - Christine, as she now preferred to be called, realised that with a small child it would be impossible to follow in Mel's footsteps in becoming a fully qualified Vet. She began by studying part time with a view to becoming a qualified Veterinarian Assistant like Peter, but then realised even that was scarcely practicable, calling as it did for several weeks full time attendance at a College, and she had to reconcile herself to just being as helpful to Mel as possible in the practical care of the ever growing number of animal patients who were brought to Roussanne. She loved Gus, her husband, and adored their baby, but she had always been the clever one at school as well as the prettiest girl in her year and would have loved the academic challenge of a University degree.

Mel comforted her with the thought that when Lisa was older she was sure they could manage as a family to look after her during the week, enabling her to attend College. But both knew that, if at all, it was a long way into the future and there was nothing anyone could do about it in the meantime. 'But you are very young' Mel comforted her. 'Even if you can't go with Peter now, you can learn an awful lot in the mean time that'll give you a flying start when the time comes'.

There were no lack of volunteers to be going on with to help look after Lisa: Mayer and Bridgette liked nothing better than to take the little girl off Christine's hands, releasing her to work with Mel, and there was also Mayer's son Saeed, who was delighted to take Lisa under his wing when he came back from pre-school, and this she loved best, waiting anxiously during term time for him to appear.

It was his idea for them to have rides on Shamus the donkey, who resigned himself to being led round the paddock with first one then the other on his back - although to begin with, an adult had to walk alongside when it was Lisa's turn. And knowing he would be rewarded with snacks after his stint of child carrying was over, even Shamus began to look forward to these sessions.

Mel's twins, Phillipe and Dale Junior might also have been expected to participate in leading Shamus when they got back from school, but although still only six, they had already been infected by their Uncle Andrew's passion for Soccer and usually came home too late from practice or school games, or from watching him play.

And so life might have continued at Rousanne and Poussan le Bas; with most content - most of the time.

*

Richard Chambers was not a particularly nice young man. He was too self centred for one thing, but that was not altogether his fault, being the only child of rich parents, both of whom had spoiled him as a child and continued to indulge him as a young adult.

Despite this, he was not very content with his lot: After leaving Exeter University - having failed to get into Oxbridge, he joined his father's office at the Baltic Exchange in London, and although he soon decided shipping was not for him, he developed a talent for computer systems, and having reorganised the family firm to its considerable benefit left, and with a loan from his father, set up his own company on the M4 corridor, and within three years had not only paid back the loan but sold out for a sum that, at the age of twenty five, could have kept him comfortably off for the rest of his life.

But although enjoying the money, having invested it safely with the help of one of his father's friends, he looked around for another challenge. He said good bye to his current girl-friend, who although disappointed, was not altogether surprised to be dumped when he decided that if he was going to make a fresh start he needed no encumbrances - certainly not one like her, who although satisfactory, and sometimes even alarmingly good in bed, had ambitions he knew of a more permanent nature. But he was grateful to her, and for all his faults, was not ungenerous, so he gave her the keys to the apartment they had been sharing and left instructions with his solicitor to draw up the necessary papers transferring it to her, which he would sign on return from the planned tour of Europe which, he decided, would not only allow him to see a lot of places he only knew about second hand - his parents having much preferred to take their vacations in their holiday home in Cornwall, but to think through which of the possibilities now open to him to pursue.

Various female companions joined him en route from time to time, but all, without exception misunderstood their purpose, and having found the hotel bed empty beside them, hurried down to breakfast to find an envelope waiting for them in Reception with enough money for them to return to where ever they had boarded the gravy train, the provider thereof having driven away in the Jaguar sports which had misled them into assuming that being an invited passenger promised more than transport!

And so it was that when he stopped for lunch at the Bridge Hotel in Les deux Demoiselles on his way South, he was unaccompanied and strolled through into the Town Square afterwards free, and at comparative ease with life and himself.

Richard had no intention of buying a property locally, or anywhere else come to that when he stopped in front of an Estate Agent's window and gazed only mildly interested in what was on offer. His eyes were immediately drawn however to a notice in the centre of the window which, unlike the others was displayed in a frame of a more permanent nature than the rest, but despite this, showed signs of age. It was in English:

'For Sale owing to illness-established bed and breakfast business with small vineyard. River views'.

He idly considered going in to inquire into this anomaly, but the office still seemed to be closed for lunch and he was about to turn and make his way back to the Hotel where he had left the car when a young woman arrived on a bicycle, and after leaning it against the wall separating the window from the door, pulled some keys from her pocket and began to unlock it. Looking at her more closely he saw she was quite attractive, and did not look local somehow, but before he could decide why exactly, the door opened and she disappeared inside taking the bike with her.

He paused for a moment, then on impulse followed her inside. He found the office empty until she reappeared, evidently having parked her bike out the back. She looked at him in surprise for a moment, then smiled -which suddenly made her look quite pretty.

'Can I help you?'

'Do you speak English?' The girl nodded and smiled again, switching immediately from French.

'Of course. What can I do for you?'

'I was wondering...'

'Yes?'

'You speak English.'

'I am Dutch. We are good at languages, Mr....?'

'Chambers. I am English.'

'Of course. Would you like to sit down Mr... Chambers?'

'Thank you'

They sat on opposite sides of the front desk'

'Now, what can I tell you?' Again, one of the most beautiful smiles he had seen since Stella.

'I was looking in your window'.

'Yes. Is there something there that interests you?'.

Now he was feeling his feet and returned the smile.

'Not till you arrived'

'The girl frowned, then coloured slightly. 'I beg your pardon?

He relaxed further.

'I was wondering where I could buy a dog'.

He smiled innocently as he watched her mind go into overdrive. Then her brow cleared and she burst out laughing, and wiping away the tears with the back of her hand, she stood up nodding.

'We don't sell dogs here I'm afraid!'

He also stood now grinning openly.

'But you do eat dinner?'

''Of course. Why?'

'I am staying at the Bridge Hotel'

The girl nodded. 'It is expensive - but very nice, I understand. I have never been able to afford to go there'.

'Then this could be your lucky day. Would you like to join me there for dinner this evening?'.

Eva hesitated. The cheek of the man was incredible... but he was very good looking as well as amusing. She hesitated only a moment longer before saying 'What time - Eight o'clock?'

'Eight will be wonderful. My name is Richard, by the way. He held out his hand smiling and she took it.

'I am Eva'

'I'm so pleased to have met you Eva. You are very pretty'.

'And you are very cheeky Mr Richard' but she was smiling too as they shook hands.

'I know. 'till eight then'.

'Eight o'clock'. Eva nodded as he bowed his head for a moment; smiled again, then she watched him turn and walk out of the door.

She immediately had feelings of doubt. Was she crazy making a date with a man she had only met a few seconds ago? But even as she considered rushing to the door and calling after him, she knew she was already excited at the prospect of meeting him again.

Richard walked back in the direction of the Hotel feeling pleased with himself. The 'dog' line always did the trick. He did not turn around, but guessed she was now standing in the doorway looking after him.

By the end of the evening Eva told herself she must be in love. It was absurd she told herself later, but they drank champagne together and he was the most entertaining man she had ever met - amusing and flattering her in turn, and possessing a natural authority that those who served them seemed to instantly recognise. She felt 'safe' with him, whatever that meant, except she already felt she could entrust herself to him. At the end of the evening, when she wondered if he would ask her to come up to his room, he ordered a taxi to take her home and arranged to pick her up in his car the following Sunday so they could spend the day together. He did kiss her before she got into the waiting cab in a way that made her disappointed he had not asked, but she was certain now that he wanted her and that soon enough they would come together,

In the course of the evening she had eventually felt at ease enough to refer to his 'where can I buy a dog?' line and they had both laughed. She told him the story behind the old advertisement in the window and mentioned that the grand-daughter of the founder of Poussin le Bas worked with her half sister as a vet's assistant just up the river, so if he really wanted a dog he didn't have far to go!

Richard slept well. It was time he had some company again and had enjoyed the evening. He knew he could easily have persuaded her to come upstairs, but like an experienced fly fisherman, there was often more fun in 'playing' the quarry for a while, and when he finally took her, she would be ready to give him whatever he asked in whatever way he decided. Sunday would be soon enough.

Over breakfast on the terrace overlooking the river, it suddenly came to him that it would be good to have a loving and submissive companion. Perhaps a dog might be an idea after all.

CHAPTER TWO

As the sun still had enough warmth in it to make a topcoat unnecessary, Richard Chambers decided to walk, and following the directions of the hotel Receptionist soon found himself at the entrance to the Farm where he had been told there was the Vet's Surgery. He paused for a few moments looking past the buildings down to the river. There was the smell of smoke in the air which he guessed came from the Estate he had also been told about on the other side of the river. He was glad he had left the car as he found the limited parking space between the road and the buildings was already full and several vehicles had been left out in the road.

The first time Christine saw him was when she took a break from the Surgery and carried the mug of coffee Bridgette had brought her to stand outside in the sun for a few moments and breath air free from the smell of antiseptics and sick animals. Looking down the field she saw Lisa was being given her morning ride on Shamus with Mayer walking alongside, but all her daughter's attention was being given to a man walking on the other side of the donkey. Bridgette came out of the kitchen with her own coffee to stand beside her and Christine turned to her.

'Who is that man walking with them?'.

The girl followed her gaze for a moment, then smiled and turned back to her.

'It's some rich Englishman. His French was so bad we couldn't understand what he was saying but he pulled money out of his pocket and held it out to Peter. Something about a dog, but he didn't have one with him. We managed to make him understand the Boss was busy and he would have to wait as you were the only other one who spoke English'.

Christine looked back down the field, and seeing her, they all waved.

'Except Lisa' her mother said, returning their waves.' I expect that's why she's listening to him so intently!' She paused for a moment, drained the mug, then gave it to Bridgette.

'Thank you. I'd better go and see what he wants'.

Christine stepped off the terrace and started down the hill to where they had stopped while the stranger was lifting the child up to settle her into the saddle more comfortably. As she drew closer, they looked up and smiled and she saw a man in his mid-twenties who, without having spoken a word yet, conveyed the air of confidence of those totally at ease with others, associated with the well to do.

As she approached Richard saw the most beautiful girl he had seen for a very long time. Obviously the mother of the little girl he had been helping to amuse while waiting for someone to come and see him who spoke English. She could not have been more than twenty, and with a short sleeved jumper, an old pair of jodhpurs and hair piled out of the way on top of her head, she was scarcely dressed to impress; but with sapphire blue eyes shining from a face tanned from days in the summer sun, as were her bare arms, the confidence he was assumed to possess was severely challenged as she came up to him smiling.

'I'm sorry to keep you waiting Mr.......?'

'Chambers...' but she had already turned away from him to lift the little girl into her arms.

'Come on Poppitt, it's time for your nap'. She spoke in English but with a slight American accent, then turned back to him.

'I'm sorry Mr Chambers, shall we go up to the house. The boss has come back now'

There was no suitable dog, but on discovering that he was by himself and at a loose end, Christine invited him to supper at Poussin le Bas that evening, and when he walked back to the hotel, although dogless, he knew the walk had done him the world of good and congratulated himself on the unexpected turn of events.

Christine greeted him at the front door that evening, her auburn hair now down to her shoulders and wearing a short pale blue summer dress which showed off both her shoulders and long legs, also lightly tanned by the sun; and as he had been invited early so she could show him the Winery in which he had shown an interest during their chat that morning over coffee, Lisa came with them and demanded afterwards that her new friend came to say goodnight in English before she would settle down.

He got on well with Holly and her husband Dale, and at the end of the evening promised Dale that he would come the following morning to see what he could suggest to bring their own computer systems up to date.

This he was able to do, and refused a fee. But being a Saturday when she did not usually work, and as Gus, who usually came home at weekends, was on a visit with the rest of his year at College to Bordeaux where they had been invited to a Chataux in the Margaux, they spent the rest of the day together.

The following day was Sunday and Richard called early in the Jaguar so they could go to a hotel further up the valley where there was a heated swimming pool and a children's play ground.

While they watched Lisa running round with some other children, and while they were waiting for lunch, Christine found herself admitting to him her frustration at having to wait so long to get a proper qualification like her half sister Mel. She did not blame anybody but herself. She was fond of Gus and adored Lisa, but if only she had waited!

*

By mid-morning, as he had not appeared, Eva put a call through to the hotel to be told by the Receptionist that M.Chambers was still staying at the hotel but had left in his car immediately after breakfast.

'Just one moment.....' There was a short pause before the Receptionist was back on the line.

'He did not dine with us last night, Madame, but my colleague who was on duty, tells me he was invited to Poussin le Bas, that's the big Estate....oh, you know where it is, of course! Well, I'm sorry. I can't tell you anymore.'

Eva held the phone for a while after he rang off. She contemplated ringing the Estate.' Who knew, one thing might have led to another' Then she replaced the receiver and took a deep breath. 'Whatever, he had forgotten all about her'.

She was right in thinking one thing had led to another.The following day, Christine asked Mel if she could have a few days off. It was not very convenient as they were busy, but she supposed she and Peter could manage, and her sister had been unusually persistent so she had little choice but to agree. Dale and Holly were less amenable when she told them. What was she going to do for a week that she did not want to discuss with them. Was it anything to do with that Englishman she had brought to the house.?

The matter was settled when they came back later in the day to find she had already gone taking Lisa with her. 'She would let them know where she was when she was settled.'

Christine was as good as her word. They had an email from her to say they were in London a she would be back by the end of the week. There was no need to say anything to Gus, she had already spoken to him on the phone.

Dale phoned him anyway, to be told there had been nothing he had been able to say to her that had made any difference. What he had said seemed only to have made her the more determined!

*

'Where is this place?'

Richard had turned off the main street into a narrow cobble stoned alley with garages on both sides and windows indicating living accommodation above.

He drew up about half way along then, leaving their bags in the car, unlocked a door at the side of one of the garages and led Christine up a short staircase carrying Lisa and finally depositing her at the entrance of a surprisingly large, airy living room which she immediately started to explore without invitation. They both watched her smiling for a moment, then he turned back to her.

'This is my parents place' he said casually 'They are still in Cornwall. It's known as a Mews. All the garages were originally stables, before conversion'.

Christine nodded, still looking round.' It looks as if someone is still here' she said doubtfully. Richard grinned.

'Don't worry. We have a woman who looks after it while they are away. I phoned before we left and asked her to open up everything and to make the beds.'

Seeing her expression he added 'I'll go in my old room and you and Lisa can have theirs. I asked her to borrow a cot - and it's got its own bathroom' He paused for a moment then added, 'there should be food in the fridge. We can go out if you prefer, but I thought Lisa would be tired'.

Christine gave him one of those smiles that always made his stomach turn over.

'You seem to have thought of everything' she said appreciatively.

'I hope so' He took a breath, then he said 'Right. If you're happy to stay here, I'll go and get the bags'.

After they had put Lisa to bed they shared a bottle of wine while watching television then Christine said she was tired herself and went to bed early.

There was no lock on his parent's bedroom door and she wondered what she would do if he came in. She had never made love with anyone but Gus.

They had not discussed the basis of their taking the trip together and she supposed he had every right to assume her body would be as available to him as his wallet had been to her, but there was no knock on the door, and apart from having to get out of bed to bring Lisa into bed with her, she slept soundly until one of the neighbours backed a car out into the Mews and drove away.

Christine had a bath and got dressed before waking her daughter, and by the time she had washed and dressed her, the caretaker, introducing herself as Dora, had arrived and set the table for breakfast, for which she had bought some croissants on the way, smiling that she hoped they would help them feel at home. She said that Mr Richard had gone out to get a paper, and although Lisa insisted that she was too hungry to wait, the two women chatted pleasantly for ten minutes until they heard the street door bang and his footsteps coming up the stairs.

Richard was in high spirits as they sat down together and Dora poured their coffee, laying out a suggested plan of sightseeing. They agreed to leave the Zoo, which was within walking distance, until the following day, and deciding to leave the car, took the Underground to Victoria Station and from there walked to Buckingham Palace and St James' Park, Lisa riding in her collapsible push chair.

Christine had been to Paris several times but that City had no Changing of the Guard or such a great number of ducks and other birds as on the lake in the Park opposite.

They had mid morning snacks at the small cafe in the Park, then took a boat from Westminster Pier up the river Thames to Teddington Lock and made their way to the riverside pub which was where, Christine told him, her great grandfather Andrew had proposed to her great grandmother Isobel.

As they sat under the trees after more snacks watching Lisa amuse herself on the small slide and sand pit attached to the pub, she added what she knew of their buying the small B&B and rundown vineyard in France which had since become one of the most successful vineyards in the Region; how he had looked after Isobel after she nearly drowned in the river and how she had finally died in a fire - probably started by herself, smoking in bed. They had met when Andrew took a room at Isobel's mother's house after his return from a trip to revisit the friends who had rescued him when he had fallen off a cruise ship near the French coast and stopped on the way home at Les deux Demoiselles when he had first seen the card in the window advertising the B&B. When they decided later to go and live in France, it was the first place they had gone to look at, and despite its run down condition, both fell in love with it on the spot.

In answer to his question, Christine said she knew where they had met was close by, but she did not know the address.

On returning to Westminster, they took a cab to Oxford Street and Richard indulged Lisa with a new teddy bear in Gamleys toy shop and Christine herself with an expensive pair of ear-rings which she had admired in the window without any intention of buying them. From then on she was hesitant to openly admire anything, but by the time he summoned a cab to take them back to the Mews he had also bought her a winter coat and a pair of shoes. When she got out of the cab her head was still spinning.

This time, Nora cooked for them, and after she had gone and Lisa had been put to bed, Richard poured two glasses of brandy and asked her to sit down as he had something important to tell her.

By then she was just about ready to give him whatever he wanted, but he went to a side table where she had seen a large brown envelope earlier in the day, then sat down beside her on the sofa with it on his lap.

'What are you going to sell me?' Christine smiled as he pulled out the contents, but he remained serious.

'I am going to offer you what I think is what you want at the moment more than anything'

Her smile faded as he started to read:

'The Royal Veterinary College, University of London, the UK's first and largest veterinarian school'

'Richard, what is this....?'

He held up a finger and continued to read 'We have a UK and International student population of one thousand eight hundred enrolled on undergraduate, postgraduate and continuing professional development programmes, delivered... 'and here he raised his hand again to emphasise 'full time, part time and by interactive e-learning'. He looked up with a smile 'well... I think we could manage one of those!'

'But...'

'If you would like to stay with me here in London, I will buy an apartment for the three of us. I will pay for a nanny to give you plenty of time to study, and a house keeper like Nora to look after us. All I ask is that you marry me'

At last Christine found her voice. 'But I am married'.

'If you go back to Gus the chances are you will always be an assistant. If you stay with me, after you graduate, I will give you all the backing you need to set up your own practice. Here... in France, America... where ever you want'

She stared at him, then suddenly burst into tears and buried her face in her hands. After a moment he took her gently into his arms and she turned to him weeping.

For the briefest of moments the thought flashed across his mind that perhaps he had just done the cruellest thing he ever had in his life, and to the first person he had ever really loved. Then he swore that he would make it up to her. He would not only open the door to her life's ambition, but look after and cherish both of them for the rest of his life.

11

CHAPTER THREE

Having resisted the temptation for weeks, Alim called into Immobilliers Cevant. He knew he and Jeaninne had no future - he just wanted to see she was alright, and was taken aback to find another young woman sitting at her desk.

She looked up smiling and said in English 'Hello. Can I help you?'

He looked around frowning then answered her in French 'Where is Jeaninne Berger?.

Eva stood up.' Jeaninne?'

'Yes'

Eva replied in French: 'She does not work here anymore. Are you a friend of hers?'

'A friend, yes. Where she go?'

Eva came round the desk to face him 'I'm afraid I can't tell you. Mr...?'

'Alim'

'Alim. Eva paused for a moment, then she said 'Didn't you used to work here too?'

'Yes. I work for Madame Nelson, but it was not good.... so I leave. For Jeaninne's sake'.

Eva frowned. 'I'm sorry. I don't understand.'

'Some people here do not want someone like me working with French girl'

Eva thought for a moment, then she nodded slowly.

'I see'

'We work happy together, but it not safe for her, so I leave. Where she go? With boy friend?'

Eva shook her head.' No. He is looking for her'.

'Looking! What means...'

''No one knows where she has gone Alim. She just left and never came back'.

They continued to face each other and Eva saw conflicting emotions coursing through him. Finally he said' Who is this boyfriend who doesn't know where she is?'

Eva hesitated for a moment, but he was obviously so upset she said finally' He is a policeman'.

'Policeman!'

'A Sergeant I think. His name is Andre Farbre. He has been in here several times to see if we have heard anything. I think he is stationed in St Fleur'.

Alim nodded for a moment, then he said 'Now I work at Poussin le Bas. For Mr Meuse'.He suddenly smiled. 'We have a machine picks the grapes now'.

He nodded once more and Eva said eventually 'I'm sorry I can't be more helpful'.

With a last nod he turned for the door but paused and looked back with his hand on the handle.

'You tell me please if you hear'.

After he had gone Eva sat down again. She knew there had been trouble just before the other girl had left. She had found a letter in her personal file which had obviously referred to what he had spoken about, and she had given this to Sergeant Fabre when he had called just after they met for the first time on Jeaninne's land on the hill overlooking the town. She had also shown him the documents which recorded its purchase by her and the attached letter from the Marie warning that the permission to build a house was about to run out. He had taken copies, but left the originals. Suddenly she decided to do something she had been thinking about ever since she found the letter.

Her boss Sara was not due back until late afternoon, but Eva reached into the bottom draw of her desk and pulled out all the relevant papers, which she then put into the new brief case Sara had given her for her birthday and went out, locking the office door behind her and after putting a notice on the glass panel that she would be back in an hour.

She started to walk the short distance to the office of Notaire Maitre Julliard who had already informed her that it was not necessary for her to own the land to apply for the Permis to build to be extended, but that there would be some tax to pay in addition to his fee. It was this that had made her hesitate before taking the matter any further, but now it was near the cut off date and she knew she had to do this for Jeaninne whom she had never met, but now knew instinctively was in trouble. She was sure her father would lend her the money.

She also hoped it would help her finally to put thoughts of Richard Chambers out of her mind.

*

He knew as soon as he walked into the Mews apartment something was wrong. He had gone to meet a colleague in the City to discuss funding for his new proposed project, leaving Christine to take Lisa to the park for a couple of hours as the weather was more like Spring than Autumn and most of the trees still clung possessively to their leaves. There was an envelope propped on the mantelpiece in the living room, but after he had walked into his parent's bedroom and seen the coat lying on the bed with the shoes he had bought her and the earrings on the otherwise empty dressing table he did not need to read it. Only Lisa's bear had gone with them and he imagined the battle that would have taken place over that.

Going back into the living room, he poured himself a large scotch before finally opening the envelope and sitting at the dining room table.

Rejection by others was something for which his upbringing and life so far had left him unprepared and waves of disappointment, incredulity and finally rage swept over him. Then he stood up and poured himself another drink. In a way, he blamed himself. He should have taken her when he could have, and with his experience of women, he knew that if he had, there would have been no envelope waiting for him. Finally, he sat down again and tried to consider the situation calmly. He had never loved anyone much before, if at all, and now realised his whole future happiness depended on getting her back.

Even so, it was more than a month before he set out after them, but calculated that would have given her enough time to realise what she had given up and start to regret her impulse.

*

Mel suggested that Christine and Lisa came to live at Roussanne until Gus came home from Montpellier and they could afford a place of their own. Her holiday in London was not referred to and Gus apparently accepted that was all it had been; unwise, in retrospect, but seemingly no harm had been done.

Christine did not refer either to the Veterinarian College nor Richard Chamber's offer to pay for her to go there. She knew to have done so would have alarmed those who loved her, above all Gus, but it was hard to forget completely that momentary glimpse of Paradise.

A car, eventually identified by the staff of the Bridge Hotel as belonging to a guest who had stayed with them the previous month was noted in their car park, but it was still there after three days without its owner appearing and the Manager reported the matter to the local Gendarmerie, indignant that the Englishman should make use of their facilities while staying somewhere else.

CHAPTER FOUR

The Vendange at Poussin le Bas was above average. Dale had to admit that apart from the incident when one of the espalier wires was accidentally cut, the picking machine had lived up to Stephane's predictions: the grapes had been scarcely more contaminated by leaves and twigs than when picked by hand and the resultant wine just as good.

He agreed that the rest of the rows be similarly adapted for the machine. It was a pity; they would then no longer need the Spanish pickers who had been coming since before both he and Stephane had arrived themselves - the end of an era. But they had to move with the times. They would still need the local regulars to walk behind the machine and pick the few bunches the machine left behind, if they wanted to.

The remaining caravan was towed over to Roussanne to act as much needed additional holiday accommodation for the B&B visitors since Christine, Gus and Lisa had come to stay.

The usual celebratory dinner was tinged with a little sadness in the knowledge that it was the last time their old friends would be with them, but these had assured Stephane that they bore no ill will. The older ones were shortly to retire anyway and the younger now mostly had families who would prefer them to look for work locally.

It came as a shock when the following morning Andrew told his father over breakfast that he had been offered a job as a reserve with the League Two football Club Clermont, one of whose Directors had seen him play for the local team, following which, he had gone for a trial. He had not told them about this before in case it all came to nothing, but now the offer had been confirmed.

Holly joined them, and Dale, having waved his hand towards Andrew, sat down while he explained over again to his mother who seemed to take it a good deal more calmly.

'Well?' Dale demanded when he had finished, and Holly reached across the table to squeeze his hand.

'I think we should be very proud of him' she said gently

'It's something I've always dreamed about Dad' Andrew said calmly.

'But what about here? his father protested.' You and Gus running the Estate together one day'.

'I'm sorry. But you have Stephane... and the two boys'.

Holly said 'He'll make a lot more money than he would here!'

'That's hardly the point! Besides... the real money is in the First Division'.

Andrew nodded.' That's true. But I'm only twenty. I have to start somewhere'.

By the time he left soon afterwards in the old Citroen they had given him for his last birthday, although Dale's mind was still in shock as he tried to reconcile himself with what was happening, let alone see a future for the Estate without his son, Dale hugged him and wished him well, then stood with Holly out in the lane smiling and waving goodbye as he drove away and out of sight round the first bend. Holly then turned into his arms and shed a few tears for no other reason than she knew how much she was going to miss him. Then, with a final hug, they separated - Holly to get ready to leave for the Clinic, and Dale to go and tell Stephane, Christine and Mel what had happened. Gus would find out soon enough. Dale wondered if he might not feel too upset.

After a few more days, what had begun as a casual check in response to the complaint of the Manager of the Bridge Hotel turned into a more serious search for a missing person. No one had seen the owner of the car and Inspector Goudon instructed Sergeant Andre Farbre to question all those who had had anything to do with him during his last visit. And reminded it was not that long since the girl who used to work at Immobliers Cevant had gone missing, Farbre was also encouraged to look for any possible connection.

Sara Cevant, as she still preferred to be known as professionally, was in the office with Eva when Farbre came into the office and asked if he might have a few words with Miss Groot. Eva recognised the young policeman from when they had met on Jeaninne's land up on the hill overlooking the town and stood up smiling, but the other hesitated momentarily before taking her outstretched hand.

'Is there somewhere we can talk' he said, and Eva glanced quickly at Sara who had also risen from her desk.

'This is the gentleman I was telling you about' she said, and Sara nodded then turned back to face him.

'You are the policeman?' she said, and Farbre nodded.

'Why do you want to speak to my assistant?'.

Farbre made a placatory gesture. 'Just a general inquiry, Madame. I have no personal objection to your hearing what I have to say. It is up to Miss Groot'

He looked back at Eva who said 'I would rather Madame Cevant was present. But I cannot tell you any more about Miss Berger. None of us have seen her since you were last here'

'Shall we sit down?' Sara said 'It's more comfortable here and you can always go in the back if anyone comes in.'

After a brief pause Farbre nodded, and they sat with Sara behind her desk, the other two half facing her and each other.

'It is not about Miss Berger 'he said as they did so. It is about an Englishman who came in here about a month ago and has gone missing.'

''Richard Chambers' Eva said, and Sara looked at her puzzled.

'Who is Richard....whatever you said?'

'Chambers' Eva told her. 'He came in while you were over at the old Winery site. He didn't want anything'.

Farbre consulted the note book he had pulled from his breast pocket. 'But you had dinner with him at the Bridge Hotel where he was staying' he said, then looked directly back at her.' And you phoned the hotel to ask for him two days later'. Eva coloured slightly.

'Yes. He invited me to dinner' She glanced at Sara.' He was very persuasive'.

'And you did phone the hotel about him later' Farbre persisted.

'Yes. He had arranged to take me out so we could spend the day together.'

'But he did not turn up?'

Eva coloured again, beginning to wish she had not agreed to Sara hearing all this.

'No'

The Policeman paused again before he said 'And how did that make you feel Miss Groot? Were you annoyed?'

'I was disappointed. No one likes to be stood up!'

Fabre smiled briefly.

'No of course not. And you haven't seen him since?'

'No'

'He has not contacted you?'

No'

'Not in the last few days?'

'She just said so' Sara put in with a touch of irritation.

Farbre nodded and made a note in his book, then put it back in his pocket and stood up.

'Thank you for your cooperation.'

The other two also stood.

'Why are you asking questions about this Mr Chambers? Sara said.

Farbre said 'Because he seems to have disappeared, Madame. His car was left in the hotel car park, but he did not check in and no one has seen him. If by any chance he does come in here - or contact you' -this to Eva- 'Please contact me on this number' He took a card from his breast pocket and put it down on the desk between them. He then turned for the door, but hesitated on reaching it and turned back 'Just one last thing Miss Groot- regarding your predecessor - I understand you have made an application through Maitre Julliard to have the building permission on her land extended... at some cost to yourself. Why did you do that?'

Conscious of Sara's eyes upon her Eva said.' Because without it the land is virtually valueless.'

Farbre paused for a moment, then opened the door.

'Well, you have my card'.

He went out closing it behind him.

Sara sat down first. Then Eva had to explain all about Jeaninne's land from the beginning.

Goudon himself visited Rousanne to talk to Christine. He was well known by both Dale and Holly and he asked both of them to be present when the interview took place while Mayer looked after Lisa.

It did not come as a surprise to either that he knew of their daughter's trip to London with the missing Richard Chambers. They never discussed it amongst themselves but were aware that

Christine's adventure had become common knowledge. Some of the things she told him were new to them however, and he was particularly interested when she admitted, without giving any details, that he had expressed his wish to marry her and that she had deliberately chosen a moment to leave when he was out for fear of his reaction when she attempted to do so... 'being someone who was more than used to getting his own way' she added.'

Goudon asked if she thought he might have followed her to try and get her to change her mind, and after thinking about it Christine said it was something she had been afraid of ever since she and Lisa got back. But she had not seen him.

Goudon thought for a moment, then he said 'what would you have done if he had suddenly appeared and threatened your daughter to get what he wanted?'

Christine hesitated, then she said 'I don't know. I don't think he would have threatened Lisa, he seemed very fond of her

'But if he had, would you have killed him?'.

'Now just a minute' Dale interrupted. 'What sort of a question...'

'Would anyone else have done so?' Goudon persisted'

Holly said 'How could she possibly know that?'

The Inspector turned to her. 'I could ask you her parents the same question'. He looked at Dale, who shrugged.

'I don't know what I would have done, but none of us saw him.'

'We didn't even know he had come back' Holly said.

The Inspector paused for a moment, then he turned back to Christine.

'Your husband is in Montpellier I understand?'

'Yes'. Christine nodded.' And before you ask, my brother is in Clermont with the Football Team.'

'Is he? Since when is this?'

'Last week' Dale said.

'He's playing?'

'Just as a reserve at present'

Goudon smiled for the first time. 'Well, congratulations on that!'

'Thank you'

The Inspector paused, then stood up.

'Well, thank you. You have all been most co-operative. Of course, we shall have to check on everyone's movements as a matter of routine'.

Dale also stood up but Holly reached across to take her daughter's hand and they both remained where they were.

Dale said 'I'll see you out'

'Thank you.'

The two men walked out into the yard in silence to where the police car was waiting. The driver got out and opened the passenger door, but before he got in Goudon turned to Dale and said 'I suppose Mr Chambers has family back in England?........... Parents?'.

Dale nodded. 'Yes. My daughter stayed in their flat in London'.

'So she knows them?'

'No. I understand they were staying in their holiday home somewhere, so Christine never met them'.

Goudon paused again for a moment, then he said 'They should be informed of what has happened'.

'I'll get the address from Christine for you'.

'Thank you' Goudon held out his hand and the two men shook hands briefly before he turned and got into the car. Dale watched it drive away, then walked back into the house where he found the two women where he had left them locked in conversation. They both looked up as he came back into the room and Holly said 'Chrissie is frightened that man may still be hanging around here somewhere'.

Dale shook his head. 'I doubt it. He would not have come all this way just to go into hiding. From what Chrissie has told us, he seems the sort who would have confronted her as soon as he got here'.

Christine nodded 'But why has nobody seen him, Dad?'

'I don't know. 'Dale shrugged, then he said 'Perhaps somebody has.'

Two weeks later, a Mr Lawrence Chambers and his wife checked into the Bridge Hotel where Inspector Goudon picked them up in his car and took them to the local police station. Neither of them had been aware their son Richard was missing until they received his phone call.

Fortunately, Joan Chambers spoke perfect French having spent two years in Paris working as an au pair and she explained that they were used to their son taking off on various trips without telling them anything. Both were concerned at what Goudon told them but her husband said he was still convinced Richard would turn up sooner or later, as he always did, and the policeman did not labour his own doubts.

It was decided to leave the car at the Bridge Hotel and the Chambers left the following day having paid the hotel for doing so. Lawrence Chambers explained that business interests needed his urgent attention. He accepted in turn the Inspector's assurance that they would continue the search and that they would be contacted as soon as there was any news. In the meantime, it was agreed there was nothing they could do to help.

*

Gus graduated from Montpellier and joined Dale and Stephane working at Poussin le Bas. It was decided that, for the time being, he would assume responsibility for the proposed extensions to the winery. He was not in the least envious of Andrew and made an effort to go and watch any home matches in which he was likely to play, often taking Dale junior and Phillipe with him. Mel and Stephane were happy for him to do this, conscious of the kudos their Uncle gave them at school and that both had vowed to try and follow in his footsteps. Stephane only hoped it was a passing phase and that they would settle to join him instead when the time came, but he was wise enough to keep these thoughts to himself.

On the surface, life returned to normal, and with Mel's encouragement Christine regained her old sparkle and put her London adventure and Richard Chambers out of her mind. Only one person seemed to have changed: Peter was as supportive of both of them as ever, but Bridgette, who loved him, alone, felt a difference in him. He was as friendly towards her as ever and often went with them when she and Mayer took the boys and Saeed swimming at the Estate over the river, but now Christine also came with them bringing Lisa and she could not help notice the way he looked at her.

At Christmas, Bridgette summoned up the courage to ask if he would like to take her to a dance at one of the hotels on the river a few kilometres downstream where her elder sister worked and had offered her tickets. She was thrilled when he agreed.

The same sister lent her a dress, and when Peter picked her up he agreed with her mother that she looked beautiful!

He seemed to enjoy himself, dancing and sitting talking with she and her sister and friends, and when he took her home she expected him to kiss her and was disappointed when he made no attempt to do so but simply saw her to the door of her parents house, thanked her for the evening, then left after giving her a modest peck on the cheek.

She lay in bed thinking about him, and by the time she finally fell asleep she had decided what she was going to do. She often took him his morning coffee and when she did so the following morning and he thanked her again for the evening she said 'Peter. Do you care for me?'.

He looked at her in surprise.

'Of course I care for you'.

'But do you love me?'

Peter frowned, then smiled. 'What sort of a question is that?'.

'But do you? I'm serious'

His smile faded as they stared at each other. Then he said quietly 'I do love you Bridge. But I'm not _in_ love with you if that's what you mean'.

Bridgette started to feel sick, but she managed. 'It's her isn't it? Christine. You're in love with her!'

Peter didn't answer immediately - just went on looking at her until he said at last 'You've no right to say that. She's married'.

'That doesn't stop anyone. If you were married, I'd kill anyone who got in the way'.

'That's stupid!'

Bridgette took a breath, then she said bitterly 'But there isn't anything you wouldn't do for her, is there?'.

CHAPTER FIVE

Sara Cevante was so happy when David phoned to say he had managed to get away for a few days, but puzzled when he told her he had decided to drive so would not need picking up at the airport.

The reason became evident when he came to the point as soon as they walked from the office, where they had agreed to meet, to the new apartment. He told her that although he still loved her, he had come to realise that their marriage was impossible.

After a long pause Sara said 'Have you met someone else?'

'I ran into Dawn'

'Your Ex. Yes, you told me'

'We met again and started talking. We both came to the conclusion... that the present situation is just making three people unhappy'.

'So you decided it would be better if it was just me!'

'No dear' He put out his hands but she backed away.

'Well, what is it, then?' She said angrily.

Her husband dropped his hands and shook his head.

'You don't want to live in Dorset and...'

'It's boring in Dorset! I've always had something to do!'

'I know. But that's where I have to live.!' He paused for a moment then tried to speak more reasonably: 'That's why it doesn't work'.

'But it will work with Dawn!'

'It might give us all a chance. As long as you're tied to me you'll never meet anyone else'.

'Oh, I don't know. I might find someone on the side to fuck me like you have!'

David looked momentarily shocked, but after he had taken a breath and said 'Let's try and discuss this like adults'

'Have you?'.

'I could easily just have written you a letter, but because I do care for you I came here'.

It was no use. Eventually he turned on his heel and walked out slamming the door behind him after telling her he wanted a divorce and needed no part of her money'.

The bravado with which she had faced him collapsed almost as soon as the door closed and she sank into one of the dining room chairs, waves of misery and despair sweeping over her.

After a while she got to her feet and went into the bath room where she washed her face and reapplied her make-up.

She stared at herself in the mirror a while longer, then went out closing the front door behind her. Her mother would tell her what to do.

Agnes Courtou was in her fifties and still lived in the house not far from the old winery she had shared with her husband Georges when he was President of the old Co-operative until it went into liquidation. She had continued to live there after he died not long afterwards despite several offers from her daughter to help her to move somewhere more comfortable.

Her last few years with him had been increasingly difficult as he raged against the English run estate of Poussin le Bas whom he held entirely responsible for the Co-op's demise and had done everything he could to get rid of them - even to the point of getting himself arrested after being caught sneaking round the Winery after dark for suspected sabotage of one of their vehicles, which had led to a fatal accident. And despite the fact that he was later shown to be innocent and released, this had only increased his hatred of the Solomon family whom he managed to persuade himself, were responsible for that whole episode as well. But her mother was a good catholic and had married for better or worse. She had nursed her husband as he sank into depression and alcohol induced ill health, and even after he died had declined to move out of the house she had come to as a young woman with its memories of happier days and neighbours of whom she was fond and who had helped her through George's last years.

Again, even when Sara came into money she still preferred to stay, but accepted the services of the local launderette and the young girl who took her clothes there and cleaned the house four hours a week.

She was not surprised to see her daughter who called often, having loyally seen her through all the bad times and helped her now as much as she would allow, but when Sara told her what David had said, she took her in her arms and held her for a long time without saying anything. Then, holding her at arm's length, she said 'Your father's life was spoiled by those people, don't let them spoil yours!'

Sara frowned, she had never heard her mother speak with such vehemence, her voice shaking with anger as she went on 'You have it in your power to do what he was never able to'.

'What?' Sara was almost frightened by the hatred she saw in her mother's face.

'Get rid of them. Send the English back where they came from!'.

*

Gus had believed Christine when she told him the whole story of the Englishman's invitation to go with him for a short holiday to London, and her assurance that nothing had happened between them. After a brief wobble, their love for each other and their daughter returned as strong as ever and Christine breathed a sigh of relief. Nothing was worth endangering that, and she determined to put all other thoughts out of her mind and make the best of the wonderful and rewarding life they had together now he was home for good.

Despite this, Gus still felt something was wrong. He sometimes cursed the ability he had first become aware of as a child to sense things other people seemed incapable of feeling and which his mother had cautioned him to keep to himself, although it had been this which had drawn them together as her own life had slipped away. He had tried to describe them once to Christine before they moved to Rousanne. They had lain in each other's arms after making love listening to a nightingale singing on its usual branch of the tree just outside their bedroom window - one planted by her great grandfather Andrew fifty years ago, and which had been adopted by the ancestor of the present occupant. He told her that the feelings he had sometimes were like being the only one able hear a particular bird singing, and after a moment, she had whispered back that when she was a little girl, her mother Holly told her she had been comforted herself after her mother was killed with the thought that the sudden arrival of the bird to fill the night with its song was her mother come to watch over her.

She had expected him to chuckle, and when he didn't, raised her head off his shoulder and saw he was nodding as if there could be no other explanation.

When he finally came home and Christine told him that Richard Chambers' car had been found -apparently abandoned in the Bridge Hotel's car park and that the police had come to question her, he assumed his unease was the aftermath of that visit and that it would soon fade. But if anything, it became stronger until he became convinced the Englishman was close by hiding somewhere. But to do what?

CHAPTER SIX

During the winter following the disappearance of the Englishman the river Truyer flooded, inundating the vines on the lower part of the slope of the Estate and covering all but the top strand of the fence by the river at Rousanne. For several months it was impossible to use the stepping stones to cross from one side to the other and an early casualty was the shelter Marcus had made for the ducks on the small island, although, seeing the danger coming, Stephane had collected the ducks themselves in time and confined them in an old chicken run until alternative accommodation could be found.

It became a national sensation when, after the waters subsided, the remains of the body of a man was found caught in the roots of an overhanging tree two kilometres below the bridge at Les deux Demoiselles.

Accidental drowning was ruled out when the post mortem also revealed that the deceased had a fractured skull caused by what could only have been a deliberate blow and not as a result of the body being carried downstream.

Working carefully back upstream on both sides of the river for any signs of a struggle, Inspector Goudon and his team, which included Andre Farbre, eventually discovered the partially uncovered remains of a large bull, besides which were a wrist watch, tie pin and a shoe, suggesting that a body had been thrown on top of the animal before being reburied.

Mr Lawrence Chambers arrived two days later and identified them as having belonged to his son, but Goudon decided to spare him the ordeal of attempting to confirm the identify the body itself.

He was still there when Peter Guyot was arrested and taken to Saint Fleur where he confessed to having killed the Englishman.

The mystery of his disappearance solved, Andre was deprived of an official excuse to visit Eva at the office, but they met several times by chance on 'Jeaninne's' plot, as they still referred to it, up on the hill, and eventually, by mutual consent, the meetings ceased to be by chance.

The Marie eventually notified Jeaninne's Mother - and Eva, as a registered interested party, that in another twelve months, in accordance with the law concerning missing persons, the plot's owner would be declared presumed dead, and in the absence of a will, it would become the sole property of Jeaninne's Mother - her father having died the previous year. She came into the office a few days later to tell Eva that, in that case, she would be more than willing for it to be taken off her hands completely, having long associated it with her daughter's disappearance.

After speaking to her father, Eva agreed to do so.

Andre proposed the following Spring, but they agreed to wait until the land was officially hers. In the meantime plans were drawn up so that as soon as possible, building could begin on a small house there, which both agreed, was the only place to start their married life.

When Gus was twenty-five, the Trust under which Holly had held his mother Lisa's forty per cent interest in the Estate came to an end and he became owner in his own right.

Not long afterwards, Dale's Mother in California became seriously ill and he flew to be with her. He phoned Holly after going to see her at the hospital for the first time and told her he was obviously going to have to stay for longer than they had anticipated and that he proposed asking Gus to hand over the management of the Winery to Alim, who was already familiar with what needed to be done, and to take over his own responsibility for sales and general administration.

Stephane's parents, Phillipe and Lorraine, told Holly that they had decided to retire and spend a period in South Africa near to the friends they had made over the years while they decided where they wanted to live for the rest of their lives. They thought it only fair that they should vacate the house nearby which had come with the additional land the Estate had been able to purchase when the owners had died, and where they had continued to live after Phillipe had retired. 'Whatever they ultimately decided, it would not be there and they were aware that Gus and Christine needed a place of their own.'

For them It was ideal, being almost mid-way between their two jobs. And after some work to bring the house- particularly the kitchen - up to date, they moved in, releasing the room they had been using at Rousanne back to its original purpose of accommodating the B&B visitors just in time for the summer.

Within three months Christine announced she was pregnant, but everyone's delight at this was blunted by Peter's arrest, and the necessity for her to appear in Court at Clermont at his trial on a charge of second degree murder.

He pleaded guilty to having killed the Englishman, having found him waiting for Christine to return with Madame Meuse from visiting a farming Client. An argument had ensued which had escalated into a fight, and this had ended when he had hit M.Chambers on the side of the head with the shovel he already had in his hand to clear out one of the animal pens. He had not intended to kill him - he did not know what he had intended except to stop him bothering Christine - but panicked when he realised the other was dead. He guessed he would be accused of murder, so carried him down to the river with the intention of throwing him into the water, but changed his mind and went back for the shovel where he had dropped it, then dug into the grave of the old bull and buried the body on top, knowing no one ever went near there because of the smell. He then went back up to the stable and washed the blood and bits of hair off the shovel just before his employer returned.

For her part Christine testified that the victim had been a man used to getting his own way and she had fled from him after foolishly agreeing to take a short trip with him to London. She had been afraid ever since that he would not accept her rejection and follow her.

She had confessed these fears to Peter Guyot and he had promised to keep an eye out and make sure she came to no harm. 'She felt entirely responsible for what had happened and was sure that he had only been trying to protect her'.

There was not much else to be said. The Accused had pleaded guilty but the three judges accepted Christine's evidence as crucial and reduced the verdict to guilty of manslaughter. He was sentenced to five years - three years in prison and two years on probation.

When she and Gus got back, Mel told them they had already heard what had happened in court on the evening news and that Bridgette had then collected her things and said she would not be coming back.

CHAPTER SEVEN

Although still angry, Sara was not a vengeful person and had enough sense to realise that the sort of drastic action her mother had in mind against the local English would not make her feel any better personally and could well back fire. She did not depend on the Immobillier anymore, but it was her 'baby' and most of their inquiries were from foreigners, many of them British. Eva herself was the daughter of a Dutch couple who had bought a house through the Agency before she had decided to look for a job locally. Then there was the fact that the local Mayor, Maurice Henderson, was English and not without influence. Earning a reputation for xenophobia would do no good at all. Even so...

She was happy with Eva, who had grown into the job, and was now a partner. She had forgiven her for not telling her about her application to extend the planning permission on Jeaninne's land and was pleased with the news of her engagement to the young policeman, as well as their plans to build a house up there for when they married, which should mean the management of the office was secure for the foreseeable future. But she felt increasingly restless. Having decided that now she had no one else to consider or rely on, and having sold the house on Long Island to pay the local death duties, there was no point in retaining the other interests in America she had inherited from Walter Bush and telephoned Lloyd Butler, the Lawyer she had also inherited and who had been keeping a watchful eye on her behalf to say that she wanted to take up the offers to buy her remaining American Interests from the other shareholders and within six weeks found herself on an Air France jet bound for New York. That still left the offices in Paris and part ownership of a prestigious wine Chateau in Bordeaux, but she might have use for those. 'So David wanted no part of her money!'

On being informed of the possibility of an imminent divorce, Lloyd had advised that precautions should be taken immediately to make sure her husband had nothing to gain from a change of mind, and papers awaited her to sign - not only to complete the agreed sales but to put the proceeds where he could not get his hands on them. Sara had accepted the need for this last but in a way it only added to her sadness. She still loved him and had looked forward to sharing her good fortune with him for the rest of their lives. The trip just seemed a final acknowledgment that it was now never going to happen.

Lloyd's wife Grace, whom she had met and liked very much when she had first come over with David, met her at Kennedy Airport. When they had settled into a cab which would take them into Manhattan, she put her hand over Sara's and told her how sorry they both were at the way things had turned out, but unless she felt otherwise, did not propose to mention it again;

they would leave it to her. Having squeezed her hand again, Grace sat back with a smile and said they intended this should not only be a business trip for her but that they would have a great time together.

'The first thing is, where are you going to stay?'

Sara frowned 'I thought you had booked me into the Waldorf like last time' she said, and Grace nodded.

'I did make a provisional reservation. But we wondered then if you wouldn't like to stay with us?' Sara's eyes widened as Grace went on 'It's in an old building just off Washington Square. Not so grand as the hotel of course, but we have a nice little guest room. And the staff are friendly. What do you say? We'd love to have you'.

Sara swallowed and her eyes misted over as she leant across and to kiss Grace's cheek. 'Thank you so much!' she said huskily 'I really wasn't looking forward to going back to the same place'.

Grace put an arm around her and said softly 'That's what we thought, honey'.

The building had a flight of steps up to the front door, where Grace told her the local kids liked to hang out. 'We don't object' she added as she started to open it with her key. 'I was brought up in a place like this. We don't have any kids of our own and they seem to furnish it as I always remember it!'

'Did you grow up here?' Sara asked as Grace stood back to let her enter the now open door.

'Just round the corner. Here, let me help you with that'. She took the larger of the two cases and Sara followed her inside to be met almost immediately by an attractive, fair haired young woman who came out of a door at the end of the short hallway and came towards them smiling.

'This is Sarah' Grace said 'only she spells it with an 'H'

'Hi. Welcome to New York' the girl said, relieving Grace of the bag.

Sara returned her smile.

'Thank you'.

'Would you like to come with me?'

She glanced at Grace who nodded in affirmation and turned back to Sara.

'It's just a short flight of stairs' she said.' Let Sarah settle you in then come down and we'll have coffee'.

The room was not overlarge but furnished in a modern style and with a comfortable looking double bed. It had a large bay window from which Sarah pointed out they could see the white arch in Washington Square down the end of the street. There was also a surprisingly large bathroom attached which the girl told her she thought had been created by sacrificing the bedroom next door.

She helped Sara unpack, and by the time they went down to rejoin Grace, she already had a coffee cafetiere and three cups waiting on a counter in the kitchen, at which they sat on tall comfortably moulded stools. Grace confirmed what Sarah had already told her, that she was a student at the nearby New York University where she was studying forensic science and working part time to help with the fees. She came from California and had chosen New York to be as far away from home as possible! (The reason for this was not elaborated upon.) The conversation then turned inevitably to the main purpose of Sara's trip, with most of which Grace was familiar as she still acted as her husband's principal assistant at the Firm's office on Fifth Avenue. But after a while she said 'Well, enough of this for now. You'll have quite enough of it all day tomorrow and I really think you should try to relax for the rest of today.' She glanced at her watch, then she said 'Sarah doesn't have any classes this afternoon, so she is going up to her room to do some reading, then we'll all have something to eat here.'

Sarah said 'I could cook something - or get a take out if you prefer?'.

'Good'. Grace turned to Sara with a smile. 'She's really very talented'. She glanced back at the younger woman. 'I only hope she hasn't missed her true vocation!'.

Sarah coloured slightly and shook her head. 'I don't think so' she said

'Don't be so modest!. Anyway some lucky man is going to get the benefit some day!'

Sarah laughed and said 'Not for a long time yet, I hope!.'

Grace reached over and squeezed the girl's arm then turned to Sara with another smile.

'How things have changed! Anyway, we'll see what Lloyd feels like when he gets back. He promised not to be late'.

'Of course'. Sarah slid off her stool and picked up the empty cups.' I'll just wash these then I'll be up in my room. Just give me a buzz'. She made for the sink and Grace looked back at Sara.' We've been asked to have dinner with some friends tomorrow. They actually asked us for this evening, but we felt sure you'd feel too tired.'

Sara looked at her watch. 'Well, it is six o clock already French Time.' she admitted.

Grace paused for a moment, then she said 'shall we just take a stroll down to the Square and back? It's not very far, and if you sleep now you'll never adjust to New York time!'

It was one of those deceptively mild October days when the New York weather tried to fool everyone into thinking the Fall was going on forever. The Boston Post had reported the trees in New England were past their peak, but in Washington Square the sycamores still clung possessively to their leaves.

Many of the Park benches were occupied by students from the nearby University, laughing amongst themselves between classes. Here and there some older people were doing Chinese exercises in slow motion. One young man was practising juggling, and a pretty girl with very short shorts that made the most of her long, sun tanned legs, rode around on a mono-cycle distributing leaflets advertising a 'happening' in a nearby 'loft' theatre in which she also happened to be the star. Young mothers sat in the sun watching their children at play, but Grace found them a vacant bench near the statue of Garibaldi, the Italian revolutionary.

The sun was very pleasant, as was the whole atmosphere and Grace started to tell Sara one or two ideas she had to entertain her once the business stuff was out of the way, when a man stopped in front of them and said pleasantly 'Hello Grace. No work today?'

She had to shade her eyes from the sun to look up at him, then broke into an answering smile'.

'Alan! Have you just been to see Teresa?'

'Yes'.

He nodded, and Grace turned to Sara. 'Alan's mother lives just round the corner from us' she began, then noticed that the other two were staring at each other.

'Good God!'.

Sara was the first to recover her surprise and stood up smiling.

'Alan March!'

'Sara Cevante! What on earth are you doing here?.'

Grace watched in astonishment as they shook hands, laughing in amazement, before turning to look at her as she stood up smiling.

'Can anyone join in, or this a private party?

Still laughing, the other two each held out a hand to touch her for a moment.

'How do you two know each other?'

Alan said 'Well, It's a long story! Do sit down, please' He turned to Sara smiling and they both did so while he continued to stand facing them. Then he said 'Sara found a house for me and Gus, my step-son, when I came to Les deux Demoiselles with my wife Lisa.'

Suddenly he was no longer smiling, and Sara turned to Grace who said:

'She was killed in a dreadful accident.'

March nodded. 'It was lucky we weren't all killed.' He paused for a moment, then he said 'She was the most beautiful women I have ever known.'

'Sara nodded, and glanced at Grace adding' She was a leading - 'super model' I think they would call her today'.

Sarah said 'Lisa! Not the Lisa Davis, who fronted all the Revlon advertising. I remember her'.

March said' Her first husband died in a mugging. She was left with their son Gus and an interest in a wine estate in France so they went there to live until she was persuaded to come back to New York'.

'I seem to remember Gus didn't go with her' Sara said.' I don't know why. I didn't know them that well '.

'I think he was settled in the local school and she didn't want to disturb him. The contract was only for a few months'. He shrugged 'Anyway, that's when we met each other.' He paused again before adding 'Despite the wonderful times when we were together, I sometimes regret we ever met. She would still be alive today'.

After a moment Grace said gently 'It's the first time I've heard you talk about her Alan. You can't blame yourself for what happened.'

'Maybe not'. He shrugged, then after a moment, visibly pulled himself together and turned to Sara again smiling. 'How is Gus? The last I heard he was doing great!'

Sara said 'You know he got married? To the daughter of Holly and Dale Mori who run the vineyard.'

March nodded. 'Yes. They asked me to the reception.'

Grace said 'You didn't go?!'

'No'

'Why ever not?.

He shrugged again and pulled a face. 'I guess I didn't want to be a spectre at the feast'

'That's absurd Alan! Sara said firmly. 'The accident happened years ago. They wouldn't have asked if Gus hadn't wanted you'.

'I suppose you're right. Anyway, I made some excuse. I did send them a present.'

Sara paused for a moment, then she said 'They have a little girl. They called her Lisa.'

March walked back with them to their front door, and as they were about to say good bye, Grace said suddenly 'Are you doing anything for supper tonight Alan. If not, we'd love you to join us - just the three of us, and Lloyd, of course.

He hesitated for only a moment then beamed with pleasure.

'Thank you Grace. If you're sure it won't be too much trouble?'

Grace laughed. 'Why do people always say that? No it won't. As it happens we have a student staying with us who loves to cook!'.

'Well, in that case...'

Shall we say seven- thirty?

CHAPTER EIGHT

The taxi from the airport stopped outside the Bridge Hotel in Les deux Demoiselles and the passenger got out carrying a small flight bag and with a computer case slung over his shoulder. Having glanced at the empty car park, he walked into the lobby and up to the reception desk.

'Someone's moved my car.'

'Messieur?.

'Don't you speak English?'

'But of course'

'The car, then.'

'Which car, Messieur?'

'The one I left here'

'When was that, Sir?'

'A Jaguar sports. I was in a bit of a hurry. You must have moved it'

The receptionist opened the Register.

'Your name, Monsieur?'

'Chambers. Richard Chambers.' He shook his head irritably. 'You won't find me in there. I didn't have time to register.'

The receptionist stared at him. Then his eyes widened and he reached for the phone.

'One moment Monsieur, I will ask'

Having shown his passport to the Manager, he was given a seat and asked to wait 'while somebody fetched the vehicle where it had been moved to safety'. In fact, he rang the local police station from the inner office, who immediately telephoned Inspector Goudon and sent an officer to the Hotel to make sure the man claiming to be Richard Chambers did not try to leave during the time it would take the Inspector to reach the hotel He was told not to go into the lobby, but wait outside.

Despite being offered lunch, which he declined, the newcomer became increasingly impatient at the delay in producing the car, and by the time Goudon finally reached the hotel with Sergeant Andre Farbre, whom he had collected on the way, he was in a foul temper that was not improved by being made to go into the Manager's office for questioning. But having had it explained that it had been assumed that he was dead and that a trial had taken place at which someone had admitted to his murder, he burst out laughing.

'Well, as you can see, I'm not dead. I've never heard anything so stupid! I'm sorry I had to leave the car without explanation, but as I had stayed here before I didn't think it would bother anyone for a few days'

'You have been gone for nearly a year, Monsieur!' Farbre said 'Why didn't you contact anyone?', and Chambers turned to him with a shrug.

'I was in the United States setting up a deal. I had more important things on my mind'.

Goudon said 'Can you prove where you have been?'

'Certainly. If you look in the inner pages of my passport you'll will see stamps showing the length of my stay'.

Farbre handed the document to his superior who glanced through it then nodded and handed it back to its owner. Then he said 'Your father came here and identified a number of things belonging to you which had been dropped near where a body - presumed to be yours, had been buried,'

'Chambers frowned for a moment, then he said 'My father died three years ago Inspector'.

The two policeman looked at each other, then Goudon said. 'He came here and after he had identified the watch and the other things he paid the hotel to leave the car where it was and went back to London'.

'And did - whoever it was- identify my 'body'?

Goudon shook his head, and Farbre said 'It was too decomposed'.

'I see. And about this person who is supposed to have killed me - do I know him?'

'It seems not' Goudon answered after a second. 'But you were expected by Christine Davis who had stayed with you in London'.

Chambers took a breath, then he said 'Well, she did leave in something of a hurry, and I did come with the intention of seeing her, but I never got round to it. Just before I got here, I had a call from California from people I had been in negotiation with for several months which was far more important.'

'What about the car?' Farbre said. 'Why did you leave it?'.

'That's simple. I had just driven all the way from Calais and I was exhausted. I just couldn't face the drive to Grenoble then all the hassle of parking when I got there, so I phoned for a taxi to meet me here to take me straight to the airport.'

'That must have been very expensive' Goudon observed mildly.

'It was'. Chambers stood up.' And now, if that's all, I'll be on my way'

'Please sit down, Mr Chambers. We have not finished'. After a brief hesitation, the other did so, and Gourdon continued' You say your father is dead?'

'Yes'

'Then who was it who came here with your mother after we phoned them in London? 'Farbre demanded, and Chambers turned to him.

'I have no idea - but it certainly wasn't my father or my mother, come to that'.

'We called the number of the apartment where Madame Davis told us she stayed'

'That was mine'.

'She said your parents were staying at their holiday home when she was there'.

'That's impossible. They never had a holiday home. My mother is living now with my sister in Hounslow.'

There was a moment's silence before Goudon said 'Why should someone come all the way from London to pretend to be your father?'.

'And how did they intercept the number of - your apartment?' Farbre added.

Chambers sat back in his chair, then he said calmly 'With the greatest of respect gentleman, that is your problem - as, so I would have thought, is the identity of whoever it was who was killed ....and whose body you found - evidently, too decomposed to be recognisable but assumed was me?.'

A few hours later, Richard Chambers drove away in the car he had come to collect and the Police turned their attention to his final question. There could be no doubt that Peter Guyot had thought it was the Englishman whose arrival Madame Davis had feared, and the matter of his conviction was referred urgently to the Judiciary who eventually decided that in the circumstances there had been a miss-trial. There was no doubt Guydot had killed someone who had appeared to threaten Madame Davis's safety, but in the circumstances they agreed on a compromise and ordered that the period of probation be brought forward and that he could be released immediately.

CHAPTER NINE

Stephane decided to walk along the river bank then punt himself across to the Estate in Marcus's boat rather than drive. Although early, the air was warm and filled with the scents of early summer and he had some thinking to do before meeting Gus for their morning meeting. Like Dale this was his favourite time of day -particularly at this time of year when the vines were in full leaf and the roses at the end of each row, which acted as watchmen, warning of any blight before it infected the vines themselves, were already coming into flower. Sometimes he met Dale and they chatted while strolling between the rows about the day in front of them without the necessity of the formal meeting in the office that Gus preferred. It had been a happy time when there were just the two of them and he had become increasingly uneasy since. Then, yesterday, he had received a letter from the Chateau in the Margeaux where he had worked before returning to Poussin le Bas.

In the past, he had given little thought to the time when Dale would want to retire, but these past weeks had given him a taste of what things would be like and that sooner or later Gus and Chrissie would own eighty per cent of the Estate as opposed to his twenty and be in a position to decide what happened whether he liked it or not. He had nothing against Gus and has always liked him, but it was already clear he had his own ideas, and if he stayed he would always be as a junior partner to someone ten years younger.

The letter had invited him to come and discuss the possibility of becoming the Director of the Estate. Only a small share of the actual ownership would be offered to him, but the owners - mostly English and American - lived abroad, and looked upon their interests purely as an investment, with the additional kudos of being able to visit whenever they and their friends wanted and stay in the guest rooms available to them. There would be little question of their interfering in the management as long as a reasonable annual dividend was forthcoming. In addition to all the expenses of moving into the generous living accommodation provided, he would be in receipt of a generous salary from day one and with the security of a good pension when he himself wanted to retire.

He had not discussed the letter with Mel or even told her about it, recognising the life changing choices it would entail as far as she was concerned if he were to accept. Everything was suddenly up in the air. What if their sons really did become professional football players And even if they didn't, what would there be to offer them?

Stephane seriously considered tearing up the letter without saying anything, but the thought of a free hand in one of the outstanding Estates in France - as good as saying the world, made him realise that to turn it down without seeing if the two of them could not work something out might be a missed opportunity he would regret for the rest of his life. But what right had he to turn Mel's life upside down? Even to raise the possibility might have unforeseen consequences, not only for themselves, but all who depended on them.

Even while he was still agonising over whether or not to tell Mel, Christine gave birth to a son...and heir. They called him William - Billy, for short. It was possible he would be boss one day.

Gus was thrilled He had already discovered how precious was the adoration of a small daughter, and that to wait with arms outstretched for her to run laughing into his embrace, then sweep her up into the air while she shrieked with excitement, was to experience a joy he could never have imagined. And now a son - someone who would grow to stand at his side and learn to appreciate all the things that one day would be his....The thought of Stephane never crossed his mind.

CHAPTER TEN

He eventually decided he had to show Mel the letter - waiting until after supper, the boys were in bed, and the guests had gone out. He had no idea how she would take it and waited anxiously as they sat beside each other on the sofa in the living room. Finally, she lowered it to her lap, then lent across smiling and kissed him on the cheek.

'Is that all?'

'All! I thought...'

'I knew something was bothering you. I was afraid it was something serious... you were ill, or fancied another woman' Seeing his expression she chuckled, then lent over again and put her arm around him.

'I love you so much' she said softly. 'I can cope with anything as long as we're together'.

Despite this assurance, Mel realised, not only how such a move would affect their family, but a lot of other people as well - her father and Holly, and of course everyone whose jobs were tied to Rousanne. They all had to be considered.

The guests - Sean and Brenda Kennedy, an Irish couple came back sooner than expected and were in a mood to sit in front of the fire in the living room -lit for conviviality rather warmth at this time of year, and Stephane, now in need of a stiff one himself, poured Brandy for them all and he and Mel t sat with them while their visitors told them about Killiney where they lived just outside Dublin and their two grown up children, a boy and a girl, neither of whom had expressed any wish to take over the Pharmacy in Dun Laoghaire the two of them had built up over the years, the elder, Sean, having already announced that as soon as he had graduated from Trinity College Dublin, they intended to travel until they had each made up their minds what they really wanted to do.

Mel was outwardly sympathetic, but became conscious of the growing thoughtfulness of her husband, and knowing they were unlikely to get any sleep until some sort of decision had been made, after the two guests had gone upstairs, they talked for over an hour.

Mel pointed out that they did not want to end up like Sara Cevante and her husband. If he was to accept the offer, they would all go. Then Stephane hugged her and they went upstairs to celebrate how much they meant to each other.

Stephane realised that any sort of decision without Mel going along for his visit to the Chateau Coulet was pointless. This presented a problem as they had agreed that to tell anyone else who might be affected at this stage would only raise premature and possibly unnecessary alarm. It was by no means certain they would want to accept the offer of the Estate' owners once they had seen it, and even then, they would need to think through very carefully what to do about Mel's Practice and to protect, as far as possible, those who would be left behind.

It had been some time since they had taken a vacation together - none since boys had been born, and no one thought it strange when they announced they were going for a long week-end to stay in the Chateau where Stephane had worked so he could show it to her. 'Though economical with the truth, it was no lie.

Mayer was happy to bring Saeed over to sleep at Rousanne for the three nights they would be away and Mel was satisfied that Christine would be able to cope with the Practice while she was away. She was still hoping that Peter would come back now he had been released, but his Grandfather had told her that he had gone to look for work out of the district. He also said that Bridgette had been offered a job as an au pair in Paris. How he knew this, she did not inquire, but Les deux Demoiselles was a small town. Most people seemed to know everybody else's business!

Interest in the disappearance of Jeaninne Berger was replaced by following the romance between her Danish replacement and policeman boyfriend. This reached fever pitch when in the course of excavating the foundations for the house they planned to live in on the plot up on the hill overlooking the town came to an abrupt halt when the remains of a woman were unearthed, and this time there could be no mistaking its identity as the clinic were able to match the DNA of the corpse with that held with Jeaninne's records.

CHAPTER ELEVEN

Chateau Coulett was on the left bank of the Gironne Estuary and Stephane told Mel its reputation had been revived by the Manager, a Monsieur Ginster, who had taken charge between the two world wars, and with strict adherence to traditional methods, including forbidding any grapes to be picked early in the morning when they were still covered in dew, he had turned a watery pink wine that became progressively weaker in store into the deep strong Grand Vin of today: 'delimitred to the AOC of Margeax '.

They drove up the long avenue with vinyards on either side and eventually drew up in front of the Chateau itself, an imposing building which Stephane told her dated back to the seventeenth Century but had been considerably enlarged to its present size in 1815 despite a significant skirmish in the North which had seen the departure of the Emperor and the temporary return of the Monarchy.

'But none of that was allowed to interfere with the far more important local development which ensured the growing importance of the Chateau's reputation' Stephane added with a grin.

They got out of the car, but as they reached the foot of the steps leading up to the front door, two large hounds came bounding round the side of the house and practically knocked Stephane over in the enthusiasm of their greeting before turning their attention to Mel, who although smiling, ordered them to sit with a stern voice which they instantly obeyed so she could stroke their ears unmolested. A moment later they were joined by a sprightly looking older man wearing a leather apron tied round his middle who immediately came forward to embrace Stephane chuckling with delight and slapping him on the back.

'Stephane my boy! The dogs heard you before I did, but I knew it must be you!'.

He stood back holding Stephane at arm's length beaming with pleasure.' And how are you? You've put on weight!' He then turned to Mel. 'And this must be your beautiful wife who's been feeding you up '.The two shook hands, joined politely now by the two dogs and the old man glanced down at them for a moment.' Stephane said you were a vet. I can see they knew at once whose in charge!'

Mel laughed and Stephane said 'This is Monsieur Simon, darling. He was my boss when I worked here'

'I've heard my husband speak of you many times Monsieur' Mel said smiling.

'Henri, please'

'And you must call me Mel'

'I shall be honoured. You are an American are you not?'

Mel nodded 'It's a long story.'

'Well, come along inside.' He glanced at Stephane.' Don't bother with your bags now.- Marcel will bring them in' He turned back to Mel, and resting his hand on her arm, started to conduct her back up the steps while turning to Stephane who followed.

'I don't suppose you expected me to still be here?'

'Of course' Stephane smiled back' You will go on for ever'.

Simon nodded' Well, that would be nice'. He back to Mel as they reached the top of the steps 'Sometimes, when I wake up in the morning in the summer, with the sun shining through my window and the birds singing outside, I think perhaps I died in the night and was already in Heaven. It could not be any better than this!'

He let go of Mel's arm to step in front of her to push open the half door then stood back and gestured for her to enter, then waited for Stephane before following them inside.

A light lunch consisting of cold chicken, jambon cru and salads had been set out for them on the broad terrace at the rear of the house with its view down to the river over seemingly endless rows of vines.

To the right, their host pointed out the Winery and other out buildings.

'Stephane told me he has gone in for that refrigerated fermentation business' he said as they stood looking down to the river before sitting down. Well, you won't find anything like that here!'

Mel said 'I didn't think so somehow!' And they all laughed.

Over lunch. Simon told them that he had agreed with the owners to stay on until his replacement could be found. He then wanted to visit his brother and his family in New Zealand, but he had been told that he could then have one of the cottages on the Estate for as long as he wanted on his return.

'I was the one who suggested they approach you' he said, turning to Stephane. I never married as you know, and it would be a comfort to have someone take over I knew and who wouldn't mind if I helped from time to time!'.

Little had changed since Stephane had worked at the Chateau, but realising the importance of Mel's impression, Simon went out of his way to stress the extent and reputation of the Chateau.

He left the Cellars until last. These began immediately under the house and had gradually been extended as production had increased. Some the barrels dated back to the beginning of the twentieth century and there were shelves of ancient bottles older still, almost priceless in value.

'The last of these were sold for over a hundred thousand American dollars' Simon told her with pride. 'During the last war, they realised the danger of losing everything to the occupiers - I'm told Hermann Goering was particularly fond of the finer things in life, and well, there was no way they could be moved without destroying the very thing that made them what they were, so they bricked up this area, which holds the most valuable and distressed the new wall with dust and dirt to make it looked exactly like the rest'. He chuckled. 'They never guessed - not even the Vichy swine who were commissioned to send whatever they could find to their masters in Berlin.

Many of the Estates were not so lucky and lost everything, but no one connected with Chateau Coulett breathed a word, and although a lot of the less important stuff was taken - they were not so stupid as to try and hide everything - the best was saved. And you are looking at some of it now. Of course, that was even before my time'

Stephane and Mel did not talk much on the drive back to Rousanne. Mel knew how much her husband had enjoyed revisiting where he had found refuge and acceptance all those years ago and felt she must leave it to him to decide whether or not to accept the opportunity to become one of France's leading Vigneron. She herself had been very impressed and there was no way she was going to try and influence him. But even she was surprised when he did not get out of the car immediately after they pulled up in the yard beside their house, but turned to face her'.

'I've decided' he said calmly.'I don't want to go back there!'

'Why ever not?' Mel managed after a few seconds'

'Because it would be just that...going back. Standing on the shoulders of those who had built the place into what it is today.'

'But...'

'There is nothing I could do but just try to keep it the same...maintain the standard.' He took her hand before continuing 'I want to do more with my life than that Mel. I want to build a chateaux of our own. Pousin le Bas might never reach the standard of Coulett - at least, not in my life time, but who knows...if the boys change their minds...'

After a few seconds Mel flung herself across into his arms in a sudden upsurge of relief and love. 'Oh darling....'

'You don't think I'm being a fool?.

'No, I don't'. She pulled back to look him in the face ''But you are deciding for those reasons... not because of me?'.

Stephane nodded, seriously. 'It's the same with you' he insisted. This place is what you have made it. It would never have been the same if you had just bought it from someone else.'

'What about Marcus?'

Stephane was silent for a moment, then he said softly 'He was your Chateau Coulet. He gave you the start, but Rousanne was ...is...all yours'.

CHAPTER TWELVE

Madam Berger, Jeaninne's Mother, appeared in the Offices of Immoblier Cevante two weeks after the funeral. Eva was out showing some German visitors a small vineyard on the same side of the river as the Estate whose owners had retired without any family to carry on. They were not interested in the vines, but there was a surprisingly large house attached which, although run down, could be renovated at considerably less cost than starting from scratch, and there was a level area of land on the East side for a swimming pool.

It would not be a holiday home. Herr and Frau Keller were looking for somewhere to retire with a gentler climate than Cologne - large and attractive enough to ensue regular visits from the children and their families.

Sara stood up as soon as she saw the woman whom she had met several times when Jeaninne was alive.

'Madame Berger. How nice to see you. Would you like to sit down?'. But the other shook her head, looking around.

'Thank you, no. I just wanted a word with Eva Groot.'

Sara came round the desk to stand in front of her. 'I'm afraid she is out with some Clients. I doubt if she will be back before lunch. Is there something I can do for you?'

Her visitor frowned, then shook her head. 'I just wanted to ask her something' She hesitated. 'Perhaps you could ask her for me? She knows where I live'.

'I'll be happy to give her a message'

'Would you ask her...if she would sell me back the plot I sold to her.'

It was a moment before Sara said 'Of course'. She knew immediately what she was talking about

'I do not suppose they want to build a house there now'.

'I don't think so'

'That place meant so much to her. I would like to scatter her ashes there... and build a little memorial'

Sara thought for a moment, then she said gently 'I think that's a wonderful idea. I'll ask Eva, but I'm sure she will agree.'

'Thank you. I'll wait to hear from her, then.' She hesitated. then gave nod and turned for the door. As she opened it Sara said suddenly' Would you allow me to contribute to the cost of the Memorial? I was...so fond of her myself'.

The woman paused again, then gave another nod- which could have meant anything, and went out closing the door behind her.

Sara looked out of the window and saw her hurrying away across the Square. She remembered reading once that losing a child was the very worst thing could happen to anyone.

She wondered if what she had meant as a kind gesture had made things worse somehow. When grief was all you had.....

*

Alim thought very carefully about what he was about to do. He did not think of himself as a brave man, but when he had recovered from the immediate shock of the discovery of Jeaninne's body, he realised he was possibly the only person who might draw her murderers into the open.

He spoke to Eva and she arranged for him to meet Andre.

After describing the meeting to his immediate superior on the phone afterwards Farbre was ordered to bring Alim by car over to the Regional Headquarters at Saint Fleur, and three days later Alim found himself facing Chief Inspector Goudon whom he had first met some years previously when the Caravan he and Mayer were living in was set on fire in the middle of the night. They also met again briefly when he and Jeannine had been attacked by some hooded thugs one night on their way home from a restaurant in town.

Goudon shook hands with him warmly then invited both he and Andre to t take the seats facing his desk.

'I will come straight to the point' he said, speaking to Alim as soon as they were settled.

'I understand from my Sergeant here that you propose to draw Madame Berger's killers to reveal themselves by acting as bait?'.

Alim nodded.' They must be the same people who attacked us then threatened her if she continued her friendship with me, Monsieur'.

'You are using the word 'They'. You are sure whoever killed her was not acting alone?'

'I do not think so'.

It was the Inspector's turn to nod in agreement. 'And I think you are right', he said. 'We did not release the fact at the time for fear of distressing the girl's family still further, but evidence suggests she was raped by more than one person before she was killed'.

Alim looked stunned. Then he managed 'That is terrible!'

'Yes, it is. But please understand, that is privileged information. I am only telling you now so that you are in full possession of the facts before becoming further involved.'

Alim nodded but did not say anything, and the Inspector continued' I understand you have some idea of becoming provocative in some way?'.

'I worked in a bar for a while and there were some there who made it clear they thought I had no business taking a French person's job. Most of the customers were friendly... but there were some.' Alim paused, then went on 'I kept my head down as much as I could, and I tried to be polite to everyone. Whether the murderers were some of those who resented me, I don't know. But I'm sure they were responsible for when Jeaninne and I were attacked. I think, perhaps seeing me with a French young lady was - the last straw, I think you say'.

Andre said 'We found an anonymous letter where Mam'selle Berger lived saying that what had happened was a warning, and threatening worse if her relationship with you continued.'

'We never had a relationship' Alim protested. 'We just worked together. We only went out that one time. When we had been working late'

'But you were fond of her?'

They saw him hesitate for a moment before he said 'Yes- very. But she loved you. She was upset when you told her you were going to Paris'.

Goudon glanced at Andre for a moment before saying to Alim 'I understand you left your wife just before this happened?'

'Mayer is not my wife. I helped her to escape to Europe.' He paused for a moment, then went on "After the attack, I realised working with Madame Berger was putting her in danger and went back to work for Monsieur Stephane Meuse.'

Goudon said. 'But you did not go back to where you were living before?'

Alim shook his head, and after a moment Andre said 'Perhaps... whoever it was thought you were still having a relationship...only more discretely?'

'I don't know. But we were not'.

There was a moment's silence before Goudon said 'So, what is your idea?'.

Alim said 'I should go back to the bar I was speaking about ...and talk provocatively ...about our Government's attitude to immigrants perhaps?'.

Andre said, that might get you a punch in the face, but I doubt the sort of reaction you hope for!'.

'I agree' Goudon said 'We need the collaboration of a young woman'.

Alim stared at him, visibly shocked. 'I only know Mayer, and I would never dream...'

'I'm not talking about her' Goudon interrupted. Just a moment...' He picked up the phone and pushed a button.

'Ask Sergeant Renou to come in now please' He put down the receiver and looked at Alim.

'I thought we might get to this point!'

Almost immediately, there was knock on the door and the Sergeant came into the room.

Whatever Alim was expecting, it wasn't the slim, attractive young woman dressed in black trousers, a pink top and wearing moderately high heels who closed the door behind her, and after a brief smile at Andre, looked expectantly at Goudon.

'Chief Inspector?'

Goudon rose to his feet, prompting the other two to do the same, and gestured at a vacant chair.

'Come and sit down, Sergeant. This is Monsieur Alim I was telling you about' Then to Alim, 'this is Sergeant Avril Renou'.

The young woman smiled at Alim, but made no effort to shake hands, before they all sat down.

'Now then' Goudon began again, 'we are appreciative of your desire to help in bringing the murderers of Madame Berger to justice, Monsieur Alim, but I would not have invited you here if I had not thought through the implications of what Sergenat Farbre told me about your general idea over the telephone'.

Alim frowned, and after a moment Goudon said 'Am I speaking too fast for you? 'But Alim shook his head.

'No.But I am not sure of the word 'impli...?'

'Implications' Goudon spread his hands apologetically. 'I'm sorry. I meant to say - what might happen if we did what you suggest'

Alim nodded. 'Yes, I see'.

'We cannot allow you to put yourself in more danger than can be avoided'.

'I was hoping you would have someone follow me... or give me a gun, or something'.

Goudon smiled momentarily.' I see. But we cannot risk you shooting some innocent person by mistake, and a 'tail' could lose you, or might not be able to get to you in time if you were attacked'

'A tail. Yes. I see'.

Goudon glanced at the young woman who was sitting closest to the desk, than looked back at Alim.

'It seemed to us that Sergeant Renou here meets all our needs. Not only is she very attractive, more than enough to provoke anyone's envy of her male escort, but infuriate those whom we suspect when that escort is...not of French blood!'.

He spread is hands again as he looked from one to the other adding 'I apologise for speaking frankly, but we are not dealing with very nice people!'.

The young woman smiled.' That's alright Chief Inspector. You have explained my part in this and I am grateful of the opportunity'.

'Thank you' Goudon nodded, then turned back to Alim.

'What is far less obvious is that, far from being a vulnerable female, Sergeant Renou has reached a high level of skill in unarmed combat and won the police medal at the last contest in Paris. She is also a crack shot.' His eyes glinted.' With her at your side, you will be as well protected as by a Presidential body guard!' He allowed himself another brief smile, then stood up.

'So thank you... and the very best of luck. I suggest the three of you go now, get to know each other and decide on your exact plan of action. Sergeant Farbre here will let me know the details. He will not be directly involved for obvious reasons...but not be too far away, I hope!'

CHAPTER THIRTEEN

It was mid-summer when Stephane took the boys over the stepping stones to Poussin le Bas for a morning swim then to walk up to the house through the rows of vines where Anna would give them something to feed Shamus. They had done this many times, and with the distraction of the boys chattering about football - what else? - he almost walked past one of the rose bushes at the end of a row before noticing it had started to wilt. In fact it was Dale junior - the twin on whom his father rested his hope that at least one of them would want to follow in his footsteps - who pointed this out.

There was no doubt about it: powdery mildew, the curse of Vignerons world wide was taking hold, which meant the vines themselves were under threat.

Although immediately concerned, he did not forget to congratulate the boy before, after a quick examination at several points along the row, made for the house fifty yards from the main building where Gus and Christine were living while his parents were on their extended holiday.

He gave permission to the boys to run across to the main house to find Anna, then knocked on the kitchen door which was opened by Gus, who was in the middle of breakfast with Lisa at the kitchen table while Christine was upstairs giving Billy his morning feed.

He explained at once what he had found, and came in and sat with them while they finished their breakfast and discussed the situation until Billy had fallen asleep in mid-feed and Christine came downstairs. Thanks to the roses, and Dale Junior's eagle eye, the disease could be checked before it took further hold, but they had to act quickly.

Further examination revealed that at least a quarter of the Merlot had already been affected; not, so far, the Rousanne, but they agreed that all should be sprayed at once with phosphoric acid.

There was only one way to do this effectively and that was to walk along the individual rows and treat each plant separately - a back breaking job - with a large reservoir strapped to their backs and wearing protective overalls, breathing masks and goggles. Alim was sent to the agricultural warehouse on the outskirts of town in the Land Rover to get more chemicals while Stephane and Gus started putting everything else on hold and giving strict instructions to everyone else to stay indoors. As soon as she was finished with Billy, Christine took both of the children with her to Rousanne and phoned the school from there that the Estate's swimming area was off limits until the spraying was completed.

Not only was it back breaking, but because of the sun they were soon sweating profusely. Anticipating this, they had taken the precaution of filling a plastic container of water which could be left at the top of the two rows they were working on and moved along as the work progressed - although by mid-day it was too warm to be drinkable and had to be filled up again. They worked back to back on adjacent but separate rows to avoid the risk of spraying in each other's faces. When he had made a second journey Alim donned a spare set of protective gear and started on a third row.

They took a break at mid-day for half an hour in the Winery where they found carefully wrapped sandwiches waiting for them and several times during the afternoon for a drink or to replenish the reservoirs By six they were exhausted, but they had done half the Merlot and agreed that was enough for one day.

After an early supper, which Alim took at Rousanne, and much to Mayer and Saeed's delight he was persuaded to go home with them to the cottage they had shared not so long ago.

The following two days, the same pattern was repeated except that Alim started at the same time as the others, and finally, at the end of the third day, the last row of Rousanne was finished and Mel invited them all to a celebratory supper before an early night - contentment qualified by the knowledge that in two weeks' time they would have to do it all again, and then, two weeks after that!

*

The day after the first application was completed Gus became ill with a high fever. After tests, Holly realised it was a reaction to the phosphoric acid which, despite all precautions often managed to penetrate the breathing masks in minute quantities The fact that the other two did not display similar symptoms, meant he alone was allergic.

From a work point of view, the situation was saved by the return of Dale from visiting his mother in time for the second and third treatments.

Gus' condition deteriorated. Holly telephoned a specialist in Paris, but he only confirmed her own diagnosis that there were no drugs that could help and that his recovery was down to careful nursing and his own immune system. He was moved back home from the Clinic and with Mel's agreement, Christine gave up everything apart from the children to look after him.

Mel eventually tracked down Peter with the help of his Grandfather. She found him working as tractor driver on a farm twenty miles down the valley and asked him to come back to help her. Life had been difficult enough after he left but she had not looked for anyone else in the hope that he would come back of his own accord; but without Christine either, the practice was too big now to handle alone.

She realised he was torn between the far more rewarding occupation as her assistant and nervousness at retuning to a place where he had actually killed someone, deliberately or not. But when she explained her predicament, his sense of loyalty won the day and they went together to see the farmer, who was not at all pleased to lose someone who not only did the job he was paid for but was saving him a considerable amount in Vet's fees. But he was already a Client of Mel's, and when she offered not to charge him anything for a year, he agreed to forego the legally required notice.

He was still grumbling when they left, but as they drove down to the main road, they glanced at each other, then burst out laughing.

A week later, Peter came home after work to his grandparents house, where he had settled in again, to find a small white car parked outside. He was met at the door by his Grandmother who beckoned him in with what he thought a slightly conspiratorial smile, and when she had closed the door, she told him someone was waiting for him in the small front room. She shook her head when he asked who, and gestured instead for him to go in and see for himself.

He found his grandfather standing by the fireplace in conversation with a young woman who rose to her feet smiling when he entered, and moved forward to kiss his cheek.

'Hello Peter. I expect you're surprised to see me!'

'Bridgette! What are you doing here?'

'Doesn't she look lovely, Peter' his Grandmother said, following him into the room. 'We hardly recognised her!'. Her husband nodded smiling, then they all looked at Peter.

It would not be true to say he would not have recognised the young woman who now faced him waiting for his answer, but she looked as if she had just stepped out of the pages of one of the fashion magazines Mel bought occasionally, her hair having also been cut short in a style which gave her an air of confidence - light years, from the hesitant village girl he had known.

'You look very nice' he conceded after a few seconds, suddenly shy, and they all laughed.

'Very nice!' his Grandmother snorted. 'She looks gorgeous!'

'She certainly does' his Grandfather agreed.' That's what Paris does for you!'

Bridgette turned back to him. 'Well, if you've got the money... or in my case, an employer who seemed to enjoy taking me under her wing'. She chuckled.' I think really she was a bit embarrassed by me in front of her friends, but she is very generous. She even lent me her car to come down here'.

Recovering the power of speech, Peter said 'Why <u>are</u> you here?'

'I came down for my Sister's wedding on Saturday. You remember Julie?'.

'Of course'

'And I've brought you an invitation...if you would like to come?'

Peter nodded and held out his hand for the envelope which Bridgette took out of the bag slung round her shoulder and handed to him.

'Thank you. I would love to' he said after opening the envelope and glancing inside. 'But it doesn't give me much time for a present'.

Bridgette smiled again. 'Don't worry about that. Just come'.

'Where is it?'

'The Church in St Bedes - near where our parents live. I'm afraid I can't offer to take you.'

'I expect you are the chief bridesmaid' Peter's Grandmother said, and Bridgette turned to her nodding happily, before turning back to him.

'Julie's friend Esme lives not far from here though. She has been invited with her boyfriend Paul. I could ask them to pick you up if you like'.

'No. I'll be OK. I'm sure Madame Meuse will lend me the old car she only uses sometimes'

It was a magical evening. Bridgette met him straight after the Service, and when the photographs had been taken she arranged for him to sit with the family at the Reception. When they were not dancing they sat together and she told him about the children she looked after and the family who had been so kind to her. The father was a senior civil servant and the wife a Doctor. She had recently been told by them he was being sent to take up a senior position at the French Consulate in New York and they had invited her to go with them. Bridgette studied his face when she told him this, but he changed the subject and started to bring her up to date with the situation at Rousanne and Gus's condition.

'What about his wife?' Bridgette asked, recovering from a momentary stab of disappointment at his apparent lack of immediate interest at her news.

'Christine. She doesn't come any more. She just looks after him' Peter told her.

'So you don't see her?'

Only sometimes - when she brings the children over for a ride on the donkey'.

Then they danced again and held each other close.

Bridgette was staying with her parents, but she walked with him to his car and waited for him to kiss her, which he did.

'I hope you don't go to America' he whispered when they separated for a moment, looking at each other. He knew now she was the most beautiful girl he had ever seen. What a fool not to have realised it before, and when she had showed she loved him. How stupid to have risked losing her!

He kissed her again without waiting for an answer, and having taken off his jacket to toss it onto the passenger seat, he felt the urgency of her breasts through the thin material of her bridesmaid's dress as they clung together.

At last they separated again and he opened the car door with one hand while still holding her with the other, then turned back.

'When will I see you again?

Bridgette shook her head.

'I don't know, Peter.' She paused a moment longer then she let her arms fall to her sides.

'If you want me you will have to come to Paris and find me. My sister has my address'.

Her eyes held him for several seconds before turning to walk back to join the other departing guests without looking back as he stared after her.

CHAPTER FOURTEEN

Alim began to frequent the bar after work where he used to be employed. He kept himself to himself, drinking his beer while standing quietly at the bar watching the television. Most of the regulars remembered him, and after one or two had made some pointed remarks, which he ignored, they left him alone. That is until Avril Renou appeared.

The first time was with a male companion he did not recognise but guessed was another policeman. After they had stood next to him with their drinks for a while, the two men fell into conversation, and when the two newcomers decided to sit at one of the booths they invited Alim to join them and he spent the rest of the evening drinking and talking amicably together with them until they left separately.

Two nights later, Avril came in by herself. She looked round until she saw Alim then asked him in a voice just loud enough to carry if he had seen Michael, and when he shook his head one of the regulars offered to buy her a drink instead. But she shook her head and turned back to Alim and they stood together the few minutes until 'Michel' turned up, apologising for being late and shortly afterwards Alim left.

This pantomime was repeated a week later, but this time Michael and Avril appeared to quarrel, and after drinking up angrily, her companion stormed out of the bar leaving Avril alone with Alim.

The Michael character did not appear again, but Avril and Alim became a feature despite the evident disgust of some of the regulars.

She got into the habit of walking back with him to where he lived - something he felt uncomfortable about, but she assured him that Andre was never far away. This went on for a month without incident until Goudon eventually decided that Alim's idea was not going to work and he had better uses for Sergeant Renou. Even so, he was concerned that having exposed Alim to possible retaliation they could not just leave him to it, and Andre persuaded him to ask Stephane if he could stay at Rousanne for a while. Saying perhaps that he had fallen out with the landlord of his flat in town?

When Andre reported that Alim had agreed, his superior breathed a sigh of relief - although they were back to square one as far as Jeaninne's murder was concerned.

*

Then came the extended evenings of summer, when even the trees bordering the river added their scent to the peace of the lengthening shadows, and the water drifted slowly with scarcely a ripple.

Whenever he could, Andre went to Rousanne to meet Eva after she had finished work. Sometimes, if it had been a particularly hot day, they would join the others for a swim, but more often they walked along the river bank, hand in hand, quietly discussing their future together until it was time to turn back and go for supper at Rousanne, where Mel had assured Eva, her Fiancee was always welcome. Sometimes Andre drove them to one of the villages to explore the menu of one of the new local restaurants which were now opening up and down the valley in response to the growing tourist trade and those who had chosen to escape the winter of Northern Europe by having a holiday home constructed that could be made to pay for itself by renting to short term visitors in the summer.

One day, Eva asked Andre to meet her at the office instead, refusing to say why except that she had a surprise for him. The thought did cross his mind that she was going to tell him she was pregnant, although they had generally been careful not to allow passion over-ride caution whenever circumstances had allowed them to make love. If that were the case, he would not be displeased. One of the things they had discussed was the number of children they would like, but it would mean bringing the date of the wedding forward, which would not bother him, but as they had planned to get married in Leiden, where her parents lived in Holland with her younger brother Jan, he wondered if, in the circumstances, the Groots might decide to let Eva get married from their holiday home locally. All these thoughts had to be put on hold while he waited a bit impatiently for her to tidy up after Sara had left her to it.

Finally, she came to stand in front of the chair by the reception desk where he had been glancing idly through a list of properties currently available he had found on the desk, and pressed her knees against his.

'Are you ready?' Her eyes seemed to be dancing in amusement as Andre rose to his feet and took her into his arms.

'I don't know'.

The joking was suspended while they kissed until both came up for air and Eva managed. 'I meant about the surprise!'

Andre shook his head smiling, then he said' You're pregnant!'

'No, I am not pregnant!' She pushed him away in mock disgust.

'Well, it is possible'.

'You hope!'

'I wouldn't mind!'

'Well I would. We've got a lot more urgent things before that!'

'Like...?.

'Somewhere to live.'

'Ah, Yes. Right'. He nodded, only momentarily disappointed and gave her his attention.

'Just a minute'. Eva turned away and went over to her own desk to pick up a thin brochure before turning back to him.'

'You know I have agreed to sell Jeaninne's plot back to her mother.

Andre nodded. 'It's just as well. Even if we had carried on, we would have had such a problem selling if we had to move'.

'Which, with your job, could happen at any time'.

Andre moved to take her in his arms again, but she retreated a step, holding out the brochure between them.

'Listen to this, then you can kiss me all you want.'

Capitulating, he perched on the edge of the desk'.

'Go on then'

Eva nodded then she said 'You know Sara has turned the old Co-op Winery into a block of apartments?'.

'I know she intended to?'.

'Well, they are almost ready'

Andre frowned. 'I don't fancy living there!'.

'Not permanently, no.'

'I certainly wouldn't want to buy one '.

'Neither would I. But Sara has offered to let us live in one of them for a while - either until it's the only one left to be sold, or we have to move on. She intended to furnish one as a show flat anyway - as the rest are always easier to sell if one is occupied'.

Andre paused for a moment, then he asked a bit doubtfully 'How much rent would she want?'.

'Nothing!'.Eva smiled in triumph. 'As long as we are willing to keep the place looking good and show prospective buyers around...that would be up to me of course. Just think...'

'I am!'

'It would give us the time we need to look for something permanent. What do you think?'

He stood up 'If it's as good as it sounds...!'

Eva said 'So now you can kiss me... or if you prefer, I can lock the door and we can go in the back and arrange to risk having to bring the wedding forward. I'm afraid I don't have any means of defence at the moment!.'

It wasn't the first time they had made love there after Sara had gone home, but never before so wonderfully and all consumingly passionate.

Afterwards, they rested in each other's arms until long after it had grown dark, then they walked back to Rousanne arms around each other and kissed for the last time, promising to meet at the office the following evening so Eva could show him the flat Sara had offered.

But he was not able to make it. After she had waited for over an hour he phoned to apologise that he had been sent to a farm where half the farmer's sheep had been stolen, and Eva started to walk home disappointed. Then she changed her mind and decided to go and have another look at the apartment anyway.

By the time she started for home again it was dark.

It was mid-morning before Sara picked up the phone to dial Rousanne. It was so unusual for Eva to be late she wondered what was keeping her. When she had left the office the previous evening, leaving her waiting for her fiancee, she had seemed bright and impatient to go with him to see the flat. She only hoped nothing had happened.

Mayer told her that Eva had not come home and they had assumed she had spent the night with her boy friend.

Sara would have tried to contact Andre immediately, but even as she picked up the phone the office door opened and Alan Marsh walked in. Everything else went out of her head until much later.

CHAPTER FIFTEEN

Gus regained consciousness but was still too weak to get up and drifted in and out of normal sleep for several days.

Then he woke up to find his step-father sitting by the bed. Alan smiled as soon as Gus opened his eyes and stretched out his hand to rest it on Gus's shoulder.

'Hello, Son'.

Gus frowned and squeezed his eyes shut for a second.

'Alan?'

'That's me'

Gus closed his eyes again for a moment, then turned his head awkwardly to look at Alan more closely. 'Alan. What are you doing here?.'

''I heard you were sick and decided it was time I came to see you'.

Gus considered this for a moment, then he said 'Have you just got here?'

The other shook his head. 'No. I arrived about a week ago. I've been here every day'.

Gus nodded then managed a weak smile. 'I thought it was you. But Mother came too, and I thought I was imaging it'.

'Well, I'm here OK.' After a brief squeeze he took his hand away.' You've been pretty sick.'

'I know'.

Alan stood up. 'I'd better go and tell Holly and Chrissie you're awake. They've been pretty worried.'

'Don't go away'.

'Don't worry, I'll be back.' He smiled again.' We've a lot to catch up on!'

He opened the bedroom door but before he went out Gus said 'How did you know I was sick?'

'Sara Cevante sent me an e-mail. She guessed I'd want to know'.

When Alan had gone, promising to return the following day, and Christine had brought in the children for a few minutes to see him, Holly came and sat on the edge of the bed and told him that she had spoken again to the Specialist in Paris and he had advised that as he had obviously suffered an anaphylactic shock as a result of an extreme allergic reaction he advised that as soon as Gus felt well enough he and Christine should take the children on a long vacation as far away from vineyards as possible as a repetition could prove fatal.

Over the following days Gus began to feel stronger and he and Christine discussed where they could go, but without coming to any conclusion.

'I'm not bothered about where to go on a trip' he told her eventually, but what to do when I get back. How can I be of any use here if I can't go near the vines?!'

Christine thought for a moment, then she said 'You could work in the office...or on sales'

But Gus shook his head. 'I don't want to do that Chrissie. I'd rather leave here altogether' he added unhappily'

'But this is our home! What could we do if we left here?'

Gus considered this, then he said 'Well, you always wanted to go to college and get proper qualifications. We could go and live somewhere like London. You could go to school in the day while I looked after the children.'

Christine looked at him frowning then she burst out laughing and bent forward to kiss him. 'No darling, I don't think I would condemn you to that, much as I might enjoy it!'.

*

'Though badly frightened and left in the dark tied to a chair in a room next to where she could hear her kidnappers arguing, it became obvious to Eva that all was not well with them either. Her French was still basic, but as the argument continued, she understood enough to register that some of those arguing where blaming the others for making - what sounded like a 'cul de cochon!'

Eventually the door opened and one of them came into the room and switched on the light.

'You are the Dutch girl' he said without preamble.

Eva looked up at him squinting as her eyes adjusted to the light and nodded.

The other paused for a moment, then he said 'That is bad luck for you!'

Eva didn't answer, but went on looking up at him as he went 'They thought you were the tart who went with the illegal to the bar in the evening'.

Eva swallowed, then she said huskily' What bar? I have never been...'

'But you know the illegal' the man interrupted.

Eva thought for a moment then she said 'Do you mean Alim'

'If that is his name'.

'We both live at Rousanne '.

'That was the problem.'

'But I have nothing to do with him. He's only just come to live there. Apart from that...'

'We know' the man interrupted again. 'But now you know who we are, and if we let you go you could identify us, and then they would assume we were responsible for that other bitch'.

'Weren't you?'

'We roughed her up a bit to teach her a lesson...but someone else killed her'.

Suddenly Eva's anger mastered her fear.

'You call gang rape just teaching her a lesson!' she said accusingly.

Taken aback by her vehemence, the one standing in front of her paused, then shrugged.

'Well...it did get a bit out of hand'.

'So did killing her!'

'I've told you. That was somebody else'.

'And who's going to believe that?'

Even as she spoke, Eva realised the significance of what she had said, and kicked herself mentally as the man nodded.

'That is what I just said' He agreed quietly. 'And that is why we can't let you go.'

Eva stared at him, fear taking hold again.

'You can't keep me here for ever' she managed eventually, while the other seemed to be looking right through her. Then he said calmly 'That is why the others think we have no choice but to put you out of harm's way'.

Eva swallowed again then she managed 'I wouldn't tell anyone'.

He frowned for a moment, then burst out laughing; turned, then left the room, switching off the light and shutting the door behind him, leaving her in the dark again.

Then she knew she was going to die.

CHAPTER SIXTEEN

The Specialist phoned Holly at the Clinic.

'Following our more recent conversation concerning your Son-in-Law Madame, I have been talking to my colleagues and explained the particular difficulties of his situation. There is, as you know, no 'cure' for such extreme allergies but there is a private clinic here in Paris who can reduce an allergy over a period of time by means of miniscule exposure to whatever is causing the reaction. It must be tightly controlled of course, but if the patient has the time and the money, success is usual'.

Holly thought for a moment, then she said 'How long does the treatment take?'

She sensed him shrug.

'It depends. Several months at least, during which time daily monitoring must take place. It is not usually necessary for the patient to stay at the Clinic, even so, it is not cheap, and unless whoever it is lives within easy commuting distance, the cost of suitable nearby accommodation must also be taken into account'.

Holly thought for a moment, then she said 'is there anyone nearer to us'.

'I don't know of any. You might care to look on the internet'.

Gus was delighted at first that something could be done, but the thought of living in Paris by himself for no one knew how long was a depressing prospect as clearly it would be totally selfish of him to uproot Christine and the children for an indefinite period.

Holly had to agree, but a search on the internet showed the Clinic in Paris to be the only one in France. There were institutions in Switzerland and Germany but they were even further away.

It was Alan Marsh who suggested they look at New York. Although further in distance, Gus could stay with him during the treatment and it would take little longer in time by air for Christine to visit than Paris.

There were in fact two specialist clinics on the east coast: one in Connecticut and one in Manhattan itself. The second was considerably more expensive, but taking the other factors into account Christine agreed it seemed by far the best choice. 'And having Alan to keep an eye on you, I won't worry about you so much!' she said nodding firmly.

As far as the expense was concerned, Gus still had most of the money his mother had left him and Holly said she was sure Lisa would have been delighted for him to use it in such a way.

Within three weeks a place had been reserved and Christine said a tearful farewell to both of them at the airport in Toulouse where she, Holly and Sara went to see them off.

During the following weeks, Christine threw herself back into her work with Mel. She missed Gus dreadfully, but the release from his sick room back into the world she loved made her feel a whole person again- even if, sometimes, she felt a bit guilty when she stopped to think about it. Even Lisa regained the playful naughtiness that had had been suppressed during her father's illness and pestered her Grandfather Dale for more trips to Roussanne to ride on Shamus and other requirements.

*

It was still dark when the door banged open again and the room flooded with light.

A man she recognised came towards her, and after untying her from the chair helped her to her feet. He then took one of her arms and firmly steered her to the door'.

'Where are you taking me? Please don't hurt me...'

The man did not answer but pushed her through the door and outside where the car she had been brought in was waiting, it's engine running, and where a third man was standing by an open rear door. Pushing her inside, she found herself next to the one who had come in to see her and the door was slammed shut.

A moment later, the front passenger door opened and the third man got in beside the driver who at once put the car into gear and accelerated into the darkness. Eva was terrified, but before she said anything, the man sitting in front of her turned and said 'If you do as you are told, no one is going to harm you.'

Taking some small comfort from this, Eva shrunk back into herself, and tiring of trying to recognise where they were going closed her eyes. She was exhausted, and eventually half dozed - she did not know for how long - but suddenly there were the street lights of a small town and the car pulled up outside a railway station.

The driver cut the engine, but stayed where he was while the other two got out; and pulling her out of the car, walked on either side, guiding her towards the ticket office, which was not yet open, but there was an automatic machine just to the side where they stopped and the one who had been sitting in the front handed Eva her own bag, which she had dropped when they had bundled her into the car in the first place.

'Thank you' she managed after a moment, conquering her surprise, while the other smiled thinly.

'Everything is still there. We are not thieves!' Eva took the bag from him but did not risk his anger by opening it to check until he said 'Take your credit card and buy a one way ticket to Paris. The first train will be here in twenty minutes'

Eva nodded, and after a few seconds, did as she was told while the others watched her until she had taken the ticket from the machine and put the card back in her bag.

'What now? I don't know anyone in Paris.'

'When you reach Paris, buy yourself a ticket to where ever you live in Holland'

'And don't come back' the other said menacingly. 'You are a nice girl, and it was bad luck for you, you became involved. We wish you no harm, but if you ever come back...'

'Or contact anyone in Les Deux Demoiselles - next time you will not be so lucky!'

Eva paused then nodded.

They waited until the train arrived then found her an empty compartment. Just before closing the door one said quietly 'Don't misunderstand, Miss Groot. If we ever see you again, you will die'.

Eva sat obediently and did not look at them again as the train pulled out but started to rummage in the contents of her bag once she was sure they could no longer see her

The train was not an Express, and stopped again after ten minutes, where Eva got out. She was still badly shaken, but they had underestimated both her courage and trust in Andre. They had also overlooked the small mobile phone tucked into a small section of the bag.

Andre was overjoyed to hear her voice.

'I think I know where you are, but leave your phone connected to this number then we'll know for sure. Now give me the registration number of that car again.

While Andre drove as fast as he dared to pick up Eva, three squad cars under Sergeant Renou set up road blocks on the outskirts of Les deux Demoisells and arrested the three men.

Recognising her, one of the three looked at her in amazement.

'You are a Poulet!' he said disgustedly, and Avril laughed.

'Hello Henri. Nice to see you too!'

The other spat in disgust and turned away to join his two companions in the waiting van.

CHAPTER SEVENTEEN

The Summer slipped into Autumn. The Vendange was not as good as recent years because of lack of rain at the right time, but the spraying, with two other treatments, had stopped the mildew in its tracks. It was hard work without Gus but both Christine and Peter helped when Mel could spare them, and when the last basket of grapes had been tipped into the press, the celebratory dinner was held in its usual place on the terrace under the plane tree planted by Andrew Solomon more than fifty years ago and set with the trestle tables brought out of the store where they lived for the rest of the year. Gus once said, he wondered if the old man ever managed to tear himself from the joys of Paradise to sit unseen at the head of the table, where by tradition a place was always set for him.

There were not as many as there used to be in those days. Since they had purchased a mechanical grape picker of their own, the Spanish pickers had ceased to be needed, but in addition to the family, there were still a dozen local stalwarts whom Dale knew looked forward to their two weeks in the vineyard, even though it now meant just following the machine and picking the bunches it left behind for one reason or another. It would never have occurred to him to disappoint them

Although his help had been invaluable, in addition to Gus, Peter was absent, and when Dale asked if anyone knew where he had gone, Mel told him she understood he had gone to Paris. Holly saw her suppress a grin as she said this but decided not to press her further.

The dinner reached the point where a few speeches were usually made, but even as she saw Dale looking round to see if everyone had refilled their glasses in anticipation, Holly heard her grand-daughter shriek, and sliding off her chair next to Christine ran towards a man and a woman, who had walked round the corner from the front of the house, squealing 'Richard... you've come!!'

The little girl flung herself into his arms and he held her aloft laughing before lowering her into a hug then turning to carry her back towards them. She saw the young woman was quite beautiful and wearing a short summer dress of pale yellow that showed off both her figure and long slim legs - but she seemed oblivious of the effect she was having as she eventually took the child into her own arms just before they reached the table, which the child accepted with easy familiarity and Holly realised she was looking at Bridgette, and a moment later, as they stopped beside them, that her companion was Richard Chambers.

Dale rose to his feet smiling and shook hands with Chambers first, then kissed Bridgette on either cheek before waving his hands at the table invitingly, and taking the cue, extra chairs were quickly produced and space made opposite Stephane and Mel and next to Christine who finally reclaimed her excited daughter.

'We won't have anything to eat' Richard said apologetically as they sat down. 'We booked into the Bridge for dinner where I'll be staying, but we heard you were all here and thought we must come and say hello first'

Bridgette nodded happily. 'We ran into each other in Paris at a party.' She reached out and took his nearest hand possessively. 'Everything happened so fast, and I wanted my Mother and Father to meet Richard...so, here we are.'

'Have you seen them yet? 'Mel asked

Bridgette shook her head. 'Richard is going to run me over there later.'

Richard laughed.' I think Bridgette's not sure how they'll take to the likes of me and needs to break the news gently!.'

Bridgette pulled a face, then smiled. 'It's not that, you know it isn't, but.... well, they're fairly traditional and I want to explain our relationship to them first'

'Are you getting married?' Stephane asked bluntly, and Richard opened his mouth to say something but Bridgette got in first.

'Not straight away. Like I said, It's all happened so fast!'.

Christine said 'So Richard will be staying at the hotel for the moment'

'Yes' Bridgette coloured a little. 'Like I said...'

'It's all happened so fast!' Dale junior, who was sitting next to his father', piped up cheekily, and everyone one laughed, including Richard and Bridgette themselves.

Mel said eventually 'Did Peter catch up with you in Paris?'

Bridgette paused for a moment, frowning, then she shook her head. 'No. Why? Was he there?'

'He went to see you. Somehow, I thought you were expecting him.'

'Oh. I didn't know' She glanced at Richard then turned back to Mel.

'I left the job after...'

'I'm afraid I rather kidnapped her' Richard put in.

'We're staying in a nice apartment at the moment overlooking the Seine' Bridgette went on. 'But we plan to move back to London when Richard's project is finished in Paris' She paused looking round a bit defensively before adding 'it's normal' with more stress than she had intended.

'So you did not see him? Mel persisted, and Bridgette shook her head.

'No. What did he want?'

'He wanted to see you'.

'Oh!' She looked down at her lap.

After a few seconds Christine said 'Well, it's not your fault if he didn't tell you he was coming'.

'What do you do during the day now you have given up your job?' Holly said, leaning across to join in the conversation.

'Richard said 'She does some research for me... and takes the dog for a walk'.

'So you got a what you wanted eventually!' Christine said laughing.

The others smiled without knowing quite what was the joke; except Richard, who stared back at her.

'But not the one I really wanted' he said levelly. Christine's smile faded before she looked away.

*

Despite being polite to her parents, Bridgette knew he was in one of his moods and hardly said a word to her during the drive back to Paris.

When they arrived, he dropped his case on the floor of the living room of their flat and told her he was going out and did not know what time he would be back.

He did not come back at all that night but arrived mid morning and again offered no explanation but shaved and took a quick shower and change of clothes, then left again only this time carrying his laptop saying he had to meet a business associate and make some arrangements.

'When will you back? Bridget said anxiously.

He hesitated by the door.

'I don't know'

'Have I done something to make you angry?'

He hesitated for a moment, before saying 'No. You can't help being who you are'.

His expression was almost one of pity, and that frightened her more than if he had sworn at her. She swallowed then she said 'Don't you want me anymore?'

'I really don't know. Don't bother me now. I've too much on my mind'

She was going to ask for some money for shopping, but he went out of the door closing it behind him and she was glad she hadn't.

He came back in time to take her out to dinner - seemingly in a better mood, but when they got back he told her to get undressed and wait for him in the bed room while he had another drink, but when he finally appeared she had fallen asleep and he woke her up by shaking her roughly. She saw he was already naked himself as he threw her back on the bed before taking her violently and satisfying himself in a way more akin to rape than love before rolling off her and falling asleep almost at once.

Bridgette turned out the bedside light then went and sat on a chair on the other side of the room and studied him by the light of the street lights outside, before getting up, and taking a robe from the bathroom, curled up on the bed in the spare room without bothering to get between the sheets.

When she woke up he had already left, but there was a note by the phone saying he would not be late and would prefer to eat in.

She took the dog for a walk in the Tuileries garden. He had never treated her like that before, and after a snack at the small cafe, eventually made her way back to the apartment having persuaded herself that, despite the ugliness of what had happened, he needed her, and with such a man she must expect to yield to his wishes, even those that required her total submission.

He did appear well in time for the dinner she had prepared but told her he had invited a business colleague and she barely had time to rearrange the table before the door bell rang. Richard went to answer it and after closing the door behind the newcomer whom he introduced as a compatriot - a good looking, pale skinned man in his late twenties who went by the name of Alistair and who stared as he handed over some lilies with an intensity that made her feel uncomfortable. But when she glanced at Richard, she saw he was smiling and the moment passed as he led his friend into the living room where he poured them both large glasses of Scotch while she turned and went back to the kitchen to put the flowers into a bowl which she then brought back and put in the centre of the dining room table before returning to fetch the pate which she knew was Richard's favourite and was to be the first course.

The two men continued to drink heavily, ignoring the wine that she had put on the side board to go with the meal in favour of continuing with the scotch. After some initial pleasantries from Alistair, they left her out of the conversation and talked in generalities throughout the meal, but somehow she got the feeling they were both waiting for something to happen.

They eventually rose from the table and the two men sat in armchairs finishing the bottle while she cleared the table, but when she came back into the room she sensed at once the atmosphere had changed.

Smiling, Richard said 'I was telling Alistair about that lingerie we bought last week.'

'I'd love to see it!' the other said pleasantly.

'With you in it, of course!' Richard added with a grin.

Bridgette looked from one to the other, then she said 'you're joking. of course'.

'Oh, I don't think so'. Richard said firmly.' I told him what a marvellous figure you have, and he's rather looking forward to seeing it. I'd hate you to disappoint him!'

After a second, Bridgette said 'I'm not taking my clothes off just to amuse your friends.!'

'Well it wasn't just that' Alistair put in. 'We thought we might play some games.!'

Richard laughed and nodded, but before either of the men said anything else Bridgette said 'You're both drunk! and turning on her heel made for the bed room and slammed the door, locking it behind her.

*

Mel contacted the family where Bridgette had worked as an au pair until she went to live with Richard Chambers. They were reluctant at first to be of any help but she eventually persuaded the mother to give the forwarding address they had been given, and she was relieved to find Peter was still at the address he had given his grandparents and left a message.

Richard was out, but Bridgette had just come back from taking the dog for her usual walk in the park when there was a knock on the door and she opened it to find Peter standing there. For a split second, he thought he must have the wrong address. The young women facing him was a ghost of the girl he had last seen when they said good bye to each other after her sister's wedding, but she forced a smile and held out her hand.

'Peter. What are you doing here?'

Still holding her hand, he stepped past her then, after a quick glance round, turned back to face her.

'Bridgette, what are you doing here? What is this place?

'It's where I live ... with Mr Chambers.'

'Mr Chambers?'

'It's what he likes me to call him now'.

Peter looked at her more closely.' What's he done to you? Has he hit you?

Bridgette hesitated before saying quietly 'Not much'

'Not much! What the hell's that supposed to mean?'

'As long as I do what he wants...with his friends'.

He stared at her as the meaning of her words sank in, and now he saw tears begin to roll down her face.

'Darling!'

He moved and took her into his arms as she began to cry in earnest.

'I feel so ashamed!' she sobbed.

Peter held her close until her weeping had subsided,. Then he held her away so they could look each other in the face.

'Why do you stay with him?'

The girl shook her head silently, then she managed 'I'm frightened of him. What he might do. He said if I tried to run away he'd follow me. He's killed someone already'.

Peter took a breath, then he said 'Come with me. Now. I'll look after you'.

Again Bridgette shook her head. 'I don't want you to risk your life for me'

Peter smiled in spite of himself. 'Is he really that dangerous?!'

'Don't underestimate him. He says he always gets what he wants, and I believe him.!'

Peter shook his head 'Not this time' He paused a moment longer then he said firmly 'Go and get your things together, If he comes back before we've gone, I'll have a word with him.'

But Bridgette still looked doubtful

'I can't go home, looking like this' she said eventually.

Peter said 'Don't worry, we'll find somewhere to stay until you feel better.'

'I've been such a fool!'.

'I'll look after you now. I love you Bridge...'

The front door suddenly opened and Richard Chambers came into the room. He paused looking from one to the other, then smiled at Peter.

'Well, it's taken you long enough! I suppose you've come to take her with you?'

Peter turned to Bridgette and said 'Do what I said. I'll deal with this'.

After a moment's hesitation, and another glance at Chambers, who was still smiling, the girl turned and disappeared into the bed room.

'Would you like a drink?' Chambers said, turning back to face Peter.

'A drink?

'Well, I'm just about ready for one'

Seeing the other's expression, he chuckled as he turned away and made for the side board.' Oh, don't worry, I'm not going to fight you for her!' He picked up the decanter and one of the glasses and poured himself a shot before replacing the glass stopper and turning back to face Peter.

'Cheers....or Sante, I believe you say.' He took a generous sip then went on.' Bridgette's really become a bit of a liability - besides, you're bigger than me.' He moved nearer to face Peter, still smiling. 'So I'll let her go with you for now.....but, one of these days, I might need a favour in return

CHAPTER EIGHTEEN

After the Vendange the focus moved from the Vineyard itself to the Winery where Stephane and Alim worked with the refrigeration plant and barrelling the fermented juice when it reached the point where it needed to rest until the following Spring at the earliest. The barrels from the previous year needed continual testing until the wine reached the optimum complexion for bottling.

Meanwhile Dale, with the help of Madeline, an ambitious young graduate from the Secretarial College at St Fleur, who lived locally with her parents, tried to deal with the ever increasing avalanche of bureaucratic requirements from both regional and national governments - and that was before the additional demands added to anyone seeking to export their products abroad, for whom were reserved the most convoluted Returns of all.

Being an American, Dale found it doubly infuriating. He read somewhere that in France, thirty per cent of the working population were civil servants - twice as many as back home, and he did not need much convincing when Madeline wrote asking for a job that he could well use the enthusiasm and local knowledge she would bring with her. Within three months, she had convinced him that the suggestions of Richard Chambers could not be fully implemented without a more up to date computer, and from then on, their relationship never looked back, and with Dale finding himself freed from most of what irked him most and with far more time to spend on the things that had drawn him into becoming a vigneron in the first place.

Madeline was not yet twenty. She was extremely shy with strangers and wore glasses, but she was a treasure and Dale wondered how he had ever managed before she arrived.

School started, but much to his twin brother Phillipe's disgust, Dale junior seemed to have lost their shared obsession with football, and while playing the required school games spent his free time now in the Winery with Alim and his father and talked about following in the latter's footsteps by going to the College of Viticulture at Montpellier University when he was old enough. Needless to say Stephane was delighted, but concern for the future, which had lain mostly dormant since Gus had been away resurfaced.

The two 'Dales' - Grandfather and Grandson - developed a strong bond and the younger liked nothing more than to walk with his Grandfather round the Estate when he had finished his home work if there was nothing for him to do in the winery and listen to the old man talk about how he used work on the Estate in California when he was about the same age before he went to the College which eventually sent him to France where he met his grandmother Holly. He promised that one day they would take a trip over there together.

If his grandfather was tied up in the office, Dale junior would often walk round the Estate by himself and dream of the day when he would be running it with Gus now his brother had set his heart on other things. He did not share his father's worries and was sure that he and Gus would work together fine - probably with him looking after the vineyard while Gus worked in the office to avoid the vines themselves. The only regret he had about that arrangement was that it would be Gus working with Madeline, who was not that older than he himself and for whom he had developed something of a crush. She had found him easier to talk to than most when they sat by the river sometimes eating their lunch together and he felt very privileged that she confided in him. He knew she had no boy friend and that surprised him.

He looked on the vines with special affection. They were living things. Most of the time they behaved themselves, but sometimes they sulked if they got too wet, and of course they got sick occasionally. In any event, it was up to those who loved them to see to their needs whatever their condition, and then, more often than not, they rewarded those who cared for them with a generous vendange.

In autumn, the skies were often clear and it was his favourite time of year. He would often pause just below the main house and gaze across to the Pic du Midi in the far distance, visible now with renewed clarity since the haze of summer had lifted Then he just felt so happy. He had only tried to share his feelings twice - with Madeline, who came and stood beside him once on her way from the office to look for his father, and earlier in the year, when a family had stayed with them for a week at Roussanne and who had included a girl his own age who had attached herself to him. He had eventually brought her up here to show her his view. But she had just looked at it for a few seconds blankly then asked if it wasn't time to go back for breakfast.

His disgust had known no bounds and had avoided her for the rest of her stay.

Madeline had not been like that. She might not be so pretty - although when she took her glasses off to go swimming - which she only did when it got really stifling in the office, not having yet persuaded his grandfather to put in air-conditioning - she didn't look at all bad, and he noticed other people looked at her differently. He did not have to explain how he felt to her. She had just stood quietly beside him, then reached out and squeezed his hand before continuing on her errand.

*

The Clinic in New York told Gus that he would be able to go home in a few weeks time- certainly in time for Christmas. Christine was delighted. They spoke on Skype frequently, which also allowed Lisa to see her father. But he told her that he had been advised to be careful not to overexpose himself to the treated vines for a while.

His relationship with his step-father had grown closer over the years and the way Alan had looked after him had deepened their friendship still further.

When Gus reported the Clinic's news, Alan could not have been more pleased. He himself had been in constant touch with Sara Cevante since his visit in the summer and he had willingly accepted her invitation to spend the holiday with her. They both knew the cliche that 'absence makes the heart grow fonder', but without saying anything, both had been aware that over the past months their continuing relationship had led each to look forward expectantly to an open declaration of their true feelings for each other. What better time than Christmas?

He and Gus agreed to travel again together, and as Gus was feeling so much better, Alan arranged several out of town trips including to Washington and Boston to show him his old stamping grounds. Hearing of this, a colleague invited them to travel down with him for a week end's fishing to his lakeside lodge in New Jersey - with the added attraction of travelling there in the seaplane which he kept on Long Island.

Gus had got to know Alan's mother well as she lived just round the corner and they too had formed a warm relationship, so both he and Alan were surprised when they went to spend an evening with her just before setting out on this last trip before leaving for Europe that the old lady was adamantly against their flying off in such a flimsy conveyance and it took some considerable assurance, and several glasses of white wine before her fears were soothed.

It was a crisp November day without a cloud in the sky when the plane took off for the short journey, and after passing over New York City, the pilot flew slightly out of his way to show them the sea of bright red and gold of a forest beneath which he explained was due to it being further South than New England and the trees holding their leaves longer. The plane landed without incident and taxied to a landing stage not far from the lodge itself and where the caretaker was waiting for them.

CHAPTER NINETEEN

The inquest held that the plane had been brought down on the return journey by a drone flying illegally into its flight path. The pilot had done his best to land but they were nowhere near water and the plane's floats caused it to somersault when it reached the ground. One of the passengers and the pilot himself were killed instantly but the other was thrown clear into some bushes bordering the field and emerged badly bruised and shaken but otherwise unharmed. The Coroner congratulated Alan on his good fortune and thanked him for the evidence he was able to give.

The owner of the drone was never traced and a story was eventually run in the Post that the collision had not been an accident, but refused to reveal the source of its information.

Alan knew he had to tell the family before they heard about it elsewhere, but he did not feel he could face Christine on Skype and telephoned Holly from the hospital.

Sara Cevante clung to Alan when he finally walked through Customs into the Arrivals Hall at Toulouse Airport two days later and they embraced with an enthusiasm which swept aside any remaining question regarding how they really felt for each other.

Gus's body was flow home, and the funeral took place in the church where he and Christine were married.

Christmas was a bleak affair with the adult members of the family making the best of it for the sake of Lisa and the boys. Mel and Stephane discussed cancelling the impending visitors to Rousanne but the Groots had booked two months earlier having rented out their own house for six months and they knew how much Eva was looking forward to seeing them and introducing them to Andre and to discussing the wedding which was planned to take place in Bruges in the Spring. Eva had already booked Christmas lunch for them all, including Andre's parents, at the Bridge Hotel, so they let the booking stand.

Apart from Jeaninne's mother and her family, only a few friends, including, Sara and Alan, Eva and Andre, stood on top of the hill above the town on Christmas Eve for the blessing of the memorial to Jeaninne. Although the sky was clear, there was a cold wind and as soon as the priest finished, those present walked back thankfully to the shelter of their cars, where after a few minutes only, they got in and drove away.

Only one figure who had stood apart from the others remained, and now Alim, oblivious of the cold, came forward to stand looking at the figure, which had been sculpted in bronze at a cost far in excess of anything Jeaninne's mother could have afforded, thanks to help from Sara.

It was of a young girl, sitting on a bench and gazing into the distance over the town to the mountains far to the South. She was dressed for summer and smiled despite the wind which blew the clouds towards her, their shadows racing up the hill and over her shoulder, but she never turned her head to follow their passage.

After standing motionless for several minutes, Alim reached out his hand to say goodbye. He felt he would never bring himself to come up here again - to be reminded of what he had lost, and he wept before turning away and walking back down the hill. After he had gone, the young girl continued to smile as she gazed into the distance and the clouds raced past her and away to... who knew where?

CHAPTER TWENTY

Christine found herself not only the owner of a forty percent interest in Poussin le Bas but a considerable fortune, being the money Gus had inherited from his mother. Perhaps, if she were ever to go to Veterinarian College, it would be now or never. Although she loved the vineyard founded by her great grandfather and where she had grown up, she had no wish to participate in its management, but she was far sighted enough to realise that if her son Billy ever wished to do so - or even Lisa - which she knew had been her husband's dream- she would have to make sure the Estate continued to prosper, and that meant making sure that whoever was responsible had an incentive to do so.

Working closely with Mel she guessed that the week end to visit the Chateau Coulett had been more than a week-end jaunt, and felt Mel's relief after she and Stephane returned. She never asked directly, but guessed the possibility of moving on had been considered, and although rejected on that occasion, might reoccur. Stephane was clearly vital for the smooth transition to the next generation - including his own sons, and she lay awake at night turning over the possibilities.

As it happened it was Alan Marsh who gave a hint of a possible solution. She had always liked Alan and they had become close during Gus's illness during which time he had got into the habit sitting out on the terrace with her over coffee after seeing Gus and being as supportive as possible, and this had continued after his death

Taking a break from writing his book, he sometimes went out with Sara to view properties which came onto the market, and she found his friendly and relaxed presence when he accompanied her with prospective clients - particularly those English speaking - a considerable asset. One day he mentioned to Christine after one such viewing with a retired Scottish couple they had taken to show a property just downstream from the Estate that he had suggested it might be possible to sell the house and vineyard separately. The house needed work but they had funds to manage that. What they did not want was the responsibility of the rundown four hectare vineyard attached

The day after, Peter phoned his grandparents, and Bridgette her mother, to let them know that they had gone together to work at a Ski Lodge in Switzerland and would be back in the Spring when they planned to get married.

*

The trial of Henri and his two accomplices was delayed by efforts to tie the abduction of Eva to the murder and rape of Jeaninne Berger, but despite the evidence she was able to give that they had boasted to her that they had 'roughed up' Jeaninne, they vehemently denied the same when questioned by the police, and even Eva had to admit that they had denied any hand in her murder, and that they had told her their main concern, when they had realised they had taken her by mistake in their plan to teach the Illegal's new 'Tart' a lesson, was that they would be blamed for the other as well, and it could not be denied that despite this, they had let her go.

In the end, as they had done her no physical harm and had held her for less than twelve hours, the Prosecution had to be content with a charge of unlawful detention, to which they pleaded guilty, and were given suspended sentences of three years.

Alim did not return to the bar, where the three were greeted as heroes who as had pulled a 'fast one' over the authorities. But the satisfaction of having done so did not last as long as their determination to keep an eye out for their original target.

CHAPTER TWENTY-ONE

Having made up her mind, Christine went to see Stephane and Mel and put a proposition. She would lend them the money to buy the unwanted vineyard which abutted the Estate. They could pay her back over a period.

'You can then sell it to The Estate in return for a thirty per cent interest in it and so end up an equal partner with me' she went on nodding, then paused to take a sip the coffee they were sharing and to let the idea sink in.

'Why would you do this' Mel said, being the first to recover.

'Or why don't you just sell me a thirty percent interest in the Estate?' Stephane added, hard on her heels.

Christine nodded again before she said.' Well, I thought about that, of course. But I've got all this money now and it seemed the best investment I could make would be to expand the Estate in such a way that it's future was secured for the foreseeable future.

'By making me an equal partner' Stephane said.

'Something like that' Christine replied seriously.

She then turned to Mel, who, before she could add anything said 'We weren't fooling anyone with that trip to Coulet, were we?'

Christine returned her smile.' Well, you didn't have to be a mind reader!'

'But what about you?' Stephane said.

'What about me?' Christine frowned, then her brow cleared 'Me... well I thought I could spend the rest getting myself an education. Then come back here and be Mel's junior partner.... if she'll have me, of course. They all looked at each other, then burst out laughing and Mel reached out to squeeze Christine's arm.

'I'm only sorry Marcus didn't live to see this'

'So am I' Stephane said nodding, then stood up. 'Or even our beloved founder Andrew'.

'But what about Holly and Dale Mel said suddenly serious.'

'They think it's a wonderful idea. Of course, I ran it past them first.'

'The three Musketeers! 'Stephane said. 'Perhaps we should drink to that. 'The two women also stood up smiling.

'I'll go and find something'. He turned on his heel and disappeared in the direction of the kitchen and Mel reached out to give Christine a hug.

'It's such a wonderful, generous idea darling' she said as they separated. 'Suddenly I can see everything so much more clearly.'

'You don't mind me going away for a while'

Mel shrugged dismissively 'We'll all miss you of course, but if Peter comes back we can manage.'

They sat down to wait for Stephane who they heard uncorking a bottle. Then Mel said 'Have you any idea where you want to go yet?'

Christine shook her head 'I thought you could help me with that. 'It's not straight forward of course, with the children. I can't just leave them during term time!'.

Mel nodded. 'Of course not. We'll think of something.'

'Christine said 'Everything depends on being able to buy the other vineyard. 'Mel nodded again and Christine added 'I've got an appointment to meet Sara Cevante tomorrow'.

'Has it got a name? The Vineyard I mean.'

'Les Hirrondelles. The Swallows.'

*

Christine duly arrived for her appointment only to be told by Sara that she was very sorry, but since they had last spoken another buyer had come forward and was bidding for the small estate.

'We've been in touch with our Scottish Clients, who are not unnaturally irritated by this development' she added apologetically. 'They're flying from Aberdeen this weekend to try and sort things out.' She then paused for a moment before continuing 'Perhaps, Christine, you could to meet them here and see if you could not put in a joint offer for both house and vineyard?'

'I suppose...' Christine began, but Sara continued 'Unfortunately, I won't be able to be here as Alan's mother has become unwell and I'm going to go with him. But Eva will see to everything. She's very competent' Sara assured her.

Assured or not, the meeting took place as soon as the Scottish Couple arrived. The mystery bidder was not present but a woman from an Agency in Les Fleur arrived just before the meeting was due to start and announced that she had been authorised to speak on his behalf.

The meeting did not last long as it soon became obvious that whatever the couple from Aberdeen, combined with what Christine agreed to contribute was going to be topped by the Agent and they had no choice but to concede defeat. Even then, the identity of the successful purchaser was not disclosed. It would become known when the conveyance was registered, but in the meantime the Agent insisted she was not at liberty to disclose anything.

The meeting broke up with the Scots expressing their extreme disappointment and blaming Eva for dragging them all this way for nothing. Unfair as this was, Eva could not help feeling sorry for them and promised to do whatever she could to find.....but they left without waiting to hear.

The Agent left after exchanging a few pleasantries with Eva and congratulating her on the sale. She then turned to find Christine had also slipped away and Eva began to lock up. She was sure Sara would be pleased with the commission they would earn - not that she really needed it, and apart from quite genuine feelings of regret on behalf of Mr and Mrs McGovern, she was sorry for Christine- although why she wanted to expand the Estate anymore was another mystery.

It was Mayer who burst into Mel's morning surgery on returning from shopping in town, a thing she would normally never dream of doing, but full of news that could not possibly wait. Having run most of the way back, she could scarcely speak.

'It's him' she gasped, holding on to the door to steady herself.

Mel looked up frowning in the middle of bandaging the paw of an injured poodle while her owner looked on.

'Who's him' she said sternly.' Can't you see...'

'The Englishman... the one Christine went ...' She stopped suddenly, aware of the way the dog's owner was staring at her, eyes bright with interest.

'The man from London' 'she ended lamely then took a deep breath and said to the woman 'I'm sorry, Madame, I should not have disturbed you.'

'No, no 'The other assured her.' Please go on'.

Mayer turned back to Mel and said 'He is the one who has bought Les Hirrondelles.'

'Richard Chambers?'

'Monsieur Chambers - from London'

'How do you know?'

'Eva told me. It's no secret now. She thought you should know!'

CHAPTER TWENTY-TWO

What Eva had not admitted to Mayer was her own astonishment when the Agent had walked into the office that morning smiling to introduce the new owner of Les Hirrondells and to collect the keys.

'Hello Eva. Nice to see you again'. Richard Chambers had smiled and held out his hand.

'What are you doing here?' The girl had managed, standing up but ignoring the outstretched hand.

'Mr Chambers is the new owner.'

'Or rather my company' Chambers explained, 'which explains your confusion! I hope you don't mind'

'Why should I mind?' Eva said recovering, but more loudly than she had intended

'Well, I do owe you an apology'.

'Oh...why is that?' Eva asked innocently.

'Well, you know, we were going to go out...'

'You mean when you kept me waiting half my day off without an explanation?!'

Chambers managed to show contrition he did not particularly feel.

'Yes, that! I really am sorry... I had to return to London...'

With a companion, I understand?'

They looked at each other for a moment before he said 'Oh dear! I really am in the dog house!'.

Eva stared at him frowning until his meaning dawned and she burst out laughing in spite of herself.

'The dog house! Yes, that is good!'

'I hope you will forgive me' Chambers said, smiling again. 'Perhaps you will let me make it up to you?'

But Eva shook her head firmly. 'There is no need for that'

'Perhaps we could have the keys?' the Agent interrupted with a touch of impatience, and after a moment Eva nodded and reached into her desk.

'Yes, of course'

'You can give them to Mr Chambers'

Eva did so, then he said 'As we shall be neighbours, I'm sure we shall see a lot of each other'

Eva nodded but did not return his smile.' I'm engaged to be married' she said pointedly, but Chambers nodded pleasantly.

'I'm delighted to hear it'.

'To Andre Farbre I think you've met him!'

Chambers frowned for a moment before his expression cleared.

'The policeman. Yes, of course I remember. Well, congratulations!'

'Thank you'.

'Did they ever find out who that Peter...whatever his name was, killed?'

'No'

'Before he could say anything else, the Agent looked at her watch and said 'We really must be going Monsieur, the Architect is waiting for us'

Chambers glanced at her and nodded before turning back to Eva.

'Well, it really was nice meeting you again Eva. I'm so glad you have forgiven me!' He held out his hand again and this time she took it while the Agent opened the door.

'It would be nice to meet your Fiancee again. Perhaps I could buy you both dinner sometime?'

Without waiting for an answer, he turned to follow his companion to the door, but just before he reached it, Eva said' I guess you are going to use the house as a holiday home?.'

Chambers turned back. 'it needs a lot doing to it' he said.

'What about the vineyard?'

'That too.'

'Would you be interested in selling it?'

He paused, then shook his head 'I haven't decided yet.' Then he grinned 'Maybe I'll take after my illustrious neighbours!'

He went out, closing the door behind him, leaving Eva staring after them through the office window as they walked to where a sports car was parked - got in, then drove away.

She turned and glanced down at the sales documents lying on her desk. She had done what she could for Christine. Perhaps he would come around. He really was the most unpredictable man. She was glad she wasn't tempted to get mixed up with him again. Even so, she had to admit to herself, he was even more attractive than she remembered. Why on earth did he want Les Hirrondelles? Suddenly she felt uneasy, and to break the mood went into the back office to make herself coffee!

*

Christine was not only disturbed to discover that a man she would rather forget was going to be a close neighbour, but unless he changed his mind, would frustrate her plan to buy the vineyard herself. She wondered, if she went to see him, she could persuade him to sell it to her. If he was still attracted to her he might, but how could she tell without walking into a situation from which she could easily find herself entangled with him again. He was that kind of man. She did not know how Bridgette had managed to extricate herself from him, but there was no Peter to help in her case.

Despite these fears, Christine finally came to the conclusion there was no alternative but to grasp the nettle. She knew he was staying at the Bridge Hotel but was spending most of the day at Les Hirrondelles with the Architect, and before she could change her mind, she drove round while Lisa was at pre-school with just Billy in the child seat.

It was not far downstream from the Estate and on the same side of the river. She was familiar with the house having borrowed the keys from Sara before she left for New York and had walked round the vineyard with her father. But when she arrived she found the entrance to the house blocked by several vehicles, which she saw did not include Richard's sports car, so she left her own out in the lane, which was a nuisance as Billy had fallen asleep, but she had no choice but to un-strap him and lift him out, which of course woke him up and started him crying.

Hearing the noise, a man in his thirties, dressed in working clothes came out to meet them, and after dropping into the English which she had unconsciously used when asking after the new owner, and introducing himself as Henry Withers, he told her he was sorry that Mr Chambers had returned to London leaving he and his partner to get on with the agreed alterations.

The partner was an older man who nodded briefly when introduced then disappeared back into the house. When the man she was talking to took off his cap, which he explained, with a chuckle, he only wore to stop his hair filling with dust, he revealed a mass of thick dark hair which he fluffed with his hand now to demonstrate its dust freeness and they both laughed. He then offered to take her into the house to see what they were doing, but although Billy had stopped crying, he was fractious and Christine said she had better take him back and give him his lunch. She paused for a moment, then said 'Are you English?'

The other nodded. 'Yes. But I've been working near here for three years. A friend of Mr Chambers in London gave him my address. Here, let me take him'.

Without warning, he reached forward and took Billy into his arms, who although surprised, accepted this development without a murmur and just stared up at the strange person who was smiling down at him.

Christine was amazed.' I've never seen him let a stranger do that before' she said 'Have you got children of your own?'.

Withers nodded, looking up for a moment, then he handed Billy back to her.

'Two - a boy and a girl - a bit older than your son. I don't see them anymore though.'

'Why is that?' Christine said, before she could stop herself. 'I'm sorry. It's none of my business!'

'That's OK.' He shrugged, suddenly serious.' We were divorced. Charlotte had already met someone else, and they got married as soon as they could'

'I'm sorry...'

'So was I.' He paused for a moment then went on 'He was a nice guy, and they made it easy for me to see the kids, although both found it upsetting - just seeing me for a short time, then having to say goodbye. But then they decided to emigrate to New Zealand - so that was that.'

Christine hesitated, then she said 'That sounds so sad!'

Withers shrugged again. 'It was. That's why I decided to come out here...give myself a new start'.

'Why here.?

'A friend of mine stayed with his girl friend at a B&B place, just up the river from here'

'Not Rousanne?!'

'A vet's place.

Christine laughed' That's my sister's place. I work there'

'Well. I'm damned!'

'They stood smiling at each other for several seconds, then Christine said 'Well, I'd better be taking this young man back. Do you know when Mr Chambers is coming back?'

'No. But you can phone him'

Christine looked doubtful, then she said 'No, I don't think I want to do that. But if you could let me know when he's back?'

'Of course. At the Vets?'

'Or at the Estate- Poussin le Bas. We live there with my parents'.

'OK.'

'My husband was killed in an accident last year. You'll find both numbers in the book'.

She drove away wondering why she had told him that.

It just seemed natural after what he had said about his own family.

CHAPTER TWENTY-THREE

After the early Spring pruning, Dale decided to make good his promise to his junior name sake to take a trip to California in the school Easter holidays. Twin brother Phillipe was also invited but was looking forward to the Easter Football competition and it was no contest!

To Dale's surprise, Holly admitted that she would also like to go with them if she would not be a gooseberry, and assured they would love her to come, she made arrangements for a locum at the Clinic and the day approached with mounting excitement when they left, leaving Christine in charge of the office, which she agreed would be good experience.

It might all have been a bit much except that Peter and Bridgette returned early from Switzerland, to be met with open arms by Mel, and they gladly accepted Christine's offer of a room in the main house until they found a place of their own.

Peter got down to work at once, taking the pressure off Mel, and with Easter came the first B&B visitors, three elderly couples from Munich who took the available guest rooms and began to explore the locality on foot carrying the lunch prepared by Bridgette in rucksacks and wearing stout hiking boots, which Mayer insisted they left in the racks in the entrance lobby on their return.

Bridgette was alarmed to hear that Richard Chambers had bought the small estate downstream but Christine assured he that he was evidently going to be away most of the time, and from her brief visit was confident he had taken on too much to bother anyone.

She was not the only one to worry about the new owner of Les Hirrondelles. Eva had not liked his attitude when he came into the office, but Andre laughed when she told him. Now he knew to whom she was engaged, she was the last person he was likely to bother! They were in the show flat looking round to see what extras they would need to buy for when they moved in after the wedding in only three weeks time when she told him, and he put his arms around her, which always made her feel safe the way nothing else ever could.

*

Christine continued to go to Rousanne as much as possible taking Lisa and Billy with her, but once her parents left for California she found herself having to spend an increasing amount of time in the office with Madeline and she soon realised what her father had meant by 'good experience!' This is what it would be like when he was no longer there, for whatever reason, and it set her thinking once more about the future - no matter what the outcome of her attempt to persuade Richard Chambers to sell he the disused vineyard attached to his new holiday home.

She only hoped that was what it was going to be - not that he was going to live there. So many people would look to her to carry the family business forward, and if she was honest with herself, how would it be possible to take herself off to Veterinarian College?!

She was in the office when Madeline took a call, then transferred it to the phone on her desk silently mouthing 'Hirrondelles!'

Christine's heart missed a beat as she picked up the receiver, but it was Henry Withers to tell her he had just taken a call from Monsieur Chambers who wanted a progress report but then, seemingly satisfied, told him he was returning to New York and probably would not be back for several weeks.

Christine felt a mixture of disappointment at not being able to put her proposal to him immediately and relief at not having to face him.

She did not say anything for several seconds, then heard him inquire cheerfully 'How is Billy?'

She pulled herself together and answered pleasantly 'He's fine'

'I never got to meet your little girl'

'Lisa'

'Lisa, yes.'

Christine smiled then, almost without a thinking, said the words that were to affect her for the rest of her life: 'Would you like to?'

He answered without hesitation 'Of course. It would be nice to meet again'.

She suddenly realised where this was going, but after a moment's hesitation, she said 'We're staying at the Estate while my parents are away. Perhaps you would like to come over one evening before I put them to bed?'.

Again, there was no hesitation on his part.

'I'd like that very much. I could come this evening if you like?'

Christine nodded and smiled again before she said 'I'll expect you about six then'.

When she put down the phone she glanced at Madeline who had pretended to be otherwise occupied until halfway through the conversation but was now looking at her quizzically.

'It was the builder I met when I went up to Les Hirrondells' Christine said in answer to her unspoken question.

'Is he nice?' Madeline said cutting to the point with the directness her boss had taken some time to get used to.

'Yes' Christine said with mock severity. 'And I'd appreciate it if you kept what you've just heard to yourself'.

The girl nodded as Christine added unnecessarily 'He has children of his own'. She paused, then added lamely: 'In New Zealand'

When he arrived, he had obviously changed into his best clothes, which made him look even bigger. She thought he was not bad looking, without being particularly handsome - just warm and....nice!

He seemed genuinely interested in the children and Lisa took to him at once - except she kept calling him 'Richard', which just amused him when her mother explained Richard Chambers was the only other strange man she had ever had anything to do with and probably thought it a generic term!

When he eventually went downstairs, Lisa having refused to settle unless he came up to say good night, Christine asked him to wait on the terrace while she tucked them in. When she appeared, it was with a tray and two glasses and an already opened bottle of Pousin le Bas Superior, and this they shared talking quietly and watching the sun sink below the hills which were a continuation Westward of the Pic du Midi to the South. In the course of this she explained why she wanted to see Richard Chambers and Henry admitted he had wondered what he was going to do with the land. His own family had been Vignerons for generations, but his father had wisely insisted that he went into some other profession as the family vineyard was no longer viable, and just before he had died he had accept the Government offer to pay a subsidy to vignerons who were only contributing to the over production of very ordinary wines, to plough up their vines and grow something else. He had already told Monsieur Chambers there was no way such a small vineyard could be made to pay. But, of course, as part of Pousin le Bas it would be a different matter. Even so, it would take a lot of hard work.

It started to get chilly and Christine stood up and said she had already laid out a cold supper in the dining room if he would like to come in and wait for just a few minutes while she reheated the soup they would have first.

He followed her into the house carrying the tray and now half empty bottle which he put on the sideboard in the dining room, but when he turned round, he saw she was standing just behind him, and it seemed the most natural thing in the world to take her into his arms.

She finally broke away, then taking him by the hand, led him back upstairs to her own bedroom where they undressed each other with mounting passion until she drew him on top of her onto the bed, gasping for a moment as he took possession of her, but a moment later her body instinctively joined the rhythmic thrusts that led them to a mutual and overpowering climax.

CHAPTER TWENTY-FOUR

Christine got into the habit of visiting Les Hirondelles, even though she knew its owner was still away and often took the children with her. She watched with fascination the development of the old farm house into a luxury five bedroom villa with a pool on the south side which she was invited to use and which she did more often as the weather became warmer. Then one day, when she arrived with her costume already on under a light summer dress and Lisa already changed, she saw the sports car at the entrance.

She was in two minds whether or not to turn round and drive back when Richard Chambers came out through the French Windows followed by Henry, who looked a bit sheepish.

She wound down the window as they approached but did not get out of the car and waited for him to reach them.

'Chrissie. How lovely to see you' Chambers said smiling, then bent down and peered in the back

'And who do we have here?'

Billy frowned at the stranger through the window and Lisa looked confused as he said 'Hello Lisa. Don't you remember me?' He then straightened up still smiling.

'Aren't you going to get out of the car? I thought you wanted to speak to me. Or have you just come for a swim?'

He opened her door leaving her little choice but to do so.

'Hello Richard.' She held out her hand but he leant forward and kissed her on both cheeks.' Yes, I do want to talk to you'.

'Well, here I am. Unless you'd rather have a swim first.? 'Christine shook her head glancing for a moment at Henry who was standing close by.

'No?. Oh well, pity!. I'm sure we should all have enjoyed that!' He also glanced briefly at Henry with a grin.' Never mind. What do you want to ask me? Would you rather go inside?'

'I wanted to ask what you intend to do with the vineyard?'

Chambers paused for a moment nodding, then he said' I thought you might'

Henry said 'It's not worth much to anyone else'

The other looked at him again with some irritation. 'That's for me to decide 'he said thinly. Then turned to face Christine again resuming his smile.

'To be honest, I have not made up mind yet. A sculptured garden leading down to the river might be nice. Or just a paddock for a couple of horses.'

Christine could not help herself snorting in derision.

'Horses! You've never been on a horse in your life!'

Chambers grinned. 'That's true' he admitted.' But I could have visitors, and either would increase the resale value'. Christine looked back at him impatiently, but before she said anything he went on 'Look. I'm not going to make up my mind here and now. I've yet to hear your offer.'

Christine opened her mouth, but again, before she could speak he said 'I've only just got here, and I'd like to go round the house with Mr Withers before anything else - then go back to the hotel to take a shower and have a rest. Why don't you join me for dinner there at - say, seven thirty, and we can go into the whole thing?'

Again, she glanced at Henry, and seeing him nod almost imperceptibly, turned back and nodded herself.

'Alright then. Seven-thirty.

So saying, she got back into the car without looking at either of them again; started the engine, and drove away, leaving both men looking after her.

'She's a remarkable young woman!' Chambers said, turning to the man beside him.

Henry did not answer, and after a few seconds, Chambers nodded and they started to walk back towards the house.

*

Christine had no intention of trying to impress her host, but the prettiest girl in her class had grown into a remarkably beautiful young woman, and although dressing deliberately low key for the meeting, her simple deep blue summer dress, slim figure and with her russet coloured hair piled on top of her head, she started to turn heads the minute she got out of the car and walked across the park and into the hotel lobby where Richard Chambers was waiting for her.

Despite her fears to the contrary, it was a remarkably pleasant evening. The food was excellent and he had chosen a wine - not of the Region, but which blended seamlessly with their meal. He spoke amusingly of some of the difficulties he had had in obtaining planning permission to make the alterations to the house and was very complimentary about Henry. He showed genuine interest in the developments at Rousanne and expressed real sympathy for the loss of Gus.

Christine became progressively more relaxed as the evening wore on, but remained determined that he should be the one to raise the real purpose of their meeting, and finally he picked up the bottle to top up their glasses - until she put a hand over the top of hers - and said 'Well, I guess we haven't got round to this land you want to buy off me!'

Christine nodded but still did not say anything and he continued 'For a start, what I propose is this, that we get a valuer in to set a price for the land as it is at present, then, bearing in mind my alternative plans, ask how much the value of the house would increase with - let's say - the establishment of a garden, and take the higher of the two sums'.

Christine said 'Well, I would need to see what that came to. I might not be able to afford...'

'Wait 'Chambers interrupted, there's more.' He picked up the wine bottle and seeing it almost empty, raised it in the direction of their waiter, who took the hint and hurried away to get another.

'I really don't want any more Richard' Christine protested, but he just smiled.

''Wait until you hear the conditions' he said mysteriously.

'What conditions?' Christine said bluntly., and Chambers held up his hand soothingly, but had to wait while the waiter returned, and after he had the go ahead, filled their glasses.

'What conditions? 'she repeated as soon as he had gone.

'Here's to us'. He raised his glass. 'If you will become my wife, I will give you the vineyard as a wedding present'.

Christine's jaw dropped momentarily before she said dismissively 'That's impossible!'

Chambers shrugged after a moment then he said 'Well, not unexpected, but I'm sorry to hear that. There is an alternative' He paused for a moment then said quietly, 'If you will spend a night with me here - I don't mean tonight, but before I have to go back to London, I will sell you the land at the agent's valuation of it in its present condition. Just think about it'.

Christine stared at him for quite a while before she said 'and if I don't do either?'

Chambers shrugged again. 'Then I hope we will remain friends, but I will not be selling the land. I don't really want to anyway' He raised his glass again and took a sip. Christine continued to stare at him for a long time before she said 'So there is no misunderstanding, when you say spend the night with you, you mean you want to fuck me?'.

He nodded. 'Oh yes, several times. I have good stamina- and who know, you might be so impressed, you want change your mind about the other as well. I could give you the testimonies of quite a few women who would jump at what I am offering you!'

Christine stood up pushing the table away from her.

'Leaving?' Chambers said mildly 'What about coffee?'

'Just let me go'.

Chambers stood up 'I'll walk you to your car.

'Don't bother'

Despite her protests, he followed her out of the lobby and across the car park to the car.

As she unlocked it he said 'Think about it Christine. Either choice is open.'

She opened the car door and got in without answering, but he held it firmly, preventing her slamming it shut.

'I would far prefer we got married. And all the things I promised you before you ran away will also be yours too.'

'Let go of the door'

'Will you think about it and let me know?'.

'I'll think about it. Now let go!'

He did so and stood back, watching as she drove away.

When Christine got home, her mind was in turmoil and she lay awake agonising over what he had said. Just as it was starting to get light and long before the children were awake she got up, dressed, and went into the office to deal with two orders that could not wait. Then she went into the kitchen and made herself some coffee before going back into the office to wait until she could make the first of the three phone calls. Now she knew what she had to do.

Mel was happy to let Mayer come over as soon as she arrived to look after the children. Her second call was to Henry Withers, who was just getting ready to go to work, but was delighted to hear from her until he heard her say 'I'm sorry to ring you so early Henry, but I have to go out soon and I needed to catch you first.'

She cut through what he was going to say.

'I can't be your girl friend anymore Henry.....no wait, it's nothing you have done. But I have become involved with someone else. I can't tell you who, he doesn't know what I have decided yet himself, but he wants me and it's something I have to do for the family as well as myself.' Christine swallowed, determined not to cry, then went on 'I'm so sorry. I can't explain any more at the moment. No, don't come over here. I'm going out. I don't know when I will be back. Good bye Henry.'

She put down the phone, then went into the kitchen to wipe away the tears that were starting down her face against her will, and when she had got a grip on herself, she went back into the office again and made her last call.

Hotel Reception put it through to Richard Chambers' bedroom as he had not yet come downstairs. After he had picked up the receiver, he sat on the edge of the bed.

'Hello?.

'Richard, I have to see you'

'Chrissie! That sounds promising! Do you want me to come over?'

'No. Its better I come to you'

'When do you want to come?'

'Now. Or as soon as Meyer comes over to look after the children' She paused for a moment, then she said 'I've decided to do what you want. It can't wait, or I will lose my nerve'.

He needed several seconds before he said 'Well, it's a bit early, but I'm willing if you are. I'll tell the maid to leave the room for the moment.'

'I'll tell you what I have in mind over breakfast'.

It wasn't often he was at a loss for words, but before he could say anything the line went dead and he was left wondering what on earth she meant.

He finished dressing, and true to her word, an hour later Christine arrived, parked the car and walked into the lobby wearing smart jeans and jacket and with her favourite day time bag slung over her shoulder, to where he was waiting. Despite the simplicity of her turn out, as he rose to greet her, he knew again she was the most beautiful girl he had ever known and that no one else would ever be good enough. If she would only be his for a few hours, he wondered momentarily, would he be making a terrible mistake in creating a memory he would look back on with a longing for the rest of his life?

They greeted each other with the usual peck on either cheek, then he took her arm and steered her out onto the terrace overlooking the river where breakfast was being served and she slipped on sun glasses and smiled as he helped her into a seat at one of the vacant tables before taking the one opposite.

A waiter came forward immediately and took their order. When he had gone Richard said 'This is a bit of a surprise - not that I'm complaining'.

'I've been doing a lot of thinking.

The waiter came back and poured coffee, and Christine waited until he was out of earshot. Then she said simply 'I've decided to marry you. That is, of course if you meant what you said last night?'

Richard spilt coffee into his saucer as he got to his feet and came round to take her hands.

'Darling! That's wonderful!' He kissed her smiling upturned face' What a wonderful surprise!'

'You'd rather that than a quickie upstairs!? Her smile turned into a cheeky grin and he immediately looked contrite.

'I'm ashamed I suggested such a thing!'

'Well, you did give me the other option first!'.

He bent forward and kissed her again.

'Something to tell our grandchildren perhaps?' she added remorselessly.

'Please. Don't!'.

They both laughed and he resumed his seat while still holding one of her hands until she deliberately withdrew it and looked more serious.

''You'd better hear a few conditions of my own'.

Seemingly untroubled, he nodded as he took some paper napkins from the holder and put them into his saucer to soak up the coffee, gesturing with his other hand for her to continue.

Christine said 'I want a Prenuptial Agreement'

Richard paused for a moment, then he said 'Fire away!' -knowing he would agree to almost anything.

She bent down to retrieve the bag resting beside her chair, opened it and took out a small note book which she flipped open and glanced at before looking up while putting the bag back to where it had been resting.

'Well, to start with, you said last night that you would give me the vineyard attached to Les Hirondelles, but I don't feel comfortable about that.

'Why ever not?'

'Because it concerns my family's business. It's not personal, and want to buy it off you at valuation as I originally offered'

Richard smiled. 'OK, if it'll make you happy. What about the house?'

Christine paused for a moment, then she said 'You can give me a half interest in that as a wedding present, and I'll live in it with you. But I won't go and live in London. When Dad retires, I will have to take over the office until the boys are old enough. Stephane is a partner, but his real interest is in running the vineyard itself - and the winery of course - and with the extra land, he will have his work cut out. In the meantime I will go on working for Mel.'

'What about going to college and getting a proper qualification as a vet?'

Christine nodded, but did not answer for a moment then smiled ruefully 'It was just a dream!'

'It was more than that, surely?' Richard protested, but Christine shook her head.

'Perhaps. But I've decided to pay for Peter instead'.

'The guy who was supposed to have murdered me!'Richard said in amazement.

'He thought he was protecting me from you!'

Richard suddenly grinned.'

'Well, perhaps I'll feel safer with him out of the way!' He paused for a moment, then he said' 'Is that all - regarding the Agreement, I mean?.

Chtristine glanced down again, then she looked up and nodded, snapping the note book shut.

'Except we agree that, in the event of a divorce, neither of us will have any right to, or legal interest in the property of the other. Apart from the house, you have no right to anything I own here, and I have no right to anything of yours in London ... America... where ever'

Richard looked solemn for a moment, then he said 'It all sounds a bit cold and clinical!'

Christine nodded. 'I know. But I'll try and make you a good wife Richard, and hope it's all unnecessary'.

Almost on cue, they suddenly reached across the table and joined hands.

'And I'll try and make you a good husband, he promised.' But if you want to go on living here, I will have to be away quite a lot.'

'I understand. And the children and I will be waiting for you when you get back'

'I do love you Chrissie!'

'I know' She suppressed a grin. 'And I'll look forward to your promised performance in bed!'.

The waiter arrived just to catch the tail end of this as he put their orders in front of them and had to make an effort not to rattle the plates.

When he had gone, they both chuckled and picked up a croissante each.

'What about children?' Richard said happily, and Christine shrugged.

'Well, we'll have to see who comes along!'

They both laughed, and again reached across the table to join hands for a moment.

*

When Dale and Holly returned from their visit to California with their grandson, Dale junior lost no time in boasting at school about the wonders of the Sunshine State and how they had been welcomed, not only in the Nappa Valley, with vineyards the size of their whole region but at the University at UC Davis where his Grandfather was remembered as a pioneer. He taunted his twin brother Phillipe for missing out on the trip, but the other shrugged this off, reminding Dale of the matches he had missed and the visit with Stephane to see his uncle Andrew representing Clermont.

But the one Dale really wanted to impress was Madeline who listened to him as always with patience and affection. She secretly wondered when he would grow out of his crush on her and knew she would be sad when he was ready to transfer his feelings to a girl his own age.

For their part, the news broken over supper on their first evening home that Chrissie was to marry the Englishman who had caused so much alarm was hard to swallow. Knowing this, their daughter spared them any more complications - there would be time enough to tell them about Les Hirrondelles - and having spent a restless night, they both told her in the morning they were sorry not to have seemed very enthusiastic when she first told them.

She put her arms round both of them and assured them that Richard loved her and that Lisa was very fond of him - despite, she admitted to herself - her continued confusion with Henry. They planned a very simple wedding at the Marie to be conducted by the Mayor, Maurice Henderson, after Richard's Easter visit to New York, to which only the family and closest friends would be invited.

*

Christine did not visit Les Hirrondelles again until it was completed and Henry Withers had left. She tried not to think about him, but it was unlikely she would ever see him again.

True to his word, Richard Chambers sold the old vineyard to her - or rather to Stephane with the aid of a loan from Christine, which he in turn exchanged for a thirty per cent interest in Pousin les Bas, giving him a share equal to Holly and Christine herself.

Whenever they could spare the time, Stephane, Dale and Alim went across and started to clear the long neglected vines at Les Hirrondelles and prepare the soil for planting the Rousanne cuttings taken during winter pruning and potted to protect them until the Spring.

As soon as the ground was prepared, the Geometric was sent for who ran wires across the vacant space and put stakes at intervals along them to support the newly planted cuttings when the time was right. Alim questioned the need to spend money on an 'expert' to do this seemingly easy task and Stephane explained that to be able to look down the new rows and see straight lines from any angle was not only necessary to be able to use the mechanical picker but a requirement for any vigneron who wanted to be taken seriously, and was a special skill handed down through the artisan's family from one generation to the next.

Christine spoke to Mel about her idea to send Peter to College at the beginning of the academic year in September. Although surprised, Mel gave it her blessing after Christine explained the impossibility of going herself in the new circumstances, after which they agreed they would certainly need to get in more help. But when she spoke to Peter himself, although both surprised and delighted, he expressed doubts about leaving Bridgette for weeks at a time, particularly as Richard Chambers had bought the neighbouring property. But Christine pointed out that the forthcoming marriage changed the whole situation, and there would be few occasions when her future husband and Bridgette were likely to see each other.

It came as a shock to Christine when she visited her future home while Richard was away, to discuss kitchen fittings with a plumber, to see Henry Withers in the distance down by the river working alongside Alim, and lost no time, as soon as the fitter had gone, in going down to see what he was doing there.

Both straightened up and smiled when they saw her approach, and after greeting Alim turned to Henry. But before she could say anything, he intervened to explain that, as she knew, he came from a family of Vignerons so often took work in vineyards when in need of a job.

He looked at her with wide eyed innocence.

Alim said 'Stephane got to know Henry when he was working up at the house, and when he knew he was available after it was finished, asked him to give us a hand'.

'I hope you don't mind?' Henry added, with a smile that could have meant anything.

Christine took a breath, then shook her head and turned to walk back up the slope without a word.

Alim looked puzzled.

'Do you know her?' he asked.

'I was working on the house'.

'Yes, of course.' He paused for a moment, then he said 'She didn't seem very pleased'.

Henry nodded. 'No, she didn't. I can't think why'.

Alim scratched his head. 'Perhaps she doesn't think the boss should have taken on anyone else?' he said.

Henry nodded. 'Yes, I expect that's it! Well, that's his problem!'

They both chuckled and Alim said 'She is a very strong lady'.

'Yes, she is.' Henry paused for a moment, then added 'But very pretty!'

Alim nodded. 'Yes, she is that too!'

They both laughed again, then Alim turned back to pick up another cutting. But Henry watched Christine walking away and his smile faded, to be replaced by an enigmatic expression that could have meant anything except amusement.

CHAPTER TWENTY-FIVE

Christine and Richard Chambers were married when he returned from New York and moved into Les Hirrodelles.

Not wanting to disappoint Andre's family and her many new friends and business acquaintances, Eva persuaded her parents to agree to her own marriage to Andre being moved to Les des Demoiselles and Saint Peter's Church was packed.

Sitting among the congregation was the other newly married couple together with the children and Christine's family. Inspector Goudon, sitting a few rows back with his wife, noted the apparent absence of any guests associated with her new husband. He knew Chamber's father was supposed to be dead - but what of the mother?

One thing he hated more than any other was to have a case just peter out. What was the identity of the man killed by Peter Goyot, and who was the man who had arrived claiming to be Chamber's father, never to be seen again?

It was none of his business whom the Mori girl chose to marry after the death of her husband, but he couldn't help wondering about that too.

*

It was not long after they moved into the house that Christine noticed her new husband was spending an increasing amount of time away, but at the suggestion of Holly, who had started to worry that her daughter was taking on far too much, she took on Marie, a friend of Bridgette's mother, recently widowed, as a house keeper, and her invariably cheerful presence each day made a great difference. For her part, Marie had no children of her own, and in addition to taking over most of the responsibility for running the house, she looked forward each morning to escaping from the loneliness of her own life to become part of a family, and was delighted that Christine encouraged the children to call her Ma Tante, and sometimes Auntie, if their mother had been speaking to them in English, which she made a point of doing fairly regularly

Richard's initial ardour had evidently cooled - which was not unwelcome- but he also became increasingly distant when he did come home and she guessed that having been frustrated in his obsession with her for so long, she could not hope to live up to his expectations, and that his previous feelings had been replaced by indifference, almost like a child tiring of a new toy. He remained seemingly fond of the children at first, but when she showed no sign of giving him a child of his own, took progressively less interest in them too, and his place was largely taken by Marie.

Unbeknown to her husband, Christine made sure that she did not fall pregnant. She was not in love with him, but tried to keep her side of their bargain. It would have been easier if she did not love someone else and had to see him most days while maintaining a front of casual friendship.

Loyalty was not the only reason she was careful: Christine suspected that although her husband's feelings for her had cooled, she was afraid what he might do if he suspected she had transferred her affections elsewhere. It was one thing to tire of something he regarded as his - quite another to allow anyone else to take it from him. After they had been married for only a short time, and while he was still willing to give her almost anything she asked, she detected in him the existence of an inner self which he was incapable of revealing to her, even if he had wanted to - someone, or even something, who's nature she could not imagine, but feared if she thought about it.

Christine was not the only one somebody worried about: with the absence of Peter, and with the attention of her sister increasingly demanded elsewhere, Stephane noticed that Mel was almost too exhausted to eat at the end of the day, and finally he sat her down after another evening of picking at her food and insisted that she sought more help. The practice was expanding, which was part of the problem, but it could well afford to pay someone else and he suggested that while she was looking, she considered taking on a newly qualified Vet as a junior partner. He knew she had Peter in mind, but he would not be available for at least another four years.

CHAPTER TWENTY-SIX

Tom Field was born in Painswick, in Gloucestershire, a village high in the English Cotswolds overlooking the plain of Evesham. His father was a small dairy farmer and his mother ran the local Post Office until it was closed as a 'cost saving' measure by those who considered such things far more important than that from then on, anyone who needed to draw their state pension, no matter how frail, had to take the long and tiring bus journey into Cheltenham, the nearest town, to stand in a line, instead of the immediate attention - and chat if things were not too busy - they were used to.

Tom was the youngest of four children and the only boy, so was spoilt by his three elder sisters who took after their mother in being very kind as well as tall and willowy but, unfortunately, not in her good looks, favouring instead their father, who although also a kindly man, was six inches shorter than his wife and of unexceptional appearance.

Tom, on the other hand, took his father's stature but was remarkably good looking, his almost feminine features as a child evolving into boyish good looks that soon earned him the attention of the girls when it was time for him to go to school and the envy and even hatred of some of his male contemporaries. But although small, and of a generally friendly nature, he was exceptionally strong for his size and after one or two incidents, they learned to leave him well alone. He also proved an able centre forward when introduced to soccer which won over most of the rest of his male contemporaries, except for the few who hated him all the more.

Tom loved the place he grew up in and helped his father whenever he could with the small herd of Gloucester cattle, learning how to milk by hand as well as using the machine, and never minded getting up in the dark in the winter before school to help put out the churns by the roadside ready for collection by the dairy. Squatting on a stool and resting his head against the warm side of a cow while he milked her if there was a problem with the machine was the most comforting thing he knew, and they always stood quietly and never gave any trouble when it was Tom. And of course, the arrival of a new calf was the most exciting of all, and sometimes, depending on his school work, he was allowed to stay in the barn overnight with his father in a sleeping bag on the straw when a delivery was imminent.

Despite their rather plain looks, his two younger sisters found husbands and settled down - 'though not too far away - but leaving Marjorie, the eldest to take increasing responsibility for running the home as their mother's increasing arthritis became more acute.

It would have been the most natural thing in the world to expect Tom to take over the Farm eventually, and that was certainly his ambition, but his father could see which way the wind was blowing with small farms becoming progressively less profitable and advised his son to look for something else.

Tom eventually moved to the Secondary school in Cheltenham and did sufficiently well at A Level Exams to gain a place at the nearby Agricultural College.

But by the time he had been there a year, he realised that the world of the scientific care of animals rather than farming was where he really wanted to be, and after a long talk with his tutor, the other recommended that he applied for a place at the Royal Veterinarian College in London.

It was only after he had graduated that a friend asked if he would be interested in working abroad. The friend came from a town in Dorset called Exton where he already had a job, but it was Twinned with a town in France not dissimilar called Les deux Demoiselles and he had heard on the grapevine that the local Vet practice there was looking for a junior partner.

Tom decided to drive to the interview. The trip would help blow away the accumulated cobwebs of five year's study and help to clear his mind. He had only been abroad once before and that was on a school exchange to Germany but only one thing was worrying him: Although his initial enquiries had been promising, he wondered how he would manage as he didn't speak a word of French. But his father had encouraged him: Cattle and sheep were the same all over the world and he would soon pick it up. His potential boss had spoken perfect English over the phone.

He finally drove into the town square of Les Deux Demoiselles and was promptly ticked off by a traffic warden for parking in the Mayor's reserved place. But having done his duty, when Tom showed him the paper on which he had written the address of Rousanne as Mel had dictated it to him over the phone, he became positively affable and told him to go back to the Pont...et de la, a gauche where he would discover Madame Meuse who was expecting him - Tom's first experience that in Les Deux Demoiselles, as in Painswick, there were few secrets!

Mayer opened the door to a short, extremely good looking young man and realised who he was immediately.

'Madame Meuse has been called out but has left instructions that he was to be shown to the room where he was to stay'.

Mel had read the detailed CV Tom had e-mailed to her, and the College had spoken highly of him, so the 'interview' would consist of him coming out with her on her rounds for the next two days which would not only enable her to assess at first hand his ability but also how they would get on together, which was equally important.

On the third evening, they sat in her office after the last visiting patient had been dealt with and discussed the situation. For her part, Mel had been impressed, not only with his skill and gentleness in dealing with the animals they had been called to attend to, but also his remarkable strength, needed from time to time in controlling those who refused at first to cooperate and who could at times be positively dangerous. She had decided before they sat down to offer him the position and hoped he would accept, but there were points of detail they needed to discuss. He was brilliant with farm animals but had less experience in dealing with domestic pets and it had to be faced that they were an important if smaller part of the Practice. And what about the language?

Without actually eavesdropping - or not much - Mayer caught snippets of conversation through the door of Mel's office as she went about the business of preparing a meal for the B&B visitors and smiled when they heard the two of them laughing together. There was no doubt in both their minds that the addition of a handsome young English Vet would be a welcome addition to the household, and when finally the door opened and the two of them came out smiling to join Stephane, who was waiting for them in the living room with an already opened bottle of champagne, both young women nodded to each other happily.

Mel told her husband that Tom had agreed to join them. He would mainly concentrate on Farm visits leaving Mel herself to chose when she wanted to go with him or stay and help Christine with the Surgery as demand required. Tom had also suggested that he could take an internet course in French Lessons designed so that he could listen to recordings as he drove around in the car.

Stephane was delighted and turned to pour the champagne before proposing a toast.

It was agreed that Tom would start in a month's time, and he drove home the following day to break the news to his family without meeting Christine.

Tom settled in comfortably. Mel and Stephane offered him a room at Rousanne on a B&B basis until such time as he chose to make other arrangements, which he was happy to accept, and after only a few weeks, it seemed as if he had always been part of the 'team' and the farming clients were sufficiently impressed with his ability, the occasional misunderstandings as a result of his still rudimentary French were good naturedly laughed off.

Christine liked him immediately. His presence came as a considerable relief, enabling her, as it did, to spend more time in the Estate office with Madeline and cease to feel guilty about the strain her encouragement of Peter to go to Collage had put on Mel.

She and Mayer often teased him about his French but he never seemed to mind and without realising it, the banter was just what he needed in addition to his regular lessons with Madame Ganz, one of the Twins' schoolteachers, to get the feel of how the locals actually spoke.

Phillipe soon discovered Tom's interest in soccer and it was not long before he persuaded him to take him over to Clermont to watch his Uncle Andrew play. One thing led to another and soon Tom was turning out most Saturdays for the local amateur team, and this in turn, led to an incident which could not have been further from his mind, but caused some who were still in two minds at the arrival of yet another 'English' to view him in a new light:

Andrew, now in the team as a regular, was playing away in the European Cup for the first time against the English team Tottenham Hotspur. None of the TVs in Rousanne or at Poussin le Bas had a channel which covered the match and Phillipe was in a frenzy of frustration until Alim mentioned that the bar in town where he used to work had such a channel. It would be necessary to ask the owner if he would mind if Phillipe came to watch, and of course he would have to have an adult with him. On balance, much as he would have liked to have seen the match himself, Alim did not think it a good idea for it to be him, but he would be happy to make the call if someone else was available.

Like it or not, Tom never had a chance, so at five o'clock he and Phillipe duly presented themselves at the bar and sat down with fifteen others.

It might have been different if Clermont had made a better job of it; but when they were down three Nil at half time, the frustration of many began to show itself with disparaging remarks about the home team, and knowing who Phillipe was, Andrew in particularly, until Tom told them all to shut up, which revealed his nationality to those who did not know it already. Tempers then frayed to the point where Tom reluctantly decided he had better take the boy outside - which he did, to the approving jeers of some of the locals. And although Phillipe was bitterly disappointed and in tears as they stood on the pavement outside, that would have been the end of the matter. But as Tom paused. trying to think what he could do to make the boy feel any better, the door suddenly burst open and two men who must have been at the back of the Bar as he did not recognise either, followed them out and started to shout and push Tom in the chest; both were at least ten inches taller.

He didn't hit either, but a moment later picked up the more aggressive as easily as a half grown bullock, and after looking round for a second, tossed him into an old horse trough by the side of the road which was still full of water.

Phillipe stopped crying and yelped with amazed delight - which solved one of Tom's concerns, and when he turned he saw the other one had thought better of it and hurried back inside.

The incident quickly did the rounds. Neither of those who had attacked Tom were much liked and the owner of the Bar went out of his way to dissociate himself from them. Tom himself was not particularly pleased by what had happened and did not mention it to anyone, but Philliope made sure everyone at Rousanne and at school heard about it - exaggerating his own part in the event of course.

CHAPTER TWENTY-SEVEN

'Who is this buffoon who is throwing his weight around?' Richard Chambers demanded as soon as he heard about it.

Christine tried to explain what had happened and who the new arrival was, but her obvious admiration of Mel's new assistant immediately aroused his suspicions. He had already become convinced that his wife was seeing someone while he was away. He had never directly challenged her about this, but her stout defence of Tom Field was all one of his nature needed to confirm his suspicions and he deliberated what he should do to protect his 'property'. A direct attack on this intruder into his affairs was considered but dismissed as too dangerous: He was well aware that the Police Inspector who had interrogated him about the corpse that was unearthed down by the river next door still viewed him with suspicion. His wife's lover was also evidently a violent man, so some other remedy was called for.

Christine sensed the further deterioration in her husband's attitude towards her. It was true she was in love with Henry, but although she knew he loved her too, she had stayed loyal to Richard since their marriage and she thought there was no way Richard could know of the longing she felt every time their paths crossed. Not in her wildest dreams did it occur to her that her husband's paranoia had led him to suspect Tom Field

Finally, she decided she could not stand his behaviour any longer, and after confessing her unhappiness to her parents and getting their reluctant approval, she asked for a divorce. Their Prenuptial Agreement covered everything but the house and she informed Richard she was quite happy to sign over her interest in that to him and move back to the Estate for the time being.

This came as a bombshell, and her husband kicked himself for not having pursued the idea of recovering the house in this way himself, having assumed that any Divorce Court would award the matrimonial home to his wife unless he was prepared to offer some considerable financial compensation, and the thought of that had stuck in his throat. To get it back so easily was a revelation and he agreed at once.

Christine and the children moved back to Poussin le Bas taking Marie with them and Richard Chambers refurnished the house as he had originally intended as a holiday home.

For most people such an outcome would have been enough, but Richard Chambers was not most people. and although it was not now at the top of his agenda, some suitable retribution would have to be found for the one who had dared to presume to take what was not his.

The children continued to call Henry 'Richard' and Christine presumed that after a decent interval there was nothing now to stop them coming together. She was happy to wait for him to make the first move and had fantasies of the scene when they would fall into each other's arms and live happily ever after. She knew she was being absurdly romantic entertaining such thoughts, but one day he came to into the office, and after asking Madeline to give them a few minutes, closed the door behind her.

Christine stood up and came round from behind her desk, eyes shining.

'This is a nice surprise' she began, but there was something in his expression that stopped her in her tracks

'What is it?' she said after a few seconds. 'What's wrong?' She took a step towards him.' Tell me for God's sake. Stop looking at me like that!'

'I'm going to New Zealand' he said at last. 'I don't know for how long, or whether I'll be coming back'.

'New Zealand! she gasped 'But why? I thought we loved each other'.

'We do'

'Then why are you going back to your wife? Just when...'

'I'm not going back to Janice, Christine. She's been killed in a car crash'

'Oh my God!!'

Christine slumped against the corner of the desk and might have fallen if Henry had not reached out then and pulled her into his arms.

'I'm so sorry' he whispered. 'The children were hurt too, but not so badly. I've got to go to them' Christine looked up at him at once, her expression flooding with relief.

'Then you will be back? Please say you will' But Henry shook his head.

'I really don't know' he said.' I don't know how badly they are injured - or what else I'm going to find'

'I'll wait' Christine insisted forcefully. 'As long as it takes. Just come back. We'll look after them here.'

*

At last Stephane reported the first grapes were ready to be gathered at Les Hirrondelles - by hand, as the vines were still too small for the machine.

It was also the twentieth anniversary of the appointment of Maurice Henderson as Mayor of Les deux Demoiselles - only one of very few Englishmen to be so honoured in France, and his wife Ester suggested they should make a special effort to ask the members of the Twinning association of Exton, their Twin Town in Dorset in the South of England, to come over for a joint celebration; not only of that, but also to participate in the first vendage of the new vineyard.

Having lost contact with the Spanish pickers, Stephane and Dale were grateful for anyone able to lend a hand, and these included those working at Rousanne when they could be spared.

It was a demanding time for Tom, whose task in the Autumn was to make sure that any remaining cattle going for slaughter were free of defects and that the others were given the necessary injections to see them through the winter. Even so, the vendange was a new experience and he eventually, and with Mel's encouragement, managed to find half a day to join the others.

During the picnic lunch provided by Marie and Anna, the latter having welcomed the younger woman with open arms in helping her to cope with the seemingly ever growing household.

Tom sat in the shade of the trees down by the river with a small group including, Madeline, Dale Junior, Phillipe and Bridgette. A short distance away was a larger group consisting of Dale Senior and Stephane together with some neighbours who always came to lend a hand.

The visitors from Exton were due to arrive the following day. Henderson knew that one of the things they always looked forward to was a morning helping in the vineyard, and of course the picnic down by the river before being taken off, this year, for a visit to a nearby monastery before returning to their hosts in time for supper and the usual evening concert in the Town Hall. Their 'help' was always equivocal as more leaves than usual had to be removed from the grapes by Alim on arrival at the Winery, but he bore the extra work good naturedly.

Leaning back against one of the trees, Tom was content to listen to his companions' conversation without joining in much. The air, touched by the scent of the leaves overhead with a perfume far too subtle to be artificially copied was comparatively cool in the shade, and in tune with the river which drifted past at this time of year in no hurry to get where ever it was going, Tom was in no hurry to resume work and felt his eyelids begin to droop until he was suddenly aware that someone was speaking to him. He opened his eyes to see Madeline had moved to sit beside him and smiled apologetically. 'I'm sorry. What did you say? My mind was elsewhere'.

'You were going to sleep' Madeline teased, 'so I thought I would wake you up!'

He returned the girl's smile and looked at her more closely. They had seen each other several times when she had come over to Rousanne with some message or other for Christine or Mel, but they had never exchanged more than a few words. She was wearing a pair of old jeans, trainers, and a white tee shirt with some inscription across it he could not read. She was very slight - one of the few adults who were not taller than he was. himself. He had always thought she looked a throughly nice young woman - not a beauty like Christine, but with wide set brown eyes, a flawless complexion and a smile which came easily, she was surprisingly pretty and he wondered why he had never noticed it before until he realised she must be wearing contact lenses instead of the unflattering tortoise shell glasses she normally wore for work.

'What?'.

'I asked. do you find it very different here from where you used to be'

'In England?'

'Of course.'

Tom thought for a moment, not wishing to brush her question to one side with a dismissive answer, then he said 'Well the animals are much the same. Different breeds of course, but the same problems'.

'What about the terrain - the countryside? Is it the same?'

Tom grinned. 'Well, there's not as much of it. I think France is about four times the size of England'

Madeline nodded, but didn't say anything, so he went on 'there are places further North and in Scotland where you get the kind of long views you have here, but where I come from it's hilly... and close, sort of..... if you know what I mean?"

Madeline nodded again, then she said 'we have places like that. Have you ever walked up by the river? You might be surprised. If you like, I can show you'.

Tom nodded and smiled 'Yes, I'd like that'

'Perhaps one Sunday...'

But there the topic had to be left because of the sudden arrival of the two boys who flopped down beside them'. Phillipe, who wanted to talk about the forthcoming football season, and his brother, who needed little excuse to be with Madeline.

CHAPTER TWENTY-EIGHT

David Nelson had not been an active member of the Exton Twinning Association for some years. He treasured happy memories of his 'apprenticeship' at Poussin le Bas and had kept in touch with Stephane for a while, but he had not visited since his divorce from Sara; besides which, the retirement of his father Patrick had cast the full responsibility for the vineyard on the Dorset Hills upon his shoulders. Even so, he had maintained his subscription and went to some of the meetings when he could spare the time. His relationship with Dawn, the reason for the divorce, had fizzled out for the second time and he realised, yet again, that he had behaved like a complete fool.

What impulse made him put his name down for the forthcoming visit to Les deux Demoiselles was a mystery, and within a few days he picked up the phone in his office intending to ask the Mayor's Secretary to take his name off the list. But the number seemed to be continually engaged and by the third unsuccessful attempt, he came to the conclusion it was an omen and decided to leave things as they were. Being further north than Pousin le bas, their own Vendange was still a few weeks away and there was not that much to do until then. A few days break would do him good

He knew his ex-wife had married an American and spent much of her time with him in New York so there was little danger of running into her. The more he thought about it, the chance to visit and catch up with his old friend was irresistible.

*

It had been a while since anyone had contacted him and he looked back with nostalga to the days of Walter Bush. He had carried out the latter's last commission to the letter and it was not his fault his client had lost his life thereby in a foolish act of gallantry in trying to rescue a young woman from the building which he himself had ordered to be destroyed. This had cost the Professional a considerable loss of face with his other clients, and his income had never recovered, even though he had arranged for the offending girl to be removed from the scene in as unpleasant a way as possible. The discovery of her body was unfortunate, but the usual precautions he had taken at the time - his fire wall - held, and no one dreamt for a second that such a pillar of the local community could have been involved.

The meeting with the new owner of the house at Hirrondelles was held by mutual consent in one of the parking lots created for tourists on the edge of the forest twenty miles out of town which were little used at this time of year. They were already familiar with each other, the Professional having arranged for an associate to impersonate the Client's father some time ago, thus totally confusing the police and this was an opportunity to restore his reputation.

The fee offered - half to be paid in advance the other on confirmation of the elimination of the offender was encouragingly substantial. The reason for the commission was not revealed - nor was it necessary to do so.

David telephoned Stephane a week before the party from Exton was due to arrive to tell him he was coming. Delighted, the other immediately invited him to stay with them at Rousanne, which he was equally pleased to accept. By coincidence, the day they arrived, Richard Chambers left for New York in order to put as much distance as possible between him and what was about to happen.

After considering the matter, the Professional decided his first reaction - that success was too critical to delegate to anyone else - was correct; anyone else would also expect a substantial part of the fee. He was not familiar with the one the client had described, but was told he was a vet from England, staying at Rousanne, and was almost certain to lend a hand with the imminent Vendange. The arrival of the visitors from England, also to participate, offered the opportunity to mingle with the pickers who would assume he was a local volunteer, and the locals would assume he was one of the visitors from England. After the first day he had discovered all he needed to know.

After the Concert, David Nelson wandered back into the Square and stopped to look into the window of Immobilliers Cevant. He was amused to see the old card which had attracted Andrew Solomon fifty years before still held pride of place. He also saw lights were on in the office and that a young woman was evidently working late, but after a few moments, he became aware that someone was standing beside him and turned to see a pleasant, middle aged man smiling at him, seemingly more interest in him than the contents of the window. But almost at once, the other nodded, and after bidding him 'good night', turned to walk away. It was only on the walk back it struck David that they had spoken to each other in English, but he immediately put that down to the other being another visitor from Exton out for a breath of air and dismissed the fact that he had not recognised him; he knew very few of the members of the Twinning Association these days.

What he did not register was that he was followed at a distance and that seeing him cross the bridge over the river and turn into the Vet's Practice his identity was confirmed.

At Stephane's suggestion David agreed to stay on for a while after the coach had taken the other's back to Exton and looked forward to the few extra day's holiday.

He rented a Renault Megane from a local garage who arranged for him to be able to leave it at Toulouse Airport in a week's time for his return trip, and planned some exploration of places he had never had the time or means to visit when he was here as a student. One of these was Montpellier down on the coast where the world famous College of Viticulture was situated and which both Gus and Stephane himself had attended.

When he mentioned this on returning to Rousanne with the car, Christine asked if she could come too. Although her husband had gone there, she herself had never visited and would love to see the place where he had spent so much of the last years of his life. David agreed at once and a trip was arranged for as soon as the vendange was over.

The acquisition of a car was duly noted by the Professional and this presented a familiar solution to fulfil his commission.

The morning after the last of the picked grapes had been safely delivered to the Winery, David drove round to Pousin les Bas to pick up Christine and Billie. She decided to leave Lisa with Marie for the day.

The road initially followed the course of the Truyer then began the steep climb out of the valley through a series of hair pin bends cut into the mountainside towards the place where it joined the Autoroute to Montpellier at the bridge of Garrabit. Unusually, there was little traffic coming in the opposite direction, but David drove with extra care in the unfamiliar car as at each corner it was impossible to see until the last minute, and despite the metal crash barriers which had been erected after several fatal accidents, the danger of being swept over the edge and down into the steep valley below by an oncoming truck could not be ignored.

The autumn sun shone from a cloudless blue sky onto the mountain tops and on the forest several hundred feet below, the trees of which still defiantly clung to their leaves, reluctant to surrender them to the approaching winter. Occasionally, there were glimpses of the river as it wound through the valley far below, its surface flashing in the sun where it penetrated the overhanging trees. It was idyllic, and only spoilt at one point when Billy became so fractious David had to pull over to let Christine go and sit in the back beside him. After this, the rest of the journey passed without incident.

The visit to the College had been arranged by Christine and they were shown round by a member of staff who remembered Gus and spoke highly of him. He told them that they had all been saddened by the news of his accident in the United States, and went on to tell them that they were working on an alternative to phosphoric acid as a treatment for powdery mildew. They had had some encouraging results so far but would not be in a position to publish the results until it could be confirmed that the substances they were now working on did not produce a similar allergic effect.

The College was on the outskirts of Montpellier, a large sprawling city with no more or less charm than the average large French metropolis, but it did have a charming old town at its centre and after finding an underground car park, they walked down into the central Place de General de Gaulle and found a cafe with an adjacent small childrens' play area where, after his mother had persuaded him to eat most of an egg sandwich, Billy was allowed to get down from the table and join some other children playing in a sandpit and on a small carousel.

After watching for a few minutes, David turned to Christine and said 'I never knew your husband. Tell me about him - if you don't mind talking about him?'

Christine smiled and shook her head.

'No. I don't mind at all. I really enjoyed listening to that man this morning.' She paused for a moment, then went on 'no matter how much you love somebody. - or how close you feel to them, there is always more. Most people who have lost someone would rather talk about them - otherwise the memory starts to fade, and that's like losing them all over again.' She paused again for a moment, then went on 'I dread not being able to remember what he looked like'.

David nodded. 'Yes, I've heard people say that -and that the best antidote to that is having children who remind you of them.'

As one, they both turned to look at Billy who had now found a girlfriend a bit smaller than himself and was showing her how to make a small castle After a few moments, Christine nodded.

'Billy does remind me of him - in so many ways' She paused for a second then looked back at him and said 'Did you know he was psychic? Gus I mean'.'

'No' David shook his head. 'In what way?'

Christine smiled. 'Well, he didn't tell fortunes, or anything like that!'.

'No, I only meant...'

'I know what you meant' she interrupted gently, and her smile faded as she remembered before continuing 'He was the kindest, most considerate person I've ever known. And he seemed to know things - logic, if you like - said he could not possibly be aware of' She paused for a second time, then went on' He kept it to himself mostly as he soon discovered, even as a child, that people began to think him 'odd' if he said anything'.

'I can understand that'.

Christine looked back at the two children then continued. 'It's one of the ways Billy reminds me of him. In a way, I hoped at first it would not be one of the ways he took after him. Gus always said it was a very mixed blessing -more a responsibility'.

David frowned 'In what way 'responsibility'? he said.

Christine glanced back at him, then she said 'it meant having to try and help people no one else knew anything about'.

David paused again, then he said 'And Billy?'

Christine looked back at the children, then she said' You remember how he suddenly became upset for no apparent reason on our way here?'

David smiled 'I just thought he'd become bored'.

'Maybe that too. But that was the place where my uncle Billy - his name's sake, and my Grandmother went off the road and were killed.'

David frowned. 'How do you know?' he said.

'Dad pointed it out to me once when he was taking Andrew and me down to visit my mother where she was convalescing in a nursing home at La Grande Motte - just along the coast from here. I've never forgotten it because from then on, whenever we went past, my brother took great delight in reminding me and giving me the shivers!'

David grinned 'Brothers do that!"

'Well I hope Billy doesn't!.'

David's smile faded 'But how could Billy have known? 'He asked softly

'I don't know. But he did. I didn't say anything at the time, but it was right there'.

When they had finished lunch, they walked back to the car then drove along the causeway to La Grande Motte with the sea on one side and a shallow salt lake on the other so Billy could see the flamingos who congregate there in their hundreds at the time of year. Christine told them both that the birds get their red side feathers from the prawns they gather in their bills, especially adapted for the purpose, and which they use to scooped up from the muddy bottom of the lake by standing in the water on their long thin legs and extending their necks in a sweeping action away from them - like a tennis player's delicate backhand.

The Nursing Home was still there, and quite a lot of late summer visitors on the sandy beach just across the road opposite where, she told him, she and Andrew used to swim with their father while Holly's father Marcus sat with her on the balcony of her room watching and waving to acknowledge some exploit or other until he nodded off.

They were able to join the Autoroute at La Grande Motte without having to go back into Montpellier and the journey back passed without incident as by the time they turned off to join the road following the river, Billy had gone to sleep. Even so, David drove with even more care.

By the time they reached the outskirts of Les Deux Demoiselles it was dark. He turned off the main road into the lane which led to the entrance of the Estate, but as he applied the brakes to slow down for the turn his foot went flat on the floor and the car kept going. He revved the engine to force the vehicle into a lower gear and when he took his foot completely off the accelerator the car began to slow, but it was still going too fast to make the entrance leaving no choice but to keep going along the lane until the car ran out of momentum up the slight incline towards the bridge.

Suddenly, by the entrance itself and where the lane was at its narrowest, the figure of a man was caught in the vehicle's headlights in the middle of the road. There was no way David could avoid him, but just when a collision seemed inevitable, the figure disappeared.

It all happened so quickly, he might have thought it an illusion - a shadow perhaps cast by the car's lights against something at the roadside, but it was all over in a second and he concentrated on forcing the engine into a still lower gear and slowing the car sufficiently to turn into the entrance of Les Hirrondelles where the engine stalled and the car came to a shuddering halt.

'Wait here!'

David flung open the car door and went running back to where the accident had almost occurred expecting to find someone by the road side they had perhaps grazed slightly or at least someone in shock from such a near miss. But there was no one.

He walked back to the car and got a torch from the glove compartment, then escorted Christine, carrying Billy who was still fast asleep, to the door of their house and safely inside.

When he told Dale what had happened the other came out with him carrying a more powerful torch and together they searched up and down the lane for anyone who might have started to walk away then collapsed, but there was no one.

David reported the incident to the garage in the morning who sent two men with a tow truck to take the car away, but they examined it first and reported that at first sight it appeared someone had deliberately loosened the pipe from the master cylinder to the front brakes. It was a miracle it had not become undone sooner. After discussing it with the mechanics before they left, David commented that someone might have interfered with the car while in the underground car park in Montpellier. ''though heaven knows why!'

When they had gone, he walked round to Poussin le Bas to see Christine was alright - which she was, except that Billy had so much enjoyed their outing he wanted to go back at once to play with his new friend in the sand pit.

He discussed with Dale whether or not he should say anything to the police, but while they were still discussing the matter over cups of coffee, there was a knock on the door and two members of the Gendarmerie who asked if they could help at all with the disappearance of a M. Germain, a wine waiter at the Bridge Hotel who had not returned to his lodgings last night nor appeared for work this morning. Dale and David exchanged glances and when the former nodded, David told them exactly what had happened the previous evening and the discovery of the tampered brakes only an hour since.

This was duly noted and David was asked not to return to England before clearance from them. 'The two incidents were not necessarily connected, but until they located M.Germain it was impossible to say.'

When he had gone back to Rousanne and brought Stephane and Mel up to date with this development, he asked if he could help in the winery as there was no where he could go until the car was repaired, and so he was there working with Alim when a police man put his nose round the door asking for M.Nelson to report that one mystery anyway was solved. The body of M. Germain had been found by a dog, walking with its owner just on the other side of the wall bordering the lane where the near accident had happened and concealed by some brambles into which he had evidently fallen. Apart from some scratches, the body showed no sign of injury and the doctor who examined the body before it was moved had expressed the opinion that the deceased had probably died of a heart attack as a result of jumping over the wall to get out of the way of the out of control vehicle.

The policeman went on to express the opinion that If this was confirmed by the autopsy no blame would attach to anyone except who ever had tampered with the brakes of the car M Nelson had been driving.

The same officer telephoned Rousanne the following day to confirm that the autopsy had indeed confirmed that M Germain had died of a heart attack and that M Nelson was therefore totally exonerated and at liberty to leave whenever he wished. He hoped he would enjoy the rest of his vacation!

A different car was delivered to Rousanne the following day as a pipe for the Megane in replacement of the one whose threads were damaged when loosened was having to be sent from the Distributors. David was over at the winery but Mel suggested they could leave the car but drive round in the one they had brought to get back to obtain his signature covering the new vehicle, and this they agreed. But before they drove away, one of the two who knew Mel asked if she had heard about the wine waiter of the Bridge Hotel and Mel answered she knew he had died of a heart attack.

'But did she know a very considerable amount of cash had been found on him - more than a year's wages? And what was he doing hanging around the entrance to Poussan les Bas after dark - as if he was waiting for someone?'.

'Or to see if they failed to return' David thought to himself after they had gone.

Despite the availability of the new car, there never seemed to be time for another day out together. But until he could not put off going home for his own vendange any longer, David and Christine met often, taking the children to the local park or just walking together down by the river after the children had been put to bed. Neither mentioned their growing fondness for each other until they met for the last time when David called round at Pousin le Bas on his way to the airport to say goodbye. He held up and kissed the children and shook hands with Dale and Holy who then left them alone together. Then he bent forward to smiling to kiss Christine lightly on the cheek, but suddenly she flung her arms around him her eyes full of tears.

'I'm going to miss you so much!' she whispered, and he was immediately plunged into a whirl pool of emotions he had tried to ignore until then.

He wasn't able to say anything as they clung together until finally he managed ''It's been wonderful!' Finally they separated to arm's length looking at each other.

'I want to kidnap you and take you with me' he said miserably after a moment.

Christine nodded. 'I know. I've thought about us so much these last few days. But it's hopeless. You have your responsibilities, and I can't leave here'

They hugged again until finally David broke away. 'I've got to go' he said unhappily. Christine nodded and they stood back looking at each other. 'It's just as well' she said, her own misery reflecting his 'We have no future together. It was just a lovely dream. Goodbye David'

After another moment's hesitation, she picked up the children and walked away with them leaving him standing at the open front door. Lisa was too young to know what was happening, but Billy looked over his mother's shoulder and waved before he was taken out of sight.

David turned away, got back into the car and drove out into the lane. A few minutes later, he joined the main road heading West in the direction of Toulouse. He knew she was right. It was hopeless and would just have been a repetition of what had happened with Sara. One or the other had to give up everything, and in the end, neither was willing.

CHAPTER TWENTY-NINE

Until the schools reopened, Saeed came with Mayer every day to Rousanne, then picked his way across the stepping stones to the Estate and spent the day with Alim in the Winery

He had accepted that his mother and father lived in different places and was old enough to know about divorce: some of his friends at school whose parents' marriage had fallen apart spoke of bitterness - even violence, but there had been none of that with them. They still seemed fond of each other, and by their actions showed how much they loved him. But as he walked up to the winery today he knew this was going to be different. As soon as he arrived he conveyed his mother's message asking his father to go home with him after work. This was not so unusual - she often invited him to a meal, particularly when there was something about Saeed himself one or the other wanted to discuss, but his mother had received an official looking letter that morning addressed to both of them and it was this, he knew, she wanted to show him.

The day seemed to last forever. During their lunch break, which they took sitting outside in the sun with Stephane and two of the Estate's other workers, it was impossible to exchange more than a few words together without these overhearing, so when the day finally came to an end, they walked along the lane speculating on the letter and could not get to the cottage where Mayer and Saeed lived fast enough.

After offering Alim a glass of wine and Saeed some homemade lemonade, Mayer invited them to sit at the small kitchen table and produced the letter which she handed Alim but suggested he gave it to Saeed to read aloud as although both of them were fluent in speaking French now, both still found the written language difficult. This had not mattered much until now.

'I think it's from the Government' he told them after struggling with the official heading. 'Someone in Paris'.

'Paris?!' both adults echoed simultaneously.

Saeed paused and looked up anxiously until Alim said 'Never mind…just tell us what it says'.

'I don't understand some of the words, Papa!'

'Just read what you can darling' Mayer said gently, and after a pause the boy looked down again and started, pulling a face from time to time when he stumbled over the 'officialese'

'Monsieur and Madame,

I am writing to inform you that……something….is due to expire at the end of the year. Your son Saeed…' the reader looked up proudly… 'that's me!'

'Go on' his father said, trying to control his growing anxiety, and after a second the boy screwed up his face again and returned to his task.

'Your son Saeed is registered as a French ...Citi......something...as he was born in France...and the purpose of this letter is to advise you that rather than re-apply for renewal of your landed resident status, you may now apply for French Citi...something yourself, which will give you the right to the National Health Service and retirement pensions in due course.

If you want to avail yourself of this offer, please telephone the special number at the top of this letter to arrange for a first interview'

Saeed hesitated for a few seconds, then passed the letter back to his father. 'The rest is who it's from and wishing you his...something or other'.

Alim nodded smiling with relief. 'That is a nice letter' he said. 'We *should* be like everyone else'

Mayer also nodded slowly, but after a few seconds she said cautiously 'There is only one problem - You are not really Saeed's father'.

'Yes, I know that' Alim said.' But how is anyone else to know? They accepted that we were husband and wife and that I was his father when we first came here. That's why I was allowed to stay.'

Mayer said carefully 'That's true Alim. But they have new ways of checking such things now. If they find out we are neither married, nor are you Saeed's father? They could send you back'.

'Send me back! Where could they send me? The whole Region is in turmol!'

There was a long silence, then Saeed said 'You could get married. That would be nice!'

CHAPTER THIRTY

In the Spring with lambing and new calves to contend with, not to mention the occasional foal, Mel and Tom's work load redoubled. They were out most days and often nights as well. There was some relief during the Easter Vacation when Peter was home from College, and they were grateful, when he had to go back, that Christine was able to spend enough time with them - leaving Madeline to help Dale -to be able to cope with the visitors to the Clinic who brought in domestic animals for attention.

At Christmas, Tom had asked Madeline to marry him, which proposal she happily accepted. Dale Junior was upset at first, but as she had hoped, Fiona, a girl in his class at school, attracted his attention and soon the two were doing their home work together and sharing a budding romance, including walking to school together, self consciously holding hands in public and snogging in private when possible Both had different ideas what they wanted to do after they had left school, but they agreed that when settled in their chosen careers they would get married and have three children.

For a while the newly engaged couple did not manage to see much of each other until Madeline asked if she could come out with him sometimes on his farm visits and this proved a great success in that they were not only able to spend more time together, but Madeline became fascinated with what he was doing and gradually moved from being a mere onlooker to another pair of hands when needed, helping the ewes who were having difficulty deliver their lambs. But it wasn't all work: Meals out, long walks, and trips in the car to such places as Saint Fleur and further afield to Clermont Ferrand where they looked at furnishings for the flat that Sara Cevant had offered in the block of the same converted from the old winery. She also introduced them to the young policeman Andre Fabre and his new Dutch Wife Eva, and the two couples became friends.

It was the first Sunday in May when Madeline suggested that instead of going out for a picnic in the car they walked up the river to where Dale junior had told her there were still the pair of Kingfishers nesting in the hole in the river bank he had shown her the previous year. He knew about them because his mother had taken Phillipe and himself to see them years ago and had told them she was taken there herself, the first time, by her Grandfather when she was about their age. Not many people knew about them, and it was probably better it stayed that way.

'It's such a special place for them' Madeline added. 'I felt I had to ask his permission to take you to see them - perhaps even take us on a guided tour, but he was quite cool about it. - Just said it was ok - 'but remember to be quiet!' Tom smiled and nodded but didn't say anything.

It was a brilliant, sunny day. The river ran down in a series of small cascades into pools where the surface turned round slowly a couple of times at first as if trying to make up its mind what to do next before being captured by the undertow and pushed forcefully on its way over the next ledge.

They took just a bottle of fizzy water and a few sandwiches which Madeline carried in a small basket while Tom brought along a rug from his car. He spread this out when Madelibe said they had reached the spot but when she pulled up her skirt to sit on it and looked up at him with that mischievous grin she put on sometimes he forgot about the kingfishers and lay down to take her into his arms. After a while She took his hand and guided it between her legs, and as they kissed lifted her pelvis momentarily so he could strip away her knickers, then pulled him on top of her.

It was not the first time they had made love, but they both agreed later it had been idylic.

'Did we make a lot of noise?' Madeline teased when she had adjusted her skirt and passed Tom one of the Sandwiches.

'I don't know' he laughed, as he took it, then looked around. 'I can't see any Kingfishers!' But even as he spoke, one flew out of a hole in the river bank opposite and took possession of a branch projecting out over the river just twenty feet away on their side, peering down into the river. A moment later, it dived like an arrow into the water, and only few seconds later re-emerged with a small fish wriggling in its beak which it hit against the branch until it stopped, then took off and dived back into the hole.

'I read they do that because fish like stickle-backs have spines along their backs' Tom whispered. 'They kill them first so the spines relax and they can swallow them whole. The chicks form a sort of line, taking it in turns to be fed after which they drag their prize to the back of the nest to eat it, and so allow the next in line to be fed.

As they watched it became obvious there were two birds at work.

'It's impossible to tell which is the male and which the female!'

'Were not all like that' Madeline stated firmly, and he glanced to see she had that look on her face again.

'Just a minute, I'll show you.'

Less than a minute later she was standing looking down at him and with everything she had been wearing on the rug at her feet.

'Well' she challenged 'Am I a boy or a girl? Go on - now it's your turn!'

They rested in each other's arms for a long time without bothering to get dressed, but eventually they did so - said goodbye and thank you to the still busy parent birds and walked back with their arms around each other.

'I agree it's a good idea not to tell people about this place' Tom observed. 'We don't want anyone else disturbing the peace!'

Madeline giggled.

*

News of the catastrophe reached him on his return from New York. Uncharacteristically, the failure of the Professional to carry out his instructions and the loss of half the fee did not send him into a fury but a steely determination to attend to the matter himself after more pressing business matters had been dealt with, and as the weeks passed, he decided not only to eliminate his wife's lover but get rid of her at the same time. Only then would he feel justice had been served.

The death of the wine waiter of the Bridge Hotel in his service did not concern him in the least except as a warning not to rely on others in future.

In two month's time, the summer season would be upon them and his appearance at les Hirrondelles for a vacation would seem the most natural thing in the world. Two months would give ample time to consider his options, and one of the first things he realised was that a female companion could only add to the appearance of normality. He therefore looked around for a suitable young woman among the staff of his various business associates. He knew from past experience that most women found him attractive, and it was not long before one the sub-editors of a technical journal he contributed to occasionally accepted his invitation to go out to lunch, and from there slipped into the role of regular girl friend.

Amy Watson was in her mid twenties; not unattractive herself but the men she had dated from time to time had shown no inclination so far to push the relationship into deeper waters. Until recently, she had shared a flat in Camberwell with a girlfriend, but when the other got married, she could no longer afford the rent by herself and no one so far had answered any of the small adverts she had put up in several newsagents for a flat mate. It would not be true to say she was becoming over anxious, about her general situation, but the marriage of her friend had been a reminder that time was ticking away. It therefore came, firstly as a surprise to be asked out by Richard Chambers, and then amazed delight when he made it plain he wanted to continue to see her. She had not got to the point of wondering where all this was going but was content for the moment to enjoy it while it lasted.

'Sleepovers' at the Mews flat - so much grander than her own - after an evening out together become a regular feature and he proved a skilled and vigorous lover who roused her to a level of pleasure she had never experienced before; and when, on top of all of this, he invited her to go with him for a holiday to his villa in France she accepted with eager anticipation.

Richard had not really thought it through yet, but he wondered from time to time in the intervening period if he might involve Amy in the fate he planned for Christine and her lover. If so, it would not only be easier to divert any suspicion towards some outsider, but relieve him of his relationship with her when he returned to London.

The more he thought about this, he came to the conclusion that if he could throw suspicion on some local who was already not well liked, their guilt would all the more readily be believed. He eventually telephoned Immobiliers Cevant who held a key to the house and asked them to arrange for it to be prepared for their arrival and to engage a housekeeper for the duration of their stay.

CHAPTER THIRTY-ONE

With no summer sport of equal popularity, the Soccer season in France never really stops, but the schools close for an interminably long summer vacation. In the days when agriculture, and wine production in particular, was a mainstay of the Economy, this was to allow both pupils and staff to participate in the work leading up to the Vendange, and of course the Vendange itself. This was no longer the case, but no government had yet managed to persuade the Unions to accept a shorter summer break, and the long exodus to the beaches of Normandy, Brittany and the South, had taken the place of work, so foreign tourists found they had Paris more or less to themselves after Bastille Day in August. Not so at Les Deux Demoiselles 'et environs'.

At Poussin le Bas and the surrounding vineyards there was plenty to do, but swimming in the river from the steps put in by Andrew Solomon fifty years ago, and open by tradition to all who wanted to use them, which usually included not only after work and mid-day swims for the family and workers of the Estate, but the B&B visitors to Rousanne, and anyone else come to that - a happy substitute for the Cote d' Azure.

With no football, Phillipe was happy to join his twin and Saeed in whatever tasks needed to be done and he accepted that wherever Dale went these days, girlfriend Fiona was sure not to be far behind. Madeline also came with her new fiancee Tom as well as Christine herself and the childre. Mayer never came at all, relying on Alim to keep his eye on Saeed as swimming had never been part of her upbringing and she far preferred to stay behind and help Mel with the B&B visitors.

After they arrived, Richard Chambers spent most of the day in his office, and when Amy came back from a visit to the shops to say she had run into Madame Meuse the Vet, who had seemed very nice, and she had invited her to join them at the Estate for a swim - which would be much nicer than just sunbathing by herself by the pool, and give her the opportunity to meet some of their neighbours.

After a momentary flash of irritation, he suddenly smiled and encouraged the idea. It would do no harm at all to learn exactly what his intended victims were doing!

Afterwards, Amy got into the habit of walking across in the early afternoon most days wearing a beach robe, having already changed and carrying a towel, but she always came back in time for the dinner laid on by the housekeeper when Richard usually emerged from whatever he had been doing. She was relieved that he was then usually in a good mood and happy to listen to her prattle away about the comings and goings of those she had met. She told him she particularly liked the fiancee of the new Vet's Assistant, who had introduced her in turn to her boss, who evidently owned much of the Estate but helped out at Rousanne when she could.

'You know you are talking about the woman I used to be married to?' he said, frowning suddenly, and Amy looked alarmed. She knew how quickly he could fly off the handle.

'I didn't know that' she said hurriedly. 'I'm sorry, would you rather...'

But just as quickly his frown turned to a smile.

'No it's fine. You were not to know' he said.

'I knew she lived over there...'

'It's fine really. We parted friends. Tell me all about her'.

After a moment's hesitation to make sure he really meant it, Amy told him everything Madeline had told her, and again, he was attentive, seeming particularly interested in Christine's work at Rousanne.

It could not have worked out better: almost the same time as he had worked out how he would rid himself of his ex-wife and her lover, Amy reported that Mel had invited them to a big evening barbecue at Rousanne. Christine and the children would be there and Mel had already checked she would not mind at all if she and Richard came along. 'If anything, she seemed relieved' Mel had told her. 'It would be good to meet and finally make peace instead of trying to avoid each other!'

On the day of the invitation, Amy was all ready to leave when Richard came out of his office and apologised that some e-mails had just come through which needed his immediate attention. But he encouraged her to go on ahead and he would follow as soon as he could. Amy was reluctant to do this, but eventually allowed him to persuade her. 'After all, she already knew most of those who would be there and it would be impolite for both of them to turn up late. He would be there as soon as he could, and she could make his apologies in the meantime.'

In fact he was a long time coming and Amy began to wonder if he had changed his mind. She thought about going back, but just at that moment, Christine came out of the house having settled the children temporarily in one of the spare rooms, and putting an arm round her, and collecting two glasses on the way, led her to one of the picnic tables and demanded to be told all about Amy's life in London and how she had come to meet her Ex'.

He waited until it was dark - that was essential, then crossed over to the Estate and down to the stepping stones over the river.

The barbecue was almost at an end when suddenly there was the sound of a shot from down by the river; particularly loud in contrast to the surrounding stillness. None of them heard the splash immediately afterwards.

The remaining guests looked at each other with varying expressions in the ensuing silence until Staphane went into the house and came out carrying a torch with which he walked down the slope to the river accompanied by Dale Senior and the twins, but when he shone the torch through the wire the river bank on both sides was empty.

'Must be a poacher' Phillipe offered, but his father shook his head.

'Not in the dark!'

Dale Senior said' they might have been aiming for a duck supper'

'They're all shut up for the night' his other grandson said'

They paused for a moment, then Stephane said' Well, whatever - there's nothing I can see. Let's go back.'

Amy rang the house but there was no reply and Richard had still not appeared by the time it was time to go. At Mel's suggestion, Stephane drove her home in his car but he was not there either, and as the house keeper had gone home, so he phoned Mel and said he was going to wait until Richard returned.

Amy made some coffee and they sat in the living room chatting together but an hour later, Richard had still not come back. Amy thanked Stephane and told him she would be fine and he should go home, but he insisted on remaining, and at his insistence she went upstairs to bed leaving him to doze in one of the arm chairs.

At 8am he phoned Andre Fabre, who had also been at the barbecue with Eva, and reported that the Englishman had apparently gone missing.

Shortly after this, a tourist having breakfast by himself on the terrace of the Bridge Hotel suddenly stood up and walked from his table to the low stone wall overlooking the river and peered down to take a closer look. Being of unemotional German stock, he did not alarm anyone else but walked inside and reported to Reception that the body of a man was caught with some other obstruction at the foot of the central arch supporting the Bridge and It was not long before a police car arrived with an Ambulance

The Medics scrambled down, and having managed to pull the body from the water, lifted it up onto the river bank where it was seen immediately that be that of a man who had obviously been shot at close range with a shot gun.

The dead man was taken to the local Clinic where Holy immediately identified him as Richard Chambers thus sparing Amy Watson the gruesome task.

It was not long before the widow of the former Wine waiter of the Bridge Hotel confessed to shooting the victim with one of her husband's guns while he was crossing the stepping stones by the Estate, but a good deal longer before Inspector Goudon, who had joined Andre in trying to piece together exactly what had happened, started to get anywhere near the truth.

'Why would she want to do such a thing?' he demanded. 'In the first place, she had used the expression 'one of her husband's guns'.

A search of their house revealed a startling collection of firearms of all kinds including some automatic weapons, most of which were illegal, and all of which were taken into safe keeping.

Further examination revealed correspondence and recorded phone calls with a number of people over several years from which it emerged that being a wine waiter had simply been a cover for a far more lucrative profession in carrying out 'commissions' of varied, and mostly unlimited unscrupulousness. Although he had a computer, her husband had apparently never used e-mails for reasons of confidentiality, but the big antique desk revealed bank deposit account books with considerable balances and diaries going back many years listing the names and details of Client; brief descriptions of the tasks carried out on their behalf and the fees earned.

The last entry was for Richard Chambers, but the nature of his request was not noted. Questioned about this, the widow remained obstinately uncooperative, so a vigorous search was instituted into the affairs of the murdered man both at Les Hirrondelles, and with the co-operation of Scotland Yard, at his flat in London. Amy was also questioned but was dismissed from any suspicion of guilt as it emerged that she had been lucky not to have been endangered herself as it emerged from both investigations that although the deceased had been a brilliant man, over the years he had become mentally unbalanced to the point where he had gradually lost any sense of responsibility towards other people until he only saw the world in terms of his own desires and needs. Goudon expressed the opinion to Andre that he had also come to the conclusion that towards the end, even this had become confused - reality giving way to pure imagination.

What had made this so dangerous was that Richard Chambers rarely betrayed any outward sign of this, apart from bouts of disproportionate anger when frustrated for some reason. He had yet to lose control of himself completely, but had he lived, his condition would have undoubtedly deteriorated still further. His laptop was also revealing: the exact nature of his instructions to 'The Professional', as they now all referred to him, and omitted from the other's last diary entry - probably because it was uncompleted - was the elimination of his former wife and her 'lover', the latter unnamed

When this was put to the widow in a further session of questioning, she admitted that for the first time he had admitted to her what he intended to do'.

'And what was your reaction on being told this?' Goudon demanded.

the woman shook her head. Then she said 'I was horrified. I had reason to hate the Solomon family - they put my father out of business, and knowing that was probably why my husband told me. He thought I would be pleased.'

'And you weren't?'

Again the woman paused, shaking her head several times before she said 'I begged him to do nothing of the kind. Then he became angry, so I said no more'.

There was a period of silence, then Andre said 'Why did you kill Richard Chambers?'

There was no hesitation this time.

'Because it was his fault my husband was killed!' she spat vehemently.

Further analysis of Richard Chamber's laptop revealed plans to construct an explosive device which could be detonated by radio.

'It may be it was his intention to leave it at the barbecue somewhere out of sight, then slip away' Goudon surmised when they had all the facts.

'What about the young English woman? Andre said, and his superior shrugged.

'From what we know now, he intended to rid himself of her at the same time'

'As well as implicating Alim'

His boss nodded. 'That's true. But that was further down the line. The whole thing was in his imagination. He never built a bomb and when he crossed the stream where he was shot he was just acting out something that was never going to happen'.

CHAPTER THIRTY-TWO

By the time Alim and Mayer were married by the Mayor, Maurice Henderson, one Saturday afternoon in June, with Stephane as best man and everyone from the Estate present, few gave a thought to the wine waiter of the Bridge Hotel - except his widow who had been found guilty of second degree murder and sentenced to five years in prison but with the possibility of being released earlier on parole.

It was to be a double ceremony, with not only the wedding, but the presentation to the newly married couple of papers confirming their being granted French Citizenship.

But Alim had something important to do first - to say goodbye again to someone he had once loved very much. He slipped away while Mayer and her bridesmaids, in the calming presence of Mel, standing in as honorary 'Mother', fussed over and all the last minute things a bride and her friends have to fuss over on the morning of a wedding.

He drove up to the small stone walled meadow on the brow of the hill overlooking the town, with its carpet of wild grass, yellow, sweet smelling broom, and wood anemones and celandine growing under the low stone walls. There was nothing now of the excavations which had revealed the tragedy from which he had thought he would never recover, but now he was to marry a woman he loved, and although that did not in any way diminish the memory of Jeannine, Alim knew it was time to move on and think only of the one he was about to marry and their son, so he put the bunch of flowers he had brought for the last time at the foot of the bronze statue of a young girl in a summer dress sitting and shading her eyes with her left hand as she gazed at the distant ridge of mountains far to the South crowned by the Pic du Midi. Up here, there was a breeze and shadows of clouds moved slowly over the ground towards her and up and over her shoulder, but she did not look up or turn to follow their continuing journey north.

Alim turned and walked back to the car and drove away. A few minutes later, the small bunch stirred, almost as though someone had picked them up, and the wind blew them away.

Among the diaries left by the 'Professional' was discovered one covering six years previously containing an entry different from most of the others in giving particulars of a 'commission' instigated by the writer himself and carried out by others - for the disposal of one Jeanette Berger. Unfortunately it gave no details of those who carried out his instructions and were still at large.

*

When Christine and the children got back from the Wedding Reception which was held at Rousanne, there was a strange car parked near the front door, and before she could open it, Maria, who had obviously been looking out for them, did so smiling mysteriously.

'There is some waiting for you on the terrace' she said, then stood to one side to let them pass.

'Who? Christine demanded, but the housekeeper only shrugged and inclined her head towards the end of the corridor, so she handed Billy to her than walked along to the door leading out onto the terrace with Lisa trotting behind her like a pet lamb.

The tall man who had been standing by one of the summer awnings admiring the view turned as soon as he heard her gasp.

'Henry! What are doing here?'

'I've come home'. He bent down smiling to pick up the little girl who immediately ran towards him laughing with pleasure'

'Richard!'

'Hello Lisa.' They hugged and he turned with the child still in his arms smiling.

'I guess I'm stuck with that name!'

'I hope not!' Christine covered the distance between them and flung her arms around them both, her eyes filling with tears.

Henry grinned.

'I don't know, you cry when I leave and now your crying co's I've come back!'

'Oh shut up!'. She raised her tear stained face to him, smiling.

'Just kiss me!'

END OF PART FOUR

PART FIVE

'Looking Across The River'

CHAPTER ONE

Fiona woke up and stared at the ceiling for a few moments then turned her head and transferred her gaze to her bed-room window, the curtains of which were light enough for even the midsummer air outside to stir gently. She could also hear the faint murmur of the river.

It had been a hot night and she had gone to sleep on top of her bed without any covering, but sometime in the night she must have pulled the single sheet over her, and she now kicked this off and sat up.

She could hear her father talking to someone outside, probably a neighbour who, being early for work, had stopped his bicycle at their gate on the narrow path which separated the row of cottages where they lived from the river, to exchange a few words before peddling on to where the path joined the road leading into Les deux Demoiselles at the bridge over the river.

Her father was the Chef at the Bridge Hotel and normally had no need to get there to prepare breakfast for the guests, which was competently dealt with by his staff, but today was Saturday when he made a point of getting there early to discuss the week-end's menus with the Manager.

Saturday! Suddenly she was wide awake and rolled onto her feet and went to the window and took a deep breath before peeking through the curtains to see if they were still there. Seeing the path empty, she pulled them fully to one side and looked across the river to the other side where she could see the extra land newly acquired by the Estate and the young vines, planted in rows running from East to West and parallel to the slope which her boy friend Dale had explained was to get maximum exposure for each plant to the sun.

Dale! This was what today was going to be all about: he had proposed to her earlier in the week and she had promised to give him her answer today.

She knew he had been surprised, and a little hurt, when she did not agree immediately, but she had hugged him and told him she loved him, and that she had always known that one day they would be together. But she wanted to be more than just a wife and mother and needed a few days to think how she was going to manage being married with her ambition to have a career. So he had hugged her back and made the best of it.

Fiona had always been good at languages and had won a scholarship to read English Literature at the University of Clermont Ferrand with a view to becoming a teacher. Her relationship with Dale had been more than helpful in this as being the son of an American Mother who had always made a point of talking to his twin brother Phillipe and himself in her native tongue, leaving it to their father to speak to them in French, they had grown up bi-lingual, and he and Fiona had got into the habit of speaking to each other most of the time in English since they were children.

Dale was the 'heir apparent' of the wine estate of Poussin le Bas, by far the largest and most prestigious in the Region. His father, Stephane Meuse, was the Estate Manager and fifty per cent owner. The other fifty per cent was owned by Christine Soloman - formally Chambers, but who had reverted to the traditional family name after the violent death of her husband. Christine was the great granddaughter of the founder of the Estate, Andrew Solomon. But she had eventually achieved her ambition to qualify as a Vet and so able help run the Practice founded by her half sister Mel, the twins' Mother, together with Tom Field, who had come to them ten years ago from England, and In the circumstances she was more than happy to give Stephane a free hand with the Estate. It was a possible that one day her own children Lisa and younger brother Billy might want to join the Family business, but they were still only fourteen and twelve respectively and such an eventuality lay well into the future.

Dale's brother Phillipe had shown no desire to spend the rest of his life in a 'French backwater' and had persuaded his Grandfather to speak to Sara Cevante, a local Immobiler who had inherited considerable wealth from her late husband but, unlike Phillipe himself, had been content to remain where she was most of the time. Nevertheless, she had retained a prominent firm of lawyers in New York to look after her American interests and these had been happy to find a place for Phillipe as a trainee at her request.

Fiona knew there had never been any such thought in Dale's mind. He loved working with his father and grandfather until the latter retired. He loved the vines as if they were his children as well as the passing of the seasons - each with it's own special pleasure. He loved the river which meandered through the Estate at this time of year allowing the guests from the B&B at Rousanne opposite, where he lived with his parents, to cross by the stepping stones put in by his father so they could reach the safe bathing place on the other side But when the melted snow from the Massive Central arrived turning the river into torrent, the only way of crossing from one side to the other was to drive up to the bridge and back down the other side

Fiona had come to know how he felt about all these things from when they were children, talking endlessly of the future they would have together. But things change. It had always been his dream, which she had been happy to share. She still loved him, and she realised that ninety-nine girls out of a hundred would leap at the opportunity of such a prospect: and yet.... she longed to reach out for something of her own.

Cursing her stupidity, but unable to help herself, she started to get dressed and ready for her Saturday job at the hotel as assistant receptionist when most of the foreign tourists arrived. She didn't bother with breakfast as she knew one of her father's assistants would bring coffee and a brioche to the two girls at the Reception desk soon after they arrived and before checking in and out got seriously under way, and within forty minutes she was cycling up the path towards the hotel.

Dale would be waiting for her when she finished work expecting an answer.

Dale had decided against following the family tradition of going to the School of Viticulture in Montpellier arguing that working alongside his father gave him all the knowledge and experience he would ever need, and although his mother had protested, Stephane was inclined to agree, and with a busy Practice to run, Mel simply did not have the time to argue with both of them.

He woke up about the same time as Fiona - got dressed quickly and went outside. It was a beautiful morning with the sun already well up, but instead of hurrying down to the vines where his father was probably already working before they walked back to the house together for breakfast, today he walked in the opposite direction up to where the land rover was parked alongside those used by his Mother and Tom Field when they went out visiting farming clients, got in and swung out onto the lane which ran alongside the river to the bridge and the hotel where Fiona would meet him. And after she had given him the answer he was expecting they would have breakfast together and start to plan the wedding. He was usually a contented young man but the thought of spending the life he already loved with the girl he adored, filled him today on the short journey with a joy he could never have expressed.

As he drove into the hotel car park he saw she was already there sitting on the low stone wall overlooking the river waiting for him with her bicycle propped alongside her.

She stood up as soon as she saw him, and by the time he had reversed into one of the marked spaces she was already beside the vehicle waiting for him to get out. She was wearing a light pale blue summer dress and the flat shoes she always wore to work. Her short dark hair shone in the morning sun almost like a halo and as he slid from the driver's seat and slammed the door behind him to take her into his arms he thought she had never looked more beautiful.

He was a surprised when she flung herself into his embrace without saying anything and clung to him until she pulled her head back and he could see she was crying.

'Darling, what on earth's the matter?'

Fiona shook her head unhappily, then she said 'It's no use Dale. I know you are going to hate me, and I don't deserve you, but I'm just not ready to get married yet.'

Before he could say anything she added 'You know why.'

Dale pulled a face and loosened his grip then, taking both her hands in his, he said 'I suppose so.'

'Imagine how you would feel!'

'I don't think I can. I only know I love you'

'Fiona squeezed his hands. 'And I love you. I just want to take this chance to make something of myself. Please let me. I'll be ever such a good wife afterwards!'.

Dale burst out laughing, despite himself

'And a much better mother!' Fiona persisted. 'It's only for three years. We can announce our engagement now, and the time will fly past!. The College has ever such long holidays!'

Dale shook his head but he was still smiling.

'Well, you know it's not what I hoped for...'

'I know, I know 'Fiona said contritely

'But if letting you go is the only way I can be sure you will come back to me...

She searched his face anxiously. 'Do you...' but before she could say anything else he suddenly grinned.

'Oh Darling, thank you! I do love you so much!

'She flung herself back into his arms'

Dale held her for a moment, then he said' I never knew grief could make you so hungry! Shall we get some breakfast?.

Fiona giggled. Then she kissed him briefly, and taking his hand again led him towards the hotel entrance bubbling with relief and excitement and suggestions for the announcement of their engagement.

CHAPTER TWO

Nichole Gosse walked across from the Estate Office to the Winery to tell Alim the Town Hall had called and would he ring them back.

Shortly after Finn was born, two years after his sister Lotte, the Vet Practice run by Mel and Tom Field had expanded to the point where they needed a part-time secretary in addition to the full time receptionist and Madeline asked Stephane if she could take the job as it would be so much easier for her to manage with the two children as she lived with Tom her husband in the same building as the practice office.

Stephane had agreed, although he had come to rely on her so much in running the Estate Office, like his father in law before him, but Madeline herself had suggested Nichole whom she knew through her brother Francis. In fact, Nichole had been married to him, but he had walked out of their flat in Lyons after a heated argument and she had not heard from him again except through a lawyer informing her that his client - her husband - wished to marry a Mademoiselle Yaron, and as there were no children, and he was willing for her to keep all the contents of the flat except for his clothes, he trusted a divorce could be amicable agreed as soon as possible. Despite this, she and Madeline had remained friends, the later agreeing that her brother had behaved very badly, and she refused to go to the wedding- hurriedly arranged, as she learned later, as her new sister in law was already in an advanced state of pregnancy - which explained a lot!.

Nichole was more heartbroken than angry, but was comforted by Madeline's continued friendship and support when she sold the lease of flat and moved back to live with her parents locally. She was twenty five years old and had worked in an accountant's office in Lyon so had little difficulty in getting a grip on what her new job called for, so both Dale, as well as Stephane himself, were delighted how quickly she settled in.

Nichole was always smartly dressed when she came to work, despite Madeline having told her 'casual' was the norm, except when they were expecting buyers or other important visitors... She was not particularly beautiful in the way of Fiona, who often called into the office when she and Dale were going out somewhere after work, or simply for a swim in the summer, or even Madeline herself, but she was slim and had a good figure, and when she smiled or laughed she became a different person - younger and vulnerably attractive.

Despite the fact that now he and his wife Mayer, who ran the B&B at Rousanne, were both French Citizens, Alim picked up the phone to return the call with some trepidation. Within seconds he had been connected to the Mayor's male Secretary.

'Mr Alim, good of you to call back so promptly: the Mayor has asked me to phone you as he was wondering if you could help us with something - or rather someone.'

Trying not to betray his relief, Alim hastened to assure M.Dubon that nothing would give him greater pleasure than to assist his superior ....

Cutting short further protestations, Dubon went on 'You may know the Department agreed with the Government to accept a certain number of refugees, and all towns within the Auvergne have been asked to accept a certain number - in our case, three.

Alim did not comment on what seemed to him not much of a problem, and after a moment the other continued 'People have been most helpful and we have already been able to find placements for two. The third has expressed a desire to work in the wine industry and needless to say, we immediately thought of the Estate, not only because of its size, and, may I say, 'Prestige', but because we know your native tongue is Arabic, and we wondered that, if you could find a position, they would settle in more easily.

Alim hurried to explain that any such decision was up to the Boss - Monsieur Stephane Meuse, but he promised to ask him at the first opportunity.

When the conversation ended, Doubon replaced the receiver, but picked it up again and dialled another number. As soon his there was an answer, he said without preamble 'I think they will agree'. then replaced the receiver without waiting for a response: You never knew who might be listening!.

After pausing for a few seconds more he picked up the papers on his desk still requiring his attention., conscious of a job well done.

Stephane was not exactly overjoyed by the Mayor's request, but had to agree with Mel that with the News still full of reports of the suffering caused by the ongoing conflicts in the Middle East, they had a duty to help if they could. Alim was willing to shoulder the responsibility of looking after him and further inquiry confirmed that accommodation in the town was available. And so, the following Thursday, there was a knock on the door of Rousanne - at 6am.

Mel was the only one up but was still in her robe when she opened the door fully expecting to find someone with an injured pet requiring emergency attention, and was surprised to find a dark, tall young man wearing faded blue shorts and a white T shirt waiting expectantly. He took off his peaked cap as soon as he saw her revealing a surprising mop of blond curls - so fair as to be almost white.

'Good Morning Madame. I am Amasa. I have come for work. I think you are expecting me' He gave her a dazzling smile and held out his hand.

Recovering, Mel took his hand. 'Amasa. Yes. But not quite so early!" She returned his smile to soften her words then, letting go his hand, opened the door wider and stood to one side. 'You had better come in' But he hesitated, uncertainly.

'I can come back later?.' But Mel smiled again and beckoned him in.

'It's alright. I was in the kitchen making coffee.'

He followed her into the house and she shut the door behind him.

'I expect you'd like some?'

'Oh, yes please. I did not like to disturb lady who owns where I am staying'.

'Come on then. Follow me'

'Thank you' He followed her into the kitchen and took the chair indicated at the table while Mel busied herself pouring two cups from the large jug keeping warm on the stove.

'Do you want milk?' she called over her shoulder

'Oh, no thank you. But some sugar please'.

'Of course'

Mel turned and came to the table smiling and put one of the mugs in front of him, then sat herself opposite and pushed the sugar bowl already on the table towards him and watched fascinated as he ladled four heaped spoonfuls into his mug and stirred vigorously 'I am sorry if I am too early' he said while doing this and smiled apologetically. 'We always started early at home before it got too hot!'

Mel nodded and took a sip of her own coffee without sugar before asking 'And where is home Amasa?' Looking at him more closely now she judged him to be in his mid twenties and was remarkably good looking, with eyes as unexpectedly blue, as was the colour of his hair - almost white- and long lashes that would have given his face an almost feminine look apart from the strong jaw line and a thin scar which ran down his cheek from just below his left ear almost to the corner of his mouth.

'I come from Syria. A village up on the Golan Heights.' he told her reaching out again to the sugar bowl 'If I may?'

'Of course'

Amasa nodded and smiled again showing perfect teeth as he reached for the bowl then went on more seriously 'We thought we would escape the fighting - almost wished for the Israelis to come, but one day some men came and took all of us old enough to fight and we never saw our families again. We heard later they too had been moved so it was no use trying to go back, and as soon as I could, I escaped to Lebanon and managed to get on a boat'.

He drank thoughtfully and Mel said 'We thought you only spoke Arabic.?'

Amasa put down his cup and shook his head.' No, I went to the Anglo- American College in Lebanon where I learned both French and English. I became a school teacher, but then I heard my father had become ill, and as the only son it was my duty to go home and help him. But he died soon afterwards and the full responsibility became mine to look after our flock.' He pulled a face - 'Before they took all our animals, leaving us to starve....'.

His story was interrupted as the door leading into the rest of the house suddenly opened and Stephane came into room. And after introductions, Amasa began all over again while Stephane joined him at the table and Mel went to get dressed.

Mayer arrived soon afterwards and produced some homemade croissants and more coffee for all of them.

Stephane took an immediate liking to Amasa and was greatly relieved that the impression given by the Town Hall that he did not speak French was incorrect. It also transpired that after their animals had been stolen and before being conscripted himself, Amasa and a few more from his village had been allowed to cross the border into Israel to work on the Vineyards which had been established on the Golan Heights with the help of the University of California, so he already had some knowledge of growing grapes, although the conditions were very different.

CHAPTER THREE

Amasa was the one who found him: Anxious to complete the last spraying before the mid-summer sun made it too hot and likely to do more harm than good, Stephane had gone across early to the new vineyard at Les Hirondelles to finish where he had left off the day before. The tractor and equipment were waiting for him and it was only a question of refilling the reservoir and putting on the protective goggles; starting the tractor, and he was away.

It had been agreed the previous evening that Dale would go straight to the office after breakfast which was in the main house of the Estate in the opposite direction, and it was not until his mother called him there to say his father was trapped under the overturned machine he knew what had happenrd.

By the time he got there, Amasa, Tom and Mel had managed to right the machine but Stephane was unconscious and apart from shielding his face from the sun, Mel insisted that no one was to do anything until the paramedics arrived.

Christine also came running across as soon as she heard what had happened, but as there was nothing she could do to help, Mel asked her to g o back with Tom and take charge of the Surgery.

Mel went with her husband in the ambulance which stopped briefly at the Clinic, but after a cursory examination, Holy ordered it to go immediately to the hospital at St Fleur and phoned ahead to warn those on emergency stand by to prepare for the multiple injuries she feared he had suffered. She promised to follow in her car as soon as she had arranged cover for herself.

By the time she got to the hospital, Stephane had regained consciousness and was in a great deal of pain. She waited with Mel in the small ward to which they had taken him while the X-Rays were being examined. He was able to speak with difficulty but only to tell Mel who was standing beside him holding his hand that he had no memory of how the accident had occurred.

After twenty minutes, a young doctor looked in and asked them to come to his office while a nurse stayed with the patient.

Without inviting either of them to sit down, he produced the X Ray negatives, and while they stood on either side of him he, started to attach them one after the other to an illuminated wall screen.

When the last one had been taken down, both women took a deep breath, then agreed with his prognosis that as well as a broken collar bone and several cracked ribs, the most serious injury Stephane had suffered was the displacement of several vertebrae in his spine, which, if not properly treated, could result in him being paralysed from the waist down for the rest of his life.

It was the doctor's opinion that care of a specialised nature was urgently required - of a kind only a few teaching hospitals in France had available. The nearest was at Clermont Ferrand. 'But to be frank, if it was someone I cared for, the only place I would want him taken to is the American Hospital in Paris' he concluded bluntly.

Holly turned to Mel after a second, and taking her hand she said 'I think he's right darling. It already had a wonderful neurological unit when I was there as an Intern.'.

Mel nodded.' Then let's get him there as soon as possible 'she said.'

The doctor momentarily looked from one to the other, then nodded himself.

'Then, if you ladies would like to go back and sit with him, I will phone Paris and see how soon we can arrange for an air ambulance.'

Alim waited until mid-morning then knocked on the door of the Estate Office. Nichole looked up from her computer and nodded with a touch of impatience which she managed to turn into a smile with an effort of will as he came in to stand in front of her desk.

'Bon jour Madame'.

'Bon jour Alim. What can I do for you? I'm afraid we are very busy reorganising things, as you can imagine'.

'I wonder if I can speak to Master Dale? (Despite the fact that Dale senior had died some years before, everyone who had known him still used the diminutive when referring his grandson).

Nichole stood up. 'I'm afraid he has been on the phone since he came in. Is there anything I can do?'

Alim hesitated for a moment, then he said 'Saeed, our son .....he is not coming.'

He looked so unhappy Nichole said more gently 'Is he not very well, Alim?'

The other shook his head, then he said. 'He is gone'

Nichole's eyes widened.

'My God, you don't mean.....'

'He has left. I don't know if we will ever see him again.'

Nichole frowned, then she said 'Why? What has happened? Look ...sit down. You look terrible!'

After a moment he did so and Nichole also sat down again. 'Has there been a quarrel?' She asked gently

Alim shook his head wearily. 'No, nothing like that'

'I mean. I don't want to pry, but we really need him now'.

'He has been very ... how do you say in French.?...'.away from us' for a long time'

'Distant?'.

'Yes. distant. He would not tell us what was troubling him, but he started going over to Clermont, to the Mosque there. We hoped he would find peace, but if anything that made it worse. Then, he just disappeared.'

'What do you mean, disappeared?'

'Last night he said he was going out to see some friends. But he never came back. His Mother found he had taken some of his clothes and a backpack I used to use on vacations when we were younger. We looked for a note he might have left. But early this morning, we had a phone call.'

'From Saeed?'

'Yes. He said he was very sorry to go without saying goodbye, but he had decided he had to go with his friends in Clermont to fight for justice for our people'.

Nichole stared at him, then she said 'My God Alim! Does that mean what I think it means?'

'He did not sound himself'.

Nichole hesitated a moment longer, then she said' Shouldn't we call the police? He is still under age and they are doing everything they can to stop young men who have been brain washed going off to Syria... or wherever?'

Alim nodded.

'That was our first thought, but then Mayer said if we did that he would never forgive us'.

Nichole spread her hands helplessly.'I really don't know,' she admitted., then glanced down at the desk and saw Dale's light was out.

'He's off the phone now. Do you still want to see him?' she asked.

After a moment Alim shook his head.

'No. You can speak to him. I will do better to go back to the Winery. There is still much to do before the Vendange.' He stood up'.

'Will you be able to manage by yourself?'

Alim nodded. Then he said 'For the moment. But unless Saeed thinks better if it, we will definitely need someone when the picking starts'.

Nichole stood up, then came round the desk to face him. 'I do so hope he changes his mind dear - for all our sakes... but mainly for his own.' She put out her hand and rested it briefly on his arm. 'He is a good boy, but he is very young'.

Alim paused, nodding unhappily.

Nichole let her arm fall to her side, then watched him turn on his heel and leave the office, closing the door quietly behind him.

Nichole sighed. You read about these things happening, never imagining that one day it might be someone you are fond of.

CHAPTER FOUR

At Fifteen Lisa had taken after her mother in being the prettiest girl in her year at school, but not in the interest Christine had always exhibited in her school work, and it was Billy, her younger brother by two years, who often did her home work leaving her free to spend her time with friends, which was much more to her liking. But she was an outstanding swimmer, having been taught to swim in the river by her grandfather by the time she was four, and was seemingly fearless off the high diving board at the new pool at the school, so she was always included in the school team in any interschool competitions. She was also a sure choice for the under sixteen regional competitions, and in the light of all this, rightly or wrongly, her teachers turned a blind eye to the obvious similarity in the writing style of many of her essays to that of her brother!

Billy loved her dearly - as she did him - but he worried about her constantly. As she was on he high diving board, it seemed she had no reservation in dealing with those who might want to take advantage of her, bestowing the same trust on all and sundry. That was not to say she was a fool, but started any relationship from the basic assumption that everyone was as well meaning as she was herself until proved otherwise, and even then, was exceptionally forgiving.

Billy's main concern was with the older boys at school and various other young men who accepted the open invitation of the Estate to the locals to swim in the Truyer from the bathing place created by its Founder half a century ago, and sun bathe afterwards on the broad stretch of grass between the vines and the river. He was not jealous. He knew no one would ever supplant him in Lisa's affections, but as well as being outstandingly pretty, she already had the body of a beautiful young women and he saw the way men of all ages looked at her. The one saving grace in his estimation was that, in addition to the periods for swimming at school, gymnastics was run alongside, which Lisa also enjoyed, and he persuaded her to take the lessons in karate which were also offered.

So far, there had been no occasion to rely on these. He knew his sister enjoyed the admiration she received and she often accepted the invitations of young men to go with them to a friend's house or a party. He knew she allowed them to kiss her when the opportunity arose, and the particularly favoured to let their hands roam when they kissed her good night, but as yet, none of these had been encouraged to claim the closer relationship of a regular boy friend. Despite this, so obvious was her genuine affection for those she held, nevertheless, at arms' length, none felt slighted and accepted her wish to remain uncommitted for the time being.

Lisa had been allowed to drive the tractor in the past for fun and now her offer to take on the hoeing of the weeds which grew obstinately between the rows of vines was gratefully accepted by Dale, but only in the Vineyard at Pousin le Bas where the land was nothing like as steep as at Les Hirondelles. Not to be outdone, Billy reported for duty at the Winery.

'It's like a plague!' Madeline said as she and Tom sat down exhausted to a late supper., Mayer having already given the children Finn and Lotte their's before putting them to bed then waiting for them to come in from the Surgery before going home.' Who else are we going to lose?'.

'At least the B&Bs have all gone home' her husband responded as they tucked into the chicken pie Mayer had left them. They did not normally drink wine during the week, but both had agreed that after such a long day coping without Mel, some additional fortification was justified and Tom had opened a bottle of the Merlot and put it on the table while Madeline was bringing in the pie, as well as and some vegetables given them that morning by the grateful owner of a large cat with an unusual liking for fruit and which had managed to get a peach stone stuck in its gullet the previous day and had been kept in overnight to make sure there were no after effects from the anesthetic.

Tom poured the wine and they clinked glasses before taking a first sip.

Tom smacked his lips, then said 'You know, I prefer this to the Rousanne!'

His wife laughed. 'Don't let Dale hear you say that!' she said with mock severity, but took another appreciative swallow.'It is very good!' she agreed after a few seconds

Tom said 'It's a pity we could not persuade Christine to stay. She looked really tired'

Madeline nodded, then she said 'I think now Dale is living over there she felt she had to go back and see he was fed and watered, not to mention Lisa and Billy.'

'Well what on earth have they got that house keeper of theirs for?'

'Helen is very good, but her husband gets grumpy if she gets back too late. Besides, you know Christine- nobody does things like she can!'

Tom nodded thoughtfully, then he brightened. 'Well, the children are asleep'

'So?'

'Let's hope I don't get called out'.

'You can do with a good rest yourself' Madeline agreed innocently, but her expression belied her words.

'Tom grinned and refilled their glasses.

'Are you trying to get me drunk Monsieur Field?' his wife challenged

'Just amenable!'

'Madeline nodded, then she said 'You know I 'm always that. Shall we finish supper first?'

Tom nodded. 'Then we can come down afterwards for desert' he said confidently.

Madeline said thoughtfully 'I've heard the English call desert 'afters'. Now I know why!'

CHAPTER FIVE

The news from Paris was not good. After a complicated procedure, Stephane remained in considerable pain, and with movement from the waist down very limited. The Surgeon told Mel it might be several months before they knew for sure if he was going to make a complete recovery.

Mel asked if he could be moved back to St.Fleur, but the other strongly advised against it for the time being. Stephane told her to go home. He was in excellent hands and was sure they needed her, but Christine assured her over the phone that they were managing, and she was sure Stephane would recover more quickly with her there to encourage him.

Fortunately, it was not a time of year when there was the same demand to visit t farming clients and Madeline had grown into the job of general assistant, so she was often able to help people who brought in injured pets if not too serious and that relieved Christine in particular who felt she ought to be spending more time over at the Estate office giving Dale and Nichole a hand.

The addition of Asmara, who quickly proved willing and able to turn his hand to most things was a God-send, and Lisa also became skilled in keeping the soil between the vines free of weeds with the harrow towed behind the tractor without damaging them. The sight of a young woman so enthusiastically at work raised the spirits of everyone else and Dale decided to teach her how to handle the machine picker - confident that she would manage that too when the Vendange started.

Not so obviously, but equally importantly, Billy became a second pair of hands for Alim as they prepared the Winery, and his company also helped Alim to put his worries to one side for most of the day.

The engagement of Dale and Fiona was advertised in the local paper, but in the light of Stephane's accident it was agreed that any celebration should be postponed until the Christmas vacation, by which time it was hoped he would be home, and Fiona left for her first term at the Teachers' Training College with the promise that she would come back for a few days at half term.

Dale was reluctant to see her go, but he had to admit to himself after a few days that he was probably better able to put his mind to his new responsibilities without her for the time being. There was also Lisa to cheer him up whenever he felt a bit overwhelmed.

As the days passed, he really came to appreciate the lightness she seem to radiate to everyone. She joined those swimming in the river after work, and at her invitation, he went with Billy and Christine to see her compete in the Regional Diving Competition in Montpellier at which she came third, only beaten by two women almost ten years older than herself and far more experienced. She was not used to being beaten, but one of the judges took her to one side and urged her to continue to practice as often as she could. She had remarkable ability for one so young and it was only a matter of time before she would be the one taking all the prizes.

Dale himself did not often swim but he came with a thermos of coffee to sit with her as she dried off in the sun and they discussed the next day's to-do list. As the Vendange was almost upon them there was plenty to talk about, but often their conversation turned to the future. Dale realised that soon she too would be going away to some college or other. but unlike Fiona she seemed to have no similar ambition and he guessed it was more likely it would not be long before some young man carried her off.

She spoke easily about 'boys' and confided her exploits with some - laughing good naturedly at the memory those who had 'tried it on', and it was as if she were talking about some naughty children.

Dale himself was conscious of the way eyes followed her as she got in and out of the water - usually with her brother, but she rarely used her towel except to lie on to dry off, and the scent of her body as the sun warmed her skin after the cold of the river was hard to ignore.

Thinking afterwards he scolded himself for the thoughts these moments engendered; even though she had the body of a woman, she was only a child - and one related to him besides ..... and he was engaged to Fiona!

He resolved that he would not sit with her again until the swimming season was over, but the after two days when he stayed in the office, she came to ask if he was unwell, or if she had done anything to upset him, giving him no choice but to resume their after work coffee breaks or risk upsetting her.

He would have been even more concerned if he had known that her feelings towards him had evolved remorselessly from growing admiration to the realisation that she was hopelessly in love with him.

The vendange was everything they had hoped for: the weather more than making up for any other difficulties. Dale kept a careful eye on Lisa as she guided the picker along the rows and he allowed Billy to drive the tractor which towed the trailer into which the machine discharged the fruit added to it from the baskets of the local helpers who came every year and who followed behind to gather the bunches missed or dropped by the machine. In the old days, professional Spanish pickers had done everything, but the machine had made the work still available not worth the journey.

Once he was satisfied that both Lisa and Billy could be left to get on with what they were doing, Dale went to help Alim and Asmara in the Winery to operate the press and the refrigeration plant which ensured that fermentation was controlled in such a way as to ensure the quality of the wine produced and more than halving the time before the finished product was ready for bottling.

The traditional dinner for all who had taken part took place on the terrace between the winery and the house, and Christine made a brief speech thanking everyone and expressing the fervent hope that next year Stephane would once more be at the head of the table with Mel at his side. Dale sat beside her this year with Billy and Lisa.

When they had cleared and the helpers had gone. Billy went willingly to bed for once, exhausted by the day's events. But despite feeling so tired, he found it difficult to sleep. Like his father before him he often sensed what was unspoken and that included hidden feelings. After nearly an hour he sat up and drank from the glass of water beside his bed, then lay back down again, but now he was wide awake.

The nightingale arrived on the branch on the tree outside his window and began to sing. Either it, or one of its ancestors had always come to sing him to sleep ever since he was very little, and he had always thought of it as 'his' ever since his mother had told him it came for just that purpose.

Billy closed his eyes, but when he finally fell asleep he dreamed that some shapeless threat was approaching and woke up sweating. The nightingale was gone, and he knew it would take him a long time now to go back to sleep. He thought of going into Lisa's room and slipping into bed with her for her to put her comforting arms around him, but no matter how he longed to do so, they were too old now. Besides, it was he who must be ready to comfort her.

CHAPTER SIX

Eva knocked on the door of Sara's office at Immobliers Cevant. and looked in, half in and half out of the doorway. 'Mr Meuse is here and would like to see you' she announced.' Mr Phillipe Meuse'

'Phillipe?! 'Sara frowned for a second, then smiled and stood up.' Well of course, show him in'.

Eva nodded, then stood to one side to admit a smiling young man in his early twenties whom many, who did not know either very well, often mistook for Dale, although slightly taller.

'Phillipe!' Sara held out her hand then glanced briefly at Eva.'This is Mr Dale's brother Eva. Please sit down, Phillipe. What a pleasant surprise!'.

After shaking her outstretched hand, he took the chair indicated opposite the desk

Trying not to stare, Eva said 'Shall I bring coffee?'.

Her employer glanced at their visitor but the other shook his head.' No thank you'

'Then no thank you Eva. but please see we are not disturbed'

'Of course.' Eva nodded, then went out, closing the door behind her while Sara resumed her seat, smiling across the desk, but before she could say anything Phillipe said 'I wanted first to thank you for getting me a place with Lloyd. It's been too long'.

Sara said.' I hear you graduated in June'.

Phillipe nodded.' I owe them a lot'.

'Have you seen Grace recently?'

'She's still with the Firm. They both said it had been too long since they saw you

Sara smiled. 'I must go over and see them soon'.

'They often mention you'.

Sara nodded. Then after a pause she said 'And what now? Do you have any immediate plans?. Are you going to set up here - or I suppose Paris would be the place'.

Phillipe shook his head., then he said 'I don't want to live here again'

'I suppose you've come back to visit your father?'

'I've already seen them in the hospital in Paris.'

Sara frowned slightly.' I see. So this is just to see the rest of the family?'

'No. I've come to see you'.

'Sara smiled.'

'I see. That's very flattering!'

Phillipe pulled his chair up closer to the desk.

'Sara, I've been offered a partnership in Lloyd's firm'.

'Have you?! I'm impressed!'

'But I need to raise some capital'.

'So is this a pitch for a loan?' Her smile faded. But Andrew shook his head.

'No. It's nice of you to think of it'

'I wasn't offering'. Sara laughed in spite of herself, and Andrew smiled.

'No, I know. But in any event, I don't want to start with a large debt hanging round my neck'.

'What then?'

Phillipe paused, then he said 'would you be interested in buying the Estate?'

Sara's eyes widened. 'Poussin les Bas?'

'I know you were interested once'

Sara paused nodding slowly, then she said 'That was a long time ago, and when I was married to David Nelson'.

Phillipe settled back in his chair, then he said 'Isn't it time to take control.? I understand it was your father's greatest ambition'.

Sara's frown deepened

'You <u>have</u> been doing your home work!'

'The Estate ruined him'.

'How do you know?'

Phillipe said 'Your mother admitted as much to my Grandfather years ago.' Sara opened her mouth to say something but Andrew went on 'I understand it was common knowledge he hated the Solomon family and wished nothing more than to see the back of them.'

It was Sara's turn to sit back in her chair and it was a some time before she said 'But your father is in charge now'.

Phillipe leaned forward: 'Was in charge. I talked to them at the hospital, and even if he manages to walk again, he will never be able to do what he used to. With his share from a sale, he could retire and live in comfort for the rest of his life'.

Sara looked him straight in the face: 'Do you think he would be happy doing that.? she said bluntly.

'Better than just having to sit and watch everything he used to do done by someone else!'

Sara paused again before she said 'What about your brother?'

Phillipe shrugged 'I don't owe him anything. He's young enough to find somrthing else.'

Sara pursed her lips, then she said 'And what are you going to get out of this? At the moment your father and Christine would get half each of any proceeds of sale'.

'That's true. But if you really would like to take over the Estate, I think I am the only one who could swing it for you.' He paused then smiled grimly before continuing 'My fee being fifteen per cent of the purchase price: five per cent on signature of the contract and ten on completion'.

CHAPTER SEVEN

Phillipe parked the Maserati he had picked up after landing at Charles de Gaulle in Paris in the space above the Surgery at Rousanne, then walked back to close the wooden gate leading onto the lane. which had been wide open when he arrived.

There were four other cars parked alongside his father's land-rover, and as he knew Dale had moved across to the main house on the Estate, he presumed the surgery was still open.

He walked round to the front door of the house and went in without knocking.- It was, after all, his home, even if he had not lived in it for more than four years. He walked into the living room but there was no one there - probably all still at work, but as he turned towards the kitchen, Mayer came out carrying some plates. She froze on seeing him, and he had the presence of mind to step forward quickly and take the plates from her before she dropped them, and put them on the table before turning back to her grinning.

'Hi Mayer.'

'Master Phillipe!'

'I'm sorry if I gave you a shock!'

'Oh...Come here!'

They hugged for a while then separated while still holding hands.

'Why did you not tell us you were coming?'Mayer demanded

Phillipe laughed, then let go of her hands with a final squeeze.

'Well, to be quite honest, I didn't know myself until a few days ago, then my priority was to stop off in Paris and see my parents'.

Mayer nodded. 'Of course. And how were they? Your mother phones but we never know if she tells us everything'

'Phillipe frowned and he shook his head briefly. 'Not good, I am afraid. He is having treatment every day but he quickly becomes exhausted it doesn't t seem to be doing much good so far'

'And your poor mother?'

'She has been on the phone to my grandmother to try and get Dad moved closer to home'.

'I understand'.

'The Hospital is reluctant - obviously- but it seems to me there is nothing they are doing now that could not equally be done here under the supervision of a specialist masseuse'. Mayer nodded and he went on 'He is becoming so depressed where he is and I'm sure that 's not helping either'.

Mayer nodded again, then she said 'It would be wonderful to have him home'. She looked round. 'We could easily make a bedroom for him here. The visitors have all gone home and Miss Christine told us not to take on anyone else'.

Phillipe nodded. 'That makes a lot of sense. Anyway', he smiled again, 'I've come to see what I can do to help'

When Fiona came home from College at the beginning of December she accepted the offer from the Manager of the Bridge Hotel of her old job as assistant receptionist over the Christmas period. Dale came to walk with her to work the first morning but she knew better than to expect him to do it every day, now the responsibility for the management of the Estate rested on his shoulders. She knew his brother Phillipe, whom she only vaguely remembered as the school's star soccer player when she first went there, had taken over the office for the moment, and Dale told her, their first evening together, that his brother had already initiated a sales drive, both locally and on the internet, and had attended meetings in Paris and Bordeaux; also, that he planned to fly to New York early in the New Year. In the meantime they had enjoyed visits from agents in Germany and London and secured orders which should ensure the prosperity of the Estate for the foreseeable future.

Nichole accepted and enjoyed the additional responsibility of running the office during her new boss's trips away. She could hardly have failed to appreciate the attendant increase in her wages, and came to regard Phillipe with something approaching awe, while he treated her on a personal level with gratitude and respect. Not even when they worked on late and alone together in close proximity did he betray any inclination to move their relationship beyond the purely professional.

Nicole herself had no wish to go beyond this, but she did sometimes wonder if she was so unattractive not to provoke some more intimate response before telling herself not to be such a fool. But she was unaware of any girl friend in the offing, and even began to wonder if he was gay. He certainly did not look it, and often commented how attractive she looked some mornings when she had made a special effort. But you could not always tell!'

Another thing she did wonder about was how content Dale seemed to be with the way things were working out, although she knew he had always found office work a bore and liked nothing more than to give all his time to the physical well being of the vineyard and working in the winery, where a vintage could be marred by a wrong decision, or made even better by the skill of an inspired Vigneron which Dale had inherited from his father

Despite the help of Asmra, Alim was relieved when Dale took charge personally of the Winery, and together they worked carefully selecting the barrels ready for bottling by the plant which had been purchased the previous year.

Lisa and her brother did not always see eye to eye. Billy sensed his sister's unspoken reservation concerning 'Uncle' Phillipe, but he was more concerned for Alim, and while he had no bad feelings about Asmara, sensed there was something more he ought to know about him.

Then they went back to school for the Autumn term and Lisa had to cope with the additional demands of the syllabus as it pushed her year relentlessly towards the Baccalaureat examinations, after which some would leave the educational system altogether, but most go on for another two years to prepare for University, or some job related training. Lisa had already decided she wanted to become a physical training instructor, but she still had to complete two more years at school before she could hope to qualify for the College in Paris.

After Christmas, pruning began, and Dale and Asmara, leaving Alim in charge of the Winery, began working steadily down the rows of vines leaving piles of prunings in small heaps to be burned, except for enough to provide fuel for next summer's barbeques and which gave the meat an unmistakable flavour.

As was often the case in early January, the skies cleared to a cloudless deep blue, unique to this time of year, and the air, devoid of the mists of autumn and the heat haze of summer, allowed a view of the mountains to the South, the Massive Central, crowned by the Pic du Midi, with unsurpassed clarity.

The river Truyer was at its lowest as the melted snow from the mountains had still to arrive, making it quite possible to wade across if you knew the right spot, and the punt. used at other times was pulled up half out of the water by the steps of the bathing place. The ducks were already in their winter quarters with a fenced pond just by the old sheep pen below the main house of he Estate, thus depriving any ambitious fox who would otherwise have paddled out quite easily to the hut built for them by Marcus years ago on a small islet midway between the two river banks.

There was no wind and the smoke from the heaps of burning cuttings rose into the air in straight columns. Dale told Asmara that the local tradition was that this denoted divine blessing and a bountiful year to come. The other laughed and said they had a similar tradition, but in their case it meant their goats would give birth to twins!

During the time before Dale started to take a direct hand, Asmara and Alim would often sit on the machinery in the Winery at mid-day to eat their lunch, and Asmra would listen sympathetically as the other poured out his concerns about Saeed, and needed little encouragement to curse those who had led his son into such danger.

Asmara did not tell him that he knew that Saeed had never left France for Syria, although he had disappeared. Such information might have offered his friend some morsel of comfort. But to others, it was deeply worrying.

At the week-ends, Billy was out of bed as soon as it got light and hurried across to the Winery as soon as he had breakfast.

Not having bothered about breakfast herself, he usually saw Lisa already in the distance wearing a thick sweater the colour of the sky and shorts - her long legs encased in rubber boots, raking the cuttings left by Dale and Asmara into heapss as they worked along the rows.

Despite the affectionate welcome home from Dale, after a few days Fiona had begun to sense something had changed, and after a week she decided to have it out with him. Had he changed his mind about their engagement? Had Nicole taken advantage of her absence to try and take her place?

Dale did what he could to reassure her, and pointed out that it was Phillipe who now had all the other's attention.

Fiona accepted what he said and was conscious that afterwards he started to make a special effort to reassure her. What she did not know was that, In a moment of inspiration, he remembered that riding and horses had been her passion since she was a little girl, but that being the daughter of a chef, she had had to be content with visits to the local livery stables where she was allowed to ride out with the owner sometimes when he took out a string of better off girls and when there was a spare pony as a reward for uncomplainingly staying behind to 'muck out' when there wasn't. Fiona had told him that this last was more often the case, but she never minded, loving almost as much to do this and look after the horses that had to stay behind because their owners had no time for them that day but did not make them available to anyone else.

This was something she had never been able to understand. She had always longed for a pony of her own, and could never understand how someone lucky enough to have one of their own could be so casual about seeing them.

Remembering this, and the sad expression on her face when she had first confided it to him not long after they started going out together, at the first opportunity after she came home, he invited her to meet him at Rousanne without saying why, then led her down to Shamus's old stables and invited her to look inside.

Nearest to the door was the old donkey, brought back from the Estate to resume his task of keeping a new friend company who was now in the further stall: a bay mare, about fourteen hands, who wheeled round and pushed him to one side so she could stick her head out over the half door to be introduced.

'I'd like you to meet Colleen' Dale said, and handed Fiona a bag that had been hanging on the outside of the door that proved to contain oats. 'She's six years old and Tom suggested her. She used to belong to the son of a Farmer he visits who is going into the army for a couple of years'.

'She's beautiful' Fiona enthused fondling the pony's ears and offering her some of the contents of the bag. 'Is Mel looking after her while he is away?'.

Without answering her question Dale continued 'He's big lad evidently and she was really getting too small for him anyway - or the other way round. Anyway, she needs riding'.

'I can do that' Fiona said turning quickly.

Unable to maintain his nonchalant expression, Dale grinned. 'I hoped you'd say that' he said.

Fiona looked back at the pony. 'I don't suppose he would sell her?' she said longingly.

'I'm afraid not' Dale said, pulling himself together

'Oh!'

'She already has a new owner'

'Oh!. I would so love to have had her!'

'You could always ask the new owner if you could ride her sometimes?'

'Could I do that do you think?'

'You already know the owner'

'Who is he?'

'She'.

'She.'

'Fiona Blanchet'

After a second Fiona's jaw dropped. 'Me!' she gasped

Dale grinned again. 'Yes., And do close your mouth. darling!'.

'But...'

'She's a late Christmas present.'

'She's really mine?!'

'And Mel says you can keep her here if you want. You don't have to, of course!'

Happy beyond words, Fiona dropped the bag and flung herself into his arms'

'Oh. I do love you so much!'

When they untangled, Fiona said 'She's the most wonderful present you could ever have given me!'

Dale said 'Perhaps you should stay and look after her?'

Fiona frowned, then she said hesitantly 'You don't mean, not go back to college?'

Dale looked serious for a few seconds then he took her into his arms again.

'Just testing! Don't worry. Tom will be happy to oblige while you are away.'

'Oh, thank God!' She pushed him away to arms length and put on a stern face.

'You are a beast Dale Meuse!'

'Aren't I just!. Perhaps he could teach Lisa and Billy? If you didn't mind of course?'

Fiona's expression relaxed immediately and she kissed him quickly on the cheek 'Of course I don't mind. And perhaps one day they can have ponies of their own and we can all go out riding together!'

Dale nodded. 'the Roussane Hunt!. Why not?'

They saddled up Colleen with the tack her previous owner had thrown in for nothing, and watched by Dale and everyone else who had been warned to stay indoors until this moment, Fiona trotted the pony round the field to show her off and everyone applauded when she finished by galloping up from the river to the stable.

When Fiona dismounted she was sure she could never feel so happy again...except perhaps until she and Colleen started to explore the surrounding countryside together.

Dale wondered how he would have felt if she had taken him seriously and decided never to go away again.

CHAPTER EIGHT

The Christmas Vacation over, Fiona had reluctantly parted both from her fiancee and the new love of her life, and Lisa and Billy went back to school.

Billy, politely for a boy declined the offer of riding lessons, having already set his heart on following in his uncle's footsteps, but as always, he took an interest in whatever his sister was doing, and when there was no match on Saturday, he walked over to Rousanne when morning practice was over to watch Lisa, who had jumped at the chance, being put through her paces by Tom, those afternoons when the demands of the Practice permitted.

Dale also drove over sometimes to watch when work in the Winery was over for the day, and so, one afternoon, when Tom had been called out leaving Lisa, who was now competent enough to exercise Colleen by herself, both he and Billy were watching when she finally thought the pony had done enough and trotted up to the stable. But when she came to dismount, she got her left foot caught in the stirrup as she swung her right leg over and yelped in alarm as the pony, thinking she was free, started to move towards the stable where she knew her tea would be waiting and leaving her hapless rider hopping on one leg. Both onlookers rushed forward just in time for Dale to catch her as the safety clip released the stirrup strap and she fell backwards, while Billy grabbed the trailing reins and brought Colleen to a halt.

He turned round in time to see his sister fling her arms round her rescuer's neck and kissed him as she gasped her thanks. She broke away almost immediately, colouring and laughing in embarrassment, then took the reins from Billy to lead the pony into the stable. Dale turned on his heel without saying anything and walked towards the house. It was all over in a moment, but Billy knew something had happened.

After a few seconds he followed his sister into the stable where she was undoing the girths and sliding the saddle off Colleen's back while the pony buried her face in the manger.

'What do you want to kiss him like that?' he demanded sternly.

Lisa did not bother to ask what he meant, but when she had put the saddle on its rest and hung up the reins and bridle she turned to face him.

'Because I love him' she said simply, and with a look that discouraged further conversation.

'I love him' Billy persisted. 'But I don't kiss him like that!'

'That's because you're a boy and I'm a girl' Lisa said defiantly

'It's more than that. You're only fifteen!'.

'That's old enough'.

'What do you mean, old enough?' Billy said angrily.' He's your Uncle!'

'No he isn't. We call him Uncle, but he's really no blood relation at all. He's just our mother's half-sister's son'

'He's engaged to Fiona then' Billy said.

As they faced each other, and Lisa was about to tell him to mind his own business, she saw there were tears in his eyes and she reached out instead and took him into her arms.

'Don't be upset darling 'she said gently

After a moment, he put his arms round her and hugged her back

'I can't help it Billy' she said softly.' I try not to think about him, then she has to go and leave him again...and he looks so sad sometimes.'

* * *

Nichole drove Phillipe to Montpellier where he caught the afternoon flight to New York after promising to stay in touch and hopefully, be back in two weeks.

She drove the car back being extra careful. She was a competent driver, but had never driven such a car before and knew how much he loved it. There was no reason why he could not have left the car at the airport and she wondered if trusting her with it was a test of some sort. If so, she was certainly not going betray his trust if she could help it. But she could not help wondering what he was going to do in New York. He had not discussed that with her at all.

The hospital in Paris finally agreed that Stephane could be transferred nearer home, and after Holly had found a specialised masseuse in Saint Fleur who was prepared to commute daily to the Clinic in Les deux Demoiselles, it was agreed that this would be a better option than Rousanne until he was even more recovered; close enough for Mel to return home and resume her responsibilities, but where his condition could be closely monitored.

The transfer was again undertaken by air ambulance and Stephane showed no signs of stress as a result of the journey as the helicopter touched down in the school soccer field - to the enormous excitement of those allowed out of class to watch - then requiring a journey of only half a mile to the Clinic.

Far from being stressed, as Phillipe had predicted, the move, and the daily visits he now received from Dale and Christine, as well as Mel herself, lifted Stephane's spirits enormously, and Holly promised that if he continued to improve at the same rate he really could go home in a few more weeks.

In the meantime, the daily visits from Dale allowed them to plan the coming year together, and this gave him the assurance that he was participating again. They discussed the possibility of extending the vineyard at Les Hirrondelles and selling off the house which was presently let to summer visitors. Of course that would depend on the agreement of Christine although there was little doubt she would agree.

Since Henry Withers had returned to Australia to be with his semi-orphaned children, having failed to persuade her to come with him, Christine had filled her life with care for Lisa and Billy and her ever increasing responsibilities as partner in the Veterinarian practice with Mel. She was still a beautiful woman, and over the years had attracted a number of those who would have jumped at the chance to join their fortunes with hers. But after the sadness of Henry's decision to put the interests of his teen aged children in front of their love for each other - no matter how much she had understood, and even admired him for it at the time - she determined never to allow herself to become so vulnerable ever again. This was not to say that she did not enjoy her admirers' attention, and even some short lived affairs, but she never allowed any to develop into anything serious, although some actually proposed marriage. She was aware that as great granddaughter of Andrew Solomon, the founder of the Pussin les Bas, she was regarded as a substantial catch and was never completely sure whether they were not more interested in her supposed fortune than her body.

Stephane did not worry that Dale seemed to have become a bit withdrawn, which he put down to the responsibilities he was having to shoulder for the time being, and just looked forward to relieving him of some of these as soon as he was able.

Nicole also visited and assured him that thanks to Phillipe, the office had never been in better shape, She looked forward to his return soon from New York when doubtless he would report direct to his father the results of his visit.

Dale made a point of not coming to watch Lisa having lessons in the paddock anymore and was relieved to hear that when Shamus died suddenly, that Tom had bought a hunter for himself, not only to keep Colleen Company, but to take his pupil out into the forest which lay between the river and mountains and which was chris-crossed by bridle ways where both riders and horses could enjoy the freedom of new surroundings every day as well as the opportunity for a full gallop where the trees opened out into a clearing. There was currently nothing Lisa could help them with work on the Estate and no excuse to call in at the office.

Fiona came back at half term and took Lisa's place during the holiday in riding out with Tom or by herself. Lisa wished sometimes her 'rival' would fall off and break her neck l, but was horrified when Colleen actually came back riderless from one of these solo outings. After a search, her body was found beside one of the paths. What was even more shocking was not that she had fallen off and broken her neck but that she had died from gun-shot wounds to her back.

Andre Fabre, promoted to the rank of Police Lieutenant when his superior, Inspector Goudon retired, together with Sergeant Moulin and the Crime Squad, combed the bushes, as well as the path itself within normal shot gun range of the dead girl but found nothing - not even a spent cartridge, and after the usual photographs had been taken, he finally gave permission for her body to be moved to the morgue of the local undertaker. It was only just over two hours since the pony had returned, thus establishing the time of death as between two and three p.m. There was no evident motive for the killing and Fabre decided that it had been a tragic accident caused by one or more people out for the afternoon after game of some sort. It was unlikely that they would have been unaware of what had happened, as even if the girl had fallen off the horse without a sound, it had dragged her for several yards before the stirrups pulled clear and the horse itself would undoubtedly have whinnied as it tried to get away. Also, the victim's injuries, although fatal, would not have killed her outright and she would have moaned or called for help. The chances were that whoever had shot her, seeing what had happened, had run and got as far away as possible.

A search of the Register of Fire Arms Certificates issued within the District was immediately instituted, and over the following days, everyone on the Register entitled to possess and use a shot gun who lived within twenty miles was visited. But so accurately had the time of death been established, that few had difficulty in establishing they were nowhere near the scene of the crime at the time it occurred, and those who could not were mostly judged to be unlikely assassins. The rest were either asleep in their beds - or somebody else's - or possessing guns that had obviously not been fired for months.

Fiona's funeral took place in the central church of Les deux Demoiselles.

Fabre and Moulin sat at the back of the Church and together they were able to identify everyone who attended. Dale was stricken with remorse on two levels: firstly, at having been the one who had bought her the pony in the first place, and secondly the feeling of relief - which was as bad, if not worse- that it had not been Lisa who had been on the horse at the time.

Lisa herself felt terrible - ever to have entertained thoughts wishing Fiona out of the way.

For several weeks, she and Dale deliberately avoided each other. Colleen was given to the livery stables by Fiona's parents in memory of all the happiness she had found there and with the hope she could be lent to other children sometimes, free of charge.

Tom decided to keep the hunter and bought another old donkey to keep him company. Lisa never rode again until years later, when her own children expressed an interest, and by then Fiona had almost been forgotten except by an old pony, who continued to look out over the half door of her stable every morning waiting for her to come and take him home.

CHAPTER NINE

Phillipe was welcomed back from New York and reported to Dale and his father the outcome of his trip. He had signed a deal with the biggest wine importer on the East Coast - Bush Associates - for the supply over the next five years of twenty-five thousand cases of their Rousanne Superior wine. The name 'Bush Associates' had no significance with either of them other than a name in the records of past dealings with a firm they had not had any orders from for more than ten years.

Conversely, the name Poussin les Bas immediately rang a bell with Sam Swann and his wife Lynda, the two directors of Bush Associates who had taken over the Firm from Sara Cevante shortly after she had inherited it on the death of Walter Bush, who had died in a fire trying to rescue Jeannine Berger, Eva's predecessor, from the flat above the Immobilier's Offices. Walter, who had been on a visit to the Les deux Demoisellesc to try once more to fulfil his mother's dying wish to seize control of the Estate by fair means or foul, had suddenly found himself totally smitten for only the second time in his life and had been horrified to discover that the object of his affection was living above the building he had ordered to be destroyed in order to eliminate evidence, which Jeannine had unwittingly revealed to him as residing in her employer's safe- not realising its significance in that it could incriminate him in the arranged fatal accident of Holly's mother and brother to prevent them from attending a vital meeting with the Ministry of Viticulture to get the embargo then in place owing to the discovery on the estate of a an infestation of phyloxera beetle, which had devastated the vineyards of Europe at the end of the nineteenth century - France, in particular - but had since been eliminated except in the Far-East.

No one had guessed how the pests had arrived, but as the beetles were discovered early, eradication had been comparatively easy. But the Ministry had still been in no hurry to lift the quarantine which had not only meant that the current year's harvest had to be destroyed, but prevented even previous years wine, already in casks and barrels from being sold.

Walter had been frustrated to learn that his comparatively simple plan to ruin the Estate and so make it 'easy pickings' might be on the verge of failure, and had given instructions for more direct action to be taken. It had not been his intention to have Ellie Solomon and her son eliminated altogether, simply put out of action for long enough for the finances of the Estate to sink beyond redemption. True, he had not felt particularly guilty when he learned they had been killed, but was terrified when Jeannine casually referred to the existence of a record of phone calls made by Sara's late husband Georges, owner of the Agency until his own accidental death, which recorded not only calls made to the one who had actually carried out the sabotage of the brake s of the Solomons' car, but to himself.

Georges Cevante had been a willing accomplice in Walter's schemes having his own reasons to hate the family and was conveniently on the spot, but he was not the brightest, and Walter had made sure there would be no connection between them - at least, he thought he had until then.

Although familiar with the name, the new owners of Bush Associates were unaware of all this and had been delighted to consider Phillipe's offer to supply them with five thousand cases a year of the Rousanne Superior for each of the next five years. This was a far bigger order than they were in the habit of giving to any one supplier, but it was a highly regarded wine and had won a number of recent awards in Paris and London thanks to Phillipe himself, and as the price put forward would enable them to supply their own customers at a price none of their competitors would be able to match, they were confident of making a record profit. However, before signing the contract themselves, they did get their Attorney to check it throughly as the sums involved would make it necessary to increase their borrowing from the bank considerably.

The lawyer reported back the following day, that as the contract was in English and the price set in US dollars he could see no reason not to go ahead with such an favourable deal.

Lisa was disappointed at the ending of her riding lessons and hurt that Dale was so obviously avoiding her. Billy told her it was all for her own good, and she really did try to put him out of her mind. It was still far too cold to swim in the river, but the heated swimming pool at school reopened and she forced herself to concentrate on preparing for the first of the inter school diving competitions in July.

She had never taken much notice of Dale's brother, and was amazed when he gave her a small emerald broach on her sixteenth birthday which he had brought back from New York and saved for the occasion. He had brought presents for everyone and had kept these too for the family celebration so no one would feel left out, but none of them were as nice - or valuable as the broach in her opinion, which she supposed was only fair, as it was her birthday. But from then on she became aware of his interest in her as he started to stop and talk to her whenever their paths crossed.

Nichole also was aware of a change in his attitude towards she herself. His previous reserve seemed to had disappeared, and on only his third day back he asked her if she would like to drive down with him in the Maserati to the newlv opened restaurant at La Butte, a small riverside village fifteen miles down the valley. She could even drive if she liked.

She agreed without even stopping to think, and he duly picked her up outside her small apartment in town at seven o'clock and smilingly held open the driver's door for her. They did not talk much during the short drive, allowing her to concentrate on her driving. She had been flattered by this invitation and was determined to show his confidence was justified, but she was nervous nevertheless and conscious that he often took his eyes off the road to look at her. She was glad she had worn the orange summer dress she had bought on-line from a firm in Paris for the first time and had managed to grab a hair appointment in town at the last minute.

They both enjoyed their meal together, the food being every bit as good as reported, and lingered afterwards over coffee and Cuviossier. Phillipe chose not discuss his recent trip, but told her about his time with Lloyd's firm in New York and how he had been offered a partnership which he hoped to take up when Stephane was completely recovered. He did not of course tell her how he hoped to finance this, and there was no reason why Nichole should have thought to ask, but he did ask her in the course of their conversation if she had ever visited New York, and there was just something about the way he said it that set her wondering if there more to this than idle curiosity.

He took the wheel on the drive home and it seemed the most natural thing in the world, when she asked if he would like to come in that they should end up in bed together.

He drove home just after mid-night.but was already in the office when she arrived for work. Nichole wondered if he might be regretting what had happened in case it should undermined his authority in some way. But before she could say anything he got up from behind his desk and closing the door behind her, took her in his arms and kissed her hard enough to take her breath away. Then he let go of her and stood politely to one side and said 'Shall we do some work now, Miss Gosse, or shall we take the rest of the day off?'.

Nichole paused, then burst out laughing. 'Are you serious? 'she demanded

'No. Not really'. Phillipe shook his head smiling, then reached out to rest his hand lightly on her upper arm.'But it's a thought!.

Still smiling, Nichole pushed him gently to one side and made for her own desk.

Phillipe's eye's followed her, then he said seriously 'It really was a wonderful evening. Thank you'.

Having gained the safety of her desk, Nichole put her small bag down and turned to face him 'If we are going to go on working together, Phillipe, don't let's spoil it' she said softly.

He nodded., then moved towards his own desk where he paused before sitting down, looking at her intently 'That's the last thing I would want' he agreed. 'But I can't help the way I feel about you'.

Nichole had no idea how her boss really felt about her, but in her eyes now he could do no wrong, and if things went according to plan, she would play the part intended for her without question.

CHAPTER TEN

Stephane continued to improve and Phillipe knew the time was not far off when he would be back in control and Dale would expect to resume spending more time in the office.

Midsummer arrived when it was too hot to work outdoors for long, but fortunately, once pruning was finished, work was reduced to simply keeping control of the weeds, mostly by Lisa running the tractor between the rows, with the broad harrow attached every so often, and keeping an eye open for any sign of disease that might call for additional spraying, and which would first be manifested by the roses planted at the end of several rows and which would show signs of any infection long before it took hold of vines themselves, so enabling remedial action early enough to stop it in its tracks.

The first B&B visitors appeared at Rousanne: this year, a Paul and Emily Blunt, friends of Lloyd and Grace Butler. Although also an Attorney, Paul having met Lloyd when they were still junior partners together in a firm in Boston, they had gone their separate ways professionally, although both had decided their future lay in New York, and they had stayed in touch. They brought with them an eighteen year old son, Julian who was waiting to go to Law School. Julian had not really wanted to come, but had been bribed by the promise of a car of his own when term started in the Fall. He was not a particularly likeable young man, his high opinion of himself being largely balanced by his low opinion of practically everyone else, but his parents hoped he would get that knocked out of him at College.

They were at breakfast when he came down the first morning, and after he had sat down with a preliminary grunt, and Mayer had brought him coffee, his mother told him they were going to drive into town after breakfast. They had been told that the Medieval Church was worth a visit and it would be nice to look round the market before driving up the valley to find somewhere nice for lunch.

Her son's answering expression was as if he had been asked to swallow poison. He had agreed to come, but that did not mean he was going to join their little jaunts.'

'Well, you can stay here if you like 'his father said 'but what are you going to do with yourself?'

Julian shrugged.

'You could go out with Tom' his mother suggested. 'He said last night he would take you with him on his farm visits if you wanted'.

'I've got all that reading to do before term starts' Julian said, quickly pulling himself together. 'I'll just stay here and go for a walk later if I feel like it'.

His father nodded approvingly. 'Good idea!'. He paused for a second, then added. 'You might like to go round to the Estate when you feel like a break. Mrs Meuse said Mayer's husband would show you round the Winery if you were interested'.

'Or you might like to go swimming' his mother put in.' Mayer said they have a place over there where it's safe to swim in the river. I think there'll be some people of your own age there'.

Julian thought about this. He was in fact a good swimmer, but he suddenly felt uncharacteristically uncertain.

'But they'll all be French' he said after a moment.

'Well, it won't do any harm to try your hand at that' his father said unhelpfully.

'You were always good at it at school' his mother added, and Julian turned to her.

'You shouldn't have let me give it up, he said reproachfully.

Julian watched their car turn into the lane then went back into the house and got the book he was supposed to be reading from his room, then he settled on one of the benches just outside the Surgery which still had the advantage of shade from several trees on the other side of the yard. But the comings and goings of pet owners and the whines and yelps from unwilling patients made it hard to concentrate on 'The law of Tort'. Then the sun rose above the tress and it became far too hot to remain where he was.

He moved to go into the living room, but a cleaner was vacuuming there and he gave up altogether. To be truthful, he wasn't all that interested in the Civil Law as practiced by his father, except for the occasional morsel he spotted from time to time from papers lying on his father's desk back home. The latter did not normally bring work home and Julian knew that, when he did, it was often something he might not want anyone else in his office to know about. He knew his father suspected that some of the junior clerks, although admirable in other ways, were not always as circumspect as they should be about discussing office business elsewhere, and for that reason, the papers he did bring home were often things of particular interest, - such as an item that had taken Julian's attention in the course of a casual snoop of the papers lying on his father's desk just before they came away concerning a Client's contract with the adjoining Estate.

Julian had no intention of swimming in the river with a load of 'frogs' so did not bother to take his costume as he set off towards the bridge, then over the river and past the Hotel on his right to turn back down the lane which led to the entrance of the Estate.

He knew the Winery was not far from the house, but just as it came in sight after he turned in through what appeared to be the main entrance, a small tractor came speeding up from an area of vines he could see now below the house and pulled up just in front of him. He found himself being examined by a young woman wearing a blue denim pinafore which left her arms and shoulders exposed to the sun, scruffy trainers and an old straw hat.

'Ce qui fait vous voulez?' She demanded sternly, then snatched the hat off to scratch her head with what he thought unladylike vigour without waiting for an answer, as if suddenly molested by a swarm of bees. He watched as a mass of long auburn hair cascaded in front of her, momentarily covering her face, until she jammed the hat back on after pushing the hair back up inside.

'What?' he managed at last and the girl sighed.

'What do you want? she said, switching into English.

Julian shook his head. 'I was told the man in charge would show me round the Winery' he said.

'Well. why didn't you say so! We can't have any Tom, Dick and Harry wandering in here.'

Julian thought he had never been spoken to like this in all his life - certainly not by a girl, who were usually flattered by his attention, but before he could say anything else, she turned off the tractor's engine and slipped off the seat to the ground to stand in front of him, taking the hat off again at the same time and leaving it on the seat. He could then see now she was about his own age, and very pretty.

'I suppose you're staying at Rousanne?' she demanded.

'Yes'

'Did you phone?'

'No'

Lisa shrugged. 'You should have. Alim's out'.

'Alim?'

'The man in charge'.

'Oh!'

the girl sighed.

'Well, I suppose I shall just have to show you round myself'.

Julian brightened. 'That would be great! 'he said.

'OK. Come with me then. Just don't touch anything!'

Despite her initial reaction, Lisa began to enjoy showing off her knowledge and her audience seemed genuinely interested - particularly, with the refrigeration plant, and listened with close attention as she explained how holding the fermentation process at a steady temperature made it possible to complete it in less than half the usual time'.

'What is the advantage of that?' he asked politely and Lisa was happy to explain.

'It guarantees the quality of the wine' she told him and takes less than half the time - which means we can beat our competitors to the market.'

'Except those who also have a plant'.

'That's true' Lisa said nodding, and beginning to quite like her student.' But it costs a lot of money and some still prefer to stick to the old ways!'

'Julian smiled. 'I guess It's the same everywhere 'he said.

'But not in America, surely?!'

Julian chuckled. 'What makes you think I'm an American' he demanded, and this time it was Lisa's turn to laugh.'

'Oh, come on!. She paused, then said smiling 'I'm a quarter American myself. My grandfather came from California'.

'I guess that's why you speak so well'.

'You mean English? 'He nodded, and she went on' We were taught at school of course, but my Mother made a point of speaking to me and my brother in English quite often at home... so did my grandfather until he died a few years ago.'

Julian paused, nodding for a few moments, then anxious to keep the conversation going with this amazingly pretty girl. who seemed to have thrown off her original coldness towards him, he said 'You say your grandfather came from California?'

Lisa smiled.

'Yes. He was sent over by UCLA in connection with some dispute with the Bush family, but fell in love with my Grandmother Holly and stayed.'.

'Sounds very romantic!'

'I suppose so'. Lisa paused for a moment, then looked up at the Refrigeration tank before turning back to him. 'I think the whole idea of controlling the fermentation process was first developed in California'. She paused again for a moment before saying with a grin.'...and that more or less concludes our tour for today, folks!'.

He returned her smile and said 'I very much enjoyed it!. Thank you'.'

'It was a pleasure - really.' She hesitated before saying more seriously 'I'm sorry I wasn't very nice to begin with!'.

'I never noticed!'

'Yes you did. I know I can be a pain sometimes!'

They looked at each other still smiling, and he said 'You are very pretty. I guess people forgive.'

Lisa frowned. 'Thank you' she said softly, 'but please don't say that. How you look is no excuse!'

Julian shrugged, obviously unconvinced, and she put out her hand to guide him gently towards the small entrance let into the big main door that could be wound up out of the way for the tractor and trailers that would use it during the vendange.

'What are you going to do this afternoon' she asked.

Julian shrugged. 'I guess I should go back and do some more reading'

'Oh. What for?' She pushed open the door and they walked out into the sunshine.

'I'm going to Law School in the Fall. Harvard, if I can pass the exams.'

LIsa smiled.' That's very impressive!'. She closed and locked the door behind them.

'My father's a lawyer' Juilian went on while she was doing this. 'As a matter of fact, one of his clients is probably your biggest customer in New York.'

'Oh?' Lisa turned back to face him, eyebrows raised slightly

'Yes. They asked him to look at a contract between them just before we flew over.' He smiled and nodded knowingly. 'I think they thought it was such a great deal, there must be a catch somewhere, but I guess it's this refrigeration thing makes it possible to offer such a low price!'.

Lisa shrugged. 'I guess so. I really wouldn't know'. They paused for a moment, looking at each other, then she said 'I don't suppose you like to come for a swim instead?. The river is deep enough to dive off the steps and it's not too cold'.

Julian said 'I *would* like to, but I don't have a costume'.

'That's alright. I was going to change in the house and I'm sure there is a spare pair of shorts somewhere'

Julian nodded.

'Well...OK;. You've twisted my arm. I guess Harvard isn't going to miss me for a few hours!'.

Lisa put out her hand again and started to lead him towards the house. 'We could get Hanna to make us some sandwiches and have a picnic'.

'Well, God bless Hanna - whoever she is'.

'She's our housekeeper' Lisa told him. 'An old friend'.

True to her word. Lisa found an old pair of shorts that belonged to Dale, and after Julian had changed, they met downstairs and waited in the kitchen for Hanna to produce the promised tomato and cheese sandwiches; and armed with these, together with a bottle of water, they made their way down to the river where several of Lisa's friends were already sitting around in groups, also picnicking under whatever shade was available, or drying off in the sun. But after greeting these, she led him to a tree bordering the river.

'Shall we go in first?' Lisa said, as they laid out their lunch on a spare towel. And without waiting for an answer, dropped the towel she had wrapped round her, and seconds later took off from the top of the steps into the water. Julian followed, and a few seconds later they had surfaced and were treading water laughing at each other.

Lisa said 'do you want to do that again, or shall we swim upstream a bit before we eat?.

'Let's go!'. Julian started to swim away with powerful strokes.

He expected to leave her behind, but no matter how hard he tried, she kept up with him, and finally he stopped to take breath while hanging onto an overhanging branch while she tread water further from the bank, grinning at him. She didn't seem to be out of breath at all.

.'What's the matter' she teased. Are you trying to lose me?'

'Not at all' He took a breath.' Shall we go on?'

'Just a bit. Let's not race'

They swam alongside each other until they reached a small cascade, then turned, and turning on their backs, drifted down with the current holding hands.

When they reached the steps, Julian waited for Lisa to go up first and he watched enthralled. She had the most amazing legs he had ever seen.

When she reached the top, she looked back down at him grinning.

'What's the matter, Mr Blunt? Haven't you seen a girl's butt before?'.

'Not like yours!'. Julian climbed up after her.' How do you know my name' he said when he reached the top. 'We haven't been introduced!'

Lisa laughed. 'It's a bit late for that now. As a matter of fact, Hanna told me your name. She and Mayer are always on the phone, *Juilian*. And my name is Lisa'

'Well, nice to meet you Lisa' he held out his hand smiling mockingly, but instead of taking it, she pushed him suddenly, and he fell back into the river, she then ran away laughing to where they had left the sandwiches'.

The vacation at Rousanne took on an entirely different aspect for the youngest member of the Blunt family, but whatever he had been expecting, the beautiful daughter of the owner of the Estate seemed to have little time between helping her uncles and practising for one diving competition after another. He persuaded his parents to stay at Rousanne for a change one day so he could borrow the car and drive her to La Grande Motte, down on the coast, for just such a competition and was almost as happy as she when she won her class - even though he had to hold his breath every time she dived. But he was thrilled when she allowed him to stand at the poolside with a large towel waiting to wrap it around her when she came up out of the water.

On their way home they never stopped talking and listened happily as a fuller picture of each emerged - including plans for the future. But the subject of Julian's father and the contract recently negotiated by Phillipe never came up again, for which Julian was relieved, realising he had said considerably more than he should. But he was mistaken in thinking that Lisa had forgotten about it.

CHAPTER ELEVEN

Billy was not unhappy at the attention the young American was paying his sister - anything that distracted her from her stupid crush on their uncle. Besides, he had something else on his mind - the murder of Fiona - and despite the accepted view now that it had been a tragic accident, he knew better. Someone had deliberately killed her, and he was determined to find out who. But he was not right in thinking that everyone else had put it down to an accident.:.

Although he decided there was nothing to be lost by the world at large believing so, Police Inspector Andre Farbre was not at all convinced, and if it had been murder, there was no harm in allowing the killer to think they had got away with it. But in that case, his first problem was to establish a motive, and there he seemed to hit a brick wall. Who could possibly have any reason to kill an innocent young girl, home from College, the daughter of the chef of the Bridge Hotel? Was she as blameless as she had always appeared?

Inquiring into such a thing was obviously an extremely delicate matter. He could hardly start to cross question her family and friends to see if Fiona had a guilty secret of some sort. It was incredible... but someone must have had a reason for wanting her dead.

He did not often discuss his work with his wife Eva, but on this occasion, both as a young woman herself and a comparative newcomer, she might be able to ask questions in apparent innocence, and without anyone attaching any particular significance thereto. Their son, Martin. had just started school, and the traditional meeting place of young Mothers, and sometimes grandmothers, at the school gates waiting for their off-spring was, as in most places, a hot bed of gossip. If his wife kept her ears open....and perhaps even pass an apparently idle remark, it might provoke something.?The only line he felt he could pursue directly was the college in Clermont.

The Principal proved both helpful and discrete and promised to make inquiries with both staff and fellow students, but she reported back in less than a week that Fiona had been a model student who had been warmly regarded by everyone. She had shared a room with three other girls but these had individually confirmed that she had worked hard and been very easy to get on with. There had never been a boyfriend on the scene as she had somebody back home. They had all been devastated by what had happened to her.

Eva also drew a blank. It was a small town and most of them knew the family, but no one had hinted at any scandal and were similarly saddened - and in some cases fearful - at what had happened.

It began to seem the police were going to have to accept that it really had been an accident, but Fabre's gut instinct would give him no peace, and despite all the evidence to the contrary, he obstinately determined t o redouble their efforts t o track down whoever had been responsible - intentional or not. They must have realised what had happened - someone with an unlicensed fire-arm? A poacher, perhaps? Or even someone from out of the district who had fancied a bit of casual sport.?

Billy did not have the knowledge, or training for such analysis. Besides, he was coming from a different direction. He just knew Fiona had been murdered and that the murderer was not far away. Not long ago he would have discussed this with his sister, who was the only one apart from his mother who had learned to listen to him, having come, from long experience, to take his instincts seriously. But his mother had quite enough to worry about at the moment, and Lisa was too busy with Julian. In any event, the only piece of additional information he had, not in possession of Farbre, was something that Lisa herself had told him, and that she herself had been told by Julian: that his father was a lawyer and had recently been asked to check a contract that a client was about to sign with Phillipe Meuse on behalf of the Estate. An odd coincidence, both agreed, but could scarcely have anything to do with what had happened to Fiona, so he turned his attention elsewhere:

Fiona had worked at the Bridge Hotel during the College vacation. Had she met anyone there who might have come to hate her? Did she do anyone out of a job, or had there been a guest who had been offended by her in some way?

None of these suggestions seemed very likely, or strong enough reasons to commit murder. But perhaps there was a way to find out.

Andre's phone rang just after eleven on Saturday night. They had had some trouble getting seven year old Martin to settle as he had a bad cold, and by the time he eventually did fall asleep, both he and Eva were tired and wanted nothing more than to go to bed themselves and curl up in each other's arms. But before they even got undressed, Andree heard the phone ring in the living room: It was Christine.

Billy was missing. He had gone out after his tea - they thought, to play with some of the children whose elder brothers or sisters had brought them for a late swim, and their first thought was that he had gone home with one or other of them without telling anybody. Although he was a considerate boy, he did tend to get some idea fixed in his head and forget everything else, and Christine had expected him to come back looking sheepish and put his arms round her to give her a hug and look up at her smiling, knowing she rarely had the heart to be cross with him. But this was different. It had started to get dark and when he still had not come in, she, Lisa, Julian and Dale went looking for him while Holly stayed by the phone. But he seemed to have disappeared into thin air.

The first thing Christine had done was to ring the homes of all those they could remember coming to swim that afternoon, but without success. The only bit of information this exercise produced was that the elder brother of one of Billy's friends remembered seeing him walking up the lane in the direction of the Bridge as he drove his younger sister home. He had not stopped as he was in a hurry to drop Ella off back home so he could go out to meet his new girl friend and take her to a dance at the school for ex-pupils.

For Holly it was all horribly reminiscent of when her own brother had been kidnapped by his grandmother and taken off to America; and the fact that he had also been called Billy made it even more terrifying. But she kept those thoughts to herself.

CHAPTER TWELVE

Billy had done some home work. There was no logical reason why anyone should have wanted to kill Fiona. She had been a lovely girl without an enemy in the world. It followed then that whoever had done it was either insane or getting at someone else through her - or both

She had been engaged to be married to Dale, on whom the on-going success of the Estate presently rested, so perhaps he was the was the ultimate target. Billy knew his family still had enemies - those who still resented the success of the Solomon Family and the Estate founded by his great grandfather, Andrew - a junior Bank Manager from London who had bought a then rundown B&B with a few vines more than fifty years ago and turned, over the years, by his descendants into the most prestigious Estate in the Region. He knew there had been attempts to undermine their success in the past - even to arranging a fatal car accident involving his great grandmother and her son Billy, after whom he was named. But who stood to benefit from harming them now?

Matha Germain had lived in a small riverside cottage in the same row as Fiona's family, but at the opposite end, ever since she was released from prison just over a year to ago. It was a considerable come down after the nice house she had shared with her husband further up into the town until he had been killed, and shortly afterwards, the police had arrived and turned the place inside out, as a result of which, they established that he had been a professional assassin, using his job as wine waiter at the Bridge Hotel as a cover - which explained why their standard of living had been so good.

Matha herself was charged with aiding and abetting. It was true she had a fair idea of her husband's extra -curricular activities, but had taken no active part. This was accepted by the police, but she had enjoyed the fruits of his projects without protest and this was enough for the Court to send her down for five years for 'aiding and abetting'. On release, she managed to sell their old house reasonably well and put enough to one side to live on after she had bought the cottage, but it would not last forever and she realised she would have to look round for some other source of income.

She kept herself to herself. Her neighbours were reasonably friendly but none of them had any idea who she really was until Fiona was killed - then it all came out. The police visited her twice, but were not able to pin anything on her, but the damage had been done. From then on, none of her neighbours spoke to her and she was shunned in the town by any who knew who she was.

Billy knew Fiona's father from when he used to watch her with him sometimes, practising for a Gymkhana. He knew where he lived, and after he had called at the hotel and found he had taken the day off, started to walk alongside the river towards the row of cottages. But as he approached., he was suddenly gripped by a sense of deep unhappiness He hesitated at the end of the row and was about to turn back when he remembered Madame Germain, whom everyone had suspected of being involved in Fiona's murder lived further along.

Inspector Farbre had immediately organised a search of the town and the surrounding countryside and it had fallen to Sergeant Moulin and Policeman Bloc to look up and down the river by the Estate, walking on opposite banks. There were one or two farm buildings on land bordering the river and these were carefully searched.

It was past midnight by the time they reached the cottages and were about to start knocking on peoples' doors despite the late hour, when they heard someone crying - a child perhaps, being held against his will?.

It took only a few moment to identify which cottage the sound was coming from and Moulin banged on the door while his companion stood just behind him with a drawn revolver.

Immediately the sound stopped and Moulin was about to bang on the door again when it was half opened and a young boy looked out at him, clearly visible by the light of the almost full moon.

'Yes?'

They had all been shown a picture of the missing child before setting out, and the Sergeant was so taken aback he froze for a few seconds. before pulling himself together.

'Are you Billy Solomon' he demanded, surprise adding a gruffness to his voice he had not intended. The lad did not look as if he had been crying.

'Yes'

Moulin stared at him even more intently, before saying 'Are you alright?'

Billy frowned.

'Why shouldn't I be?'.

'Your family are worried about you! Let me come in please'.

Without waiting for an answer Moulin pushed open the door which led straight into a small living room. He saw a fire burning in a cast iron grate, in front of which were two chairs, one of which was occupied by a middle aged woman who starred up at him in obvious fear.

'What do you want? Billy asked closing the door behind him without looking, which had the unintentionally result of preventing Bloc from following.

Moulin looked round. 'I thought I could hear someone crying.'

'You did: Madame Germain is very upset. I was trying to comfort her. She hasn't got any other friends' Billy said simply.

Moulin frowned, now feeling even more out of his depth.' And you are her friend?' he repeated weakly.

'Yes.' Billy moved to the woman's side and took one of her limp hands in his. 'I am now.'

'I see' Moulin paused again, then, trying to regain control of the situation, he said 'well, you must let me take you home now'.

The woman looked up at Billy and said 'That's alright, dear. I'm feeling better now. You run along.'

He looked back down at her and said gently.' Are you sure?'. Co's I'll stay a bit longer if you like'.

She shook her head and looked up at him smiling for the first time. 'No you had better go. I should not have kept you so long.' She let go of his hand.

'I'll come again soon' Billy promised.

'That would be lovely!'

'I don't know about that' Moulin began, but both looked at him, so he finished with a shrug.'Anyway...we must take you back now. I expect your mother will give you a good telling off!'

He turned and opened the door.

Billy bent down suddenly and kissed the woman lightly on her cheek.

'Good night Martha'.

'Good night Billy'. She stood up as they left. Moulin closing the door behind them. Then she bolted it. 'One could never be too careful!!'. She chuckled then turned to go up the short staircase, feeling more cheerful than for such a long time.

When Billy got home, he did get the promised 'talking to'. At least, Christine and Lisa started, but he looked at them with that affectionate smile they both knew so well and hugged them both before turning for the door.

'I'll go to bed now, he explained. 'I really am quite tired!'

They looked at each other helplessly, and when he was safely out of ear shot., Lisa said little devil. How does he do it?'.

CHAPTER THIRTEEN

Autumn arrived, and the Blunts prepared to return to New York, but Julian persuaded his parents to let him on stay for that climax of the year when all that men can do is either rewarded by a bountiful harvest or not - the Vendange - the most colourful, and possibly the oldest in gathering of all since men began to farm the land instead of just living on it as rootless wanders.

With mechanical pickers, powered crushers and the even more recent innovation of refrigerated fermentation, the Vignerons of the past would have barely recognised what was happening. But they would not have failed to recognise the smell of the crushed grapes from the growing heaps of skins waiting to be carted back to the vineyards to be spread at the roots of the vines, a parting blessing from one year to the next.

The celebratory dinner took place as usual underneath the lime trees on the terrace between the house and the winery for everyone who had taken part, especially blessed this year because Stephane, although still only able to take part in the physical work by helping Alim in the Winery, was back at his place at one end of the table facing Christine at the other.

After the last toast had been drunk, and all those who had helped gratefully sent on their way, including those living over on the other side of the river at Rousanne - which now included Dale who had moved back when the Blunts had gone home - Christine found Lisa waiting for her in the kitchen.

'It was lovely to see so many old friends' she said smiling as she put the last of the plates on the draining board

Lisa nodded, but obviously had something on her mind.

'Mum'

Christine turned to her.

'Julian has asked me to go back with him' she said in a rush. Her Mother frowned.

'Only for a break. Until we both have to start College' her daughter added.

'I see.'

'I've always wanted to go to New York Mum - Grandma used to talk about what a wonderful time she had!'

Christine smiled in spite of herself. 'Well... three cheers for Grandma!.But I didn't think you liked him that much?'

'Not to start with. But he's OK really. He said it was his parents suggestion that he invited me.'

Chistine paused for a moment before saying' How long is this for?'

'About a month. I'd really love to go Mum'.

Her Mother nodded. Then she said 'Well, I'm not against it in principle.'

'Oh..., thank you,!' Lisa stepped forward to give her mother a hug. 'I think it would do me good to get away for a while' she murmured into her ear.

Christine hesitated, then decided to let that one pass before saying 'But I think I ought to speak to Mrs Blunt myself just to make sure they are happy for you to go' She held her daughter at arm's length. 'After all, they will be responsible for you

Lisa nodded, the momentary shadow evidently lifted.

'That's alright. I thought you might say that. Mel has their address and phone number'.

Christine nodded again, smiling. 'When does Julian plan to leave?'

'Next Tuesday'.

'Tuesday! 'Christine dropped her arms and stepped back.' That doesn't give us much time to get things organised!.'

Lisa said 'He has an open ticket on Delta Airlines, and we checked - we can both get on a flight leaving from Paris on the Tuesday morning.'

Christine laughed, in spite of herself. 'You seem to have it all sorted out!'

'Julian said his parents will pay'.

Christine frowned, then she said 'No. I don't think that's a good idea'.

It was Lisa's turn to frown.' Why ever not' she said.' I thought you'd be pleased'

'How much are we talking about?'

Her daughter shrugged. 'For the ticket? I don't know. About two thousand Euros I guess'.

'Well. I think I can manage that'. After a moment, Christine said 'Let's sit down for a minute'.

She put out her hand and began to gently lead Lisa back out onto the terrace.

Lisa allowed herself to be led, and her mother pulled out two chairs from one of the tables, yet to be dismantled, into the last rays of the setting sun, and they both sat down before Christine went on 'It's very generous of Julian's parents to offer, but the thing is, you don't know anyone else over there, and if you are beholden to them you might find it difficult if you decided you didn't like it after all and wanted to leave'.

Lisa paused, then nodded slowly and said' I see what you mean.'

'It could be anything.'

Lisa nodded again.

'It would not matter if you were not so far from home' her mother added.

Lisa thought for a moment, then she said 'What about Alan Marsh?'

Christine looked puzzled.

'Alan Marsh?.What about him?.

Lisa said 'Doesn't he live in New York?'

Her Mother's brow cleared. 'Yes, he does...some of the time'.

Lisa went on 'He's over there now visiting his mother. I met Eva who works for Sara Cevante in town - she told me.'

Christine nodded, 'Yes, I see what you mean. That's a good idea,. In case you need any help. I'll ask Sara for his number. I'm sure he would be happy to see you anyway'.

Lisa found Dale by himself in the Winery the evening before she was due to leave. Having checked the gauges on the refrigeration tank, he was just getting ready to close the big double doors, but hearing a sound, he turned and saw Lisa standing there wearing a short, pale blue summer dress and sandals. Her auburn hair was tied back in a long pony tail. He smiled and took a few steps towards her'.

'Hello dear. You're looking very special tonight. Are you going out?'

The girl shook her head, but did not return his smile.

'I'm going away tomorrow'.

He stopped in front of her frowning.' Yes, I know.'. Then he said 'We shall miss you'.

Lisa didn't say anything for a moment, then she said 'I've come to say goodbye. Mum is driving Julian and me to the station early tomorrow to catch the train to Paris. I thought I might not see you'.

Dale paused, then he said quietly 'I'd forgotten how beautiful you are.!'

Now she did smile.' I wanted you to remember me like this - not wearing an old pair of overalls and a dirty old hat'

Dale chuckled, then he sad gently 'I was wrong. You always look beautiful no matter what you are wearing.'

Lisa nodded.

'Thank you' She paused a moment more then turned to leave.'.

'Good bye, then'.

Dale stepped forward.' Aren't you going to give me a kiss?.

Lisa looked back, paused, then shook her head'.

'Better not' And with that., she walked away.

Phillipe was surprised when he arrived at the office the day after Holly and Chrtistine had driven Lisa and Julian to catch the early train to Paris to find Stephane already at his desk. The other smiled and invited him to get a cup of coffee from the machine and come and sit with him.

'We've just had an e-mail from the Bank' he began as soon as Phillipe was settled.' The most extraordinary thing has happened: owing to some nonsense concerning various members of the E.U. falling out amongst themselves, the value of the Euro has dropped by more than fifteen percent against the US dollar.'

Phillip took a sip of his coffee frowning. 'I don't understand 'he said.' Why should the Bank want to tell us that?'

His father sat back in his chair. 'Because it's saved our bacon he said happily.'

Phillipe began to get a nasty feeling in his stomach, but he just said 'So?'

'Don't you see?' his father leaned forward again. 'That contract you signed with the Bush organisation was in dollars. It means that the payments we will now receive here in Euros will be fifteen per cent more, in effect, doubling our profits!'

Phillipe gazed at him speechless, and after a few seconds his father said 'You don't seem very pleased?'

His son pulled himself together and forced a smile.

'No... of course I'm pleased. It's wonderful! Just a bit of a shock'.

His father nodded, then went on 'Yes, it was when I phoned the Manager and he explained.' He smiled. 'So you are to be congratulated again, son!'

Stephane got up and moved to the coffee machine to re-fill his own cup, but continued over his shoulder

'I must say I wondered at the time why you arranged it like that, but I see now you knew something like this might happen, which was why you cut them such a deal!'

Having filled the cup. he turned back.

Phillipe hastily recomposed his features and said lightly 'Of course, it could have gone the other way and ruined us all!'

His father chuckled as he sat down again and shook his head. 'Oh, no. you knew better than that i know!'

His features now well under control, Phillipe smiled modestly.

'Thank's Dad.' He shrugged. 'I did speak to some of the Firm's clients while I was over there'.

His father nodded, and both sipped their coffee in silence for a few moments before Stephane put his down on the desk.

'Which brings me to the next thing: what are your plans? I can't say how much I appreciate your help over these past two months, but you have your own career to consider. What about this partnership you've been offered? Your mother and I realise that's really your ambition'.

Phillipe shrugged. 'There's no hurry' he said casually.' I'd prefer to stay on here until you are really back on your feet'.

His father nodded and smiled affectionately. 'I'd really appreciate that' he began,...but before he could say anything else the door opened and Nicole came into the room with the day's' mail. She glanced from one to the other frowning slightly, and after wishing them 'Bon Jour' put the letters on the desk.

'You both look very busy' she said. 'Shall I go and do something else until you are finished?'

Stephane shook his head. 'No, We've just had two pieces of good news, that's all'.

'Oh?'

'We've just heard the contract this young man negotiated for us has turned out to be even better than we dared to hope!' He glanced at Phillipe, before turning back to Nicole, eyes twinkling, 'And he has decided to stay on with us here a while!'

'Oh. That is good news!'

'Which?' her boss challenged innocently.

'Why, both, of course' Nichole said evenly. She paused for a moment, glancing from one to the other, then she turned to go to her own desk on the other side of the room and sat down.

Phillipe knew perfectly well what his father was thinking and returned his smile, but he guessed that although Nichole might well be glad he was to stay, and that since that first evening they had been together, it seemed he could do no wrong, he really knew very little about her, and that could be dangerous.

CHAPTER FOURTEEN

Alim reported to the police that their cottage had been broken into while both of them were at work. He and Mayer went through all their things but nothing of any value was missing. Such items that had been taken were mostly clothes Saeed had left and a pair of his shoes.

Andre Farbre was surprised a thief would have chosen such a modest target. Surely he - and it would most certainly have be a young man - would have realised they would not find anything worth risking getting caught and sent to jail for? None of the neighbours reported having seen anyone, so the odds were it was some kid taking a chance to grab a few things and possibly stock up his own wardrobe when everyone was at work.

Fabre asked for a list of everything missing on the remote chance that they might turn up at some flea market, and was reminded, when he got the list, that most of them belonged to the son who had disappeared - which must have been doubly hurtful for the parents.

Wishing to be seen to be taking the same level of care they would have given to a better off family who had lost some valuable jewellery, the crime team did their usual search for finger prints, but reported that only those of the family were in evidence

'When you say 'only those of the family', are you including the missing boy?' Fabre demanded when Sergeant Moulin put the detailed report on his desk.

The other nodded, so Fabre added 'They don't fade?'

'Not as far as I am aware'. Moulin shrugged 'Well.... I suppose over a long period ...'

'But it doesn't tell us anything really - except the possibility that it was the runaway son come back for his things.'

'Is that what you think?'

'It's a possibility'

Moulin paused for a moment then nodded slightly. and Farbre pushed the file away.' Let's see if any of the stuff does turn up at the next market in St Fleur.'

'Yes, sir' The Sergeant picked up the file and went back to his own desk on the other side of the office.

*** *** ***

Eva was very fond of Mayer. The two young women had struck up a friendship when Eva and her parents had stayed in the B&B at Rousanne when they were still looking for a holiday home in the district, and both being 'immigrants' in their different ways, a bond had quickly grown between them. She normally made a point of not asking any questions about her husband's work, but because of her concern for her friend, while they were lingering over supper, she asked if he thought there was any connection between the break-in and Saeed's disappearance, and he told her about his discussion with Moulin earlier in the day.

Eva thought about this for a while, then she said '; Don't finger prints fade?'

'I wondered about that'.

'What about dusting?'

Her husband frowned slightly, then he said 'Yes, that would do it, wouldn't it - unless there was some grease or something'.

Eva smiled faintly.' I don't think Mayer would have left dirty marks like that.! She's such a tidy person, she dusts everything to death over at Rousanne.!'

'You're saying any prints would have to be quite recent?'.

Eva nodded. Then she said 'I think it was Saeed... came back to find something specific...not just his clothes, and tried to make it look like a casual break-in'.

'Not someone looking for a clue where he might have gone?'.

Eva paused for a moment, then came to a decision.' There's something else I think I must tell you' she said cautiously.

'Oh?'

'In doing so, I 'm breaking a confidence...something Sara told me. She made me promise never to tell anyone else, but in the light of everything else that's been happening, I think it's important you should know'.

She looked so worried, Andre reached across the table and took her hand.

'Don't tell me if it's going to make you unhappy' he said gently, but Eva shook her head, and after a moment she went on 'Phillipe Meuse has told Sara that he can persuade the Solomons to sell the Estate to her'.

They looked at each other in silence while Andre digested the implications what she had just said.

'Sara told you this? 'he said eventually

Eva nodded.

'Why would they ever consider such a thing?'

She shook her head.

'Or Sara be interested?'

Eva said 'I think she thought about buying it at one time'

Her husband nodded.

'That was when she was married to David Nelson.

'Well, I don't know'. Eva shrugged'.'She said Phillipe Meuse reckoned he could persuade the family'.

'Did she say how?'

Again Eva shook her head. 'All I know is what I've told you, Andre.

Her husband nodded slowly before saying 'One last question then: what is in it for him... Phillipe, I mean?'

167

Eva paused again, looking even more uncomfortable, before she said 'Sara agreed to pay him something if he pulled it off ...and you must never repeat what I just said!'.

Andre nodded again, then he stood up suddenly and moved to put his hands on her shoulders over the back of her chair and bent down to kiss her on the cheek before he saying 'I promise. And you really did the right thing in telling me'.

Eva reached up to put her hands round his neck to pull him down gently so she could return his kiss, Then she said 'I wish I didn't feel so guilty!'

No more was said on the subject, and when Martin came back into the room, they watched a game show he was fond of then Mayer went and put him to bed. When she came back, Andre said he was ready for an early night himself.

He held her close until he knew she was asleep, then turned over into his more normal sleeping position on his right side, but it was a long time before he managed to sleep himself, turning over yet again everything his wife had told him.

There had to be some underlying plan for Phillipe Meuse to think he could persuade the Solomons -if 'persuade' was the right word - to give up where everyone else had failed.

How could he manage it? The main advantage, of course, was that he was a member of the family he planned to' persuade'.

CHAPTER FIFTEEN

The rail journey to Paris and from there out to Charles de Gaulle Airport passed quickly, with both Julian and Lisa chatting excitedly about the journey in front of them and the sort of sightseeing they would do together in the following weeks. But as soon as they passed the gate before getting on the Delta flight D440 to New York, Lisa felt Julian's attitude towards her change somehow. Only very slightly to begin with - a sense that now he was 'in charge'. But such thoughts were immediately banished in the warmth of his parents' welcome at Kennedy and the interest of the drive out to their home on Long Island.

With the six hour time difference, Lisa was ready for bed soon after supper, and by the time she woke, the following morning, Julian's father had already left to catch the commuter train into Manhattan. Julian himself was still asleep so she had a leisurely breakfast with his mother until she said she was going to turf him out of bed or he would never adjust back to New York time. In the mean time she gave Lisa the New York Times which had just been delivered and suggested she might like to sit on the veranda with its view out over the Sound and look through it to see if there were any Broadway Shows she might like to see.

When Julian finally appeared, he was not in the best of moods complaining of a headache and had to be reminded by his mother that Lisa was his guest and that it was up to him see she had a good time. Hanging out with his friends, which was all he had suggested the previous evening, did not constitute a good time.!

Lisa said tactfully that she would be happy to meet his friends, but his mother, guessing her son's principle motive was to gain points with the 'gang' by turning up with a beautiful French girl, insisted they could wait, and that he took their guest out for a proper day's sightseeing.

Although the day had not started well, by the time they got off the train at Grand Central, Jullian's headache had gone and it was difficult not to be infected by Lisa's excitement. Although the Fall already touched the air, it was still pleasantly warm, and anticipating that they would be doing quite lot of walking, Lisa was wearing light, low heeled shoes with her light, pale blue cotton skirt, cut just above the knee, and a white shirt top. At Emily's suggestion, she had brought along the light grey summer jacket her mother had insisted she packed - 'in case she went anywhere smart'. But when they got off the train Lisa took it off and looped it through the strap strung over her shoulder carrying her small hand bag.

Having worked in his father's office during vacations, Julian was well able to guide his charge to places he was sure would interest her and they began by walking along 42ⁿᵈ Street past the New York Library into Times Square, and from there up Seventh Avenue to Central Park, which seemed an appropriate place to sit on a bench to eat hot-dogs with onions bought from a nearby stand and watch a game of softball on the stretch of grass below - when the view was not interrupted by a seemingly endless succession of lunch time joggers, and kids of both sexes on skate boards.

When they had finished, they rolled up the paper into balls and both succeeded in tossing them into the bin fifteen feet away first shot.

Lisa laughed, then turned to Julian.'What now?' she demanded.

Returning her smile he said 'Well, we could take a boat on the lake, or there is a small zoo a bit further along.'

It did not take Lisa long to make up her mind. 'I'd really rather go to the zoo' she admitted. 'I've never been good on boats. We went to Lake Geneva once when I was little and my grandfather bought us all tickets for a boat trip, but I was as sick as a dog within five minutes!'

'On a lake?!'

'I only have to put one foot on the gang plank!'.

'Well, don't let's do that then!' Jullian said hurriedly.' The Zoo it is! Are you ready.?'

'Of course'.

They both got to their feet and started to walk on along the broad path between the flower beds. This time Julian took Lisa's hand, which she seemed happy with, giving his a welcoming squeeze. It was difficult for him not to notice the way most men looked at the girl beside him, but it seemed to bother him more than her - he guessed she was used to it, and soon they arrived at the small zoo which was crowded with classes of school children with their teachers.

It really wasn't a very big zoo. An attractive girl keeper was telling the children that the few large cats and the Elephant and her baby would be transferred soon to the much larger zoo in Brooklyn to spend the winter in warmer and larger accommodation. She was holding the hand of a young Ourang Outang. who was quite amenable to climbing into the arms of the braver children for a cuddle and being passed from one to the other until the keeper decided he had had enough; and telling them it was time for Bobo's afternoon nap, took him back and carried him to a cage occupied by three adults of his species, one of whom, she told them, was his mother, and installed him in the rear part of the cage which was shielded from public view.

Lisa found the children as entertaining as the animals, and when they had both distributed the small packets of permitted food on sale to the ducks, they found themselves being swept further along the path by the children to the Building of the National Art Museum, also set within the Park - evidently, their last port of call for the day.

In the larger spaces of the Museum the classes went their different ways and settled down on the floor to listen to their teachers telling them about the pictures they had selected to show them.

They eventually found themselves in the galley devoted to French Impressionists where one of the teachers had sat her class in front of some portraits by Renoir, a particular favourite of Lisa who had taken art in her last two years at school. They paused to listen for a while until the teacher glanced momentarily over the heads of her class at those standing at the back and seemed about to turn back to the picture she was standing beside when her expression suddenly changed, and after glancing hurriedly again her at the picture - of a particularly beautiful young woman with long fair hair sitting in a chair holding some croquet needles, she called out over the childrens' heads

'Excuse me'

The adults at the rear turned to look at each other.

'No you, the young lady in the white blouse'. She was pointing unmistakeably at Lisa'

'I'm sorry. Could I asked you to come over here for a second?"

'Me?' Lisa frowned, but the teacher smiled encouragingly.'

'Please. Bring your friend with you. I just want to show the children something'.

'Go on, she's not going to eat you. I'll stay here 'Julian said grinning and gave Lisa a little push, leaving her no choice but to step round the seated children to join their teacher who hushed the rising murmur of interest before turning to her.

'Your friend is happy to remain in the audience!' she said smiling and Lisa nodded, looking over to Julian with a reproachful expression, making some of the children giggle.

'Well, never mind! Thank you so much. I'm Agnes Ford, by the way. W've come from St Phillips, a school in Connecticut just for the day.' She held out her hand and the two women shook briefly.

'Welcome to New York. I'm guessing you are a visitor?'

Lisa nodded, then she said' I live in France'.

'That's wonderful!'.

'My grandfather's an American'.

The teacher nodded again, then glanced at the picture.

'Have you seen this portrait before'?

'Only in a book. But I have visited the PompIdou Musium of Modern Art in Paris. They have a whole room dedicated to Renoir.'

'Wow! I've never been there myself. I'd love to one day'. After a second's pause, she turned back to the painting.

'Now you are seeing it close to, is there anything about it that seems familiar?'

Lisa studied it, but before she could say anything, Julian called out 'She looks just like you!'

The teacher nodded immediately.

'Your friend is right. It's quite uncanny.! May I ask your name?'

Lisa was now beginning to wish she had gone for a boat trip, but she forced herself to remain calm.

'It's Lisa'

Her interrogator gasped

'What's the matter? 'Lisa said frowning.

'This is a picture of Louisa Garrond - daughter of a friend of the artist. Lisa is a diminutive both of Louise and Louisa.'

Without waiting for Lisa's agreement, the teacher beckoned the children to come up and look closer, and they crowded around, so it was quite a while before Julian was able to engineer their escape through a fire exit at the rear of the building, setting off all the alarms, while the woman rushed off to find her head teacher in another gallery. But that was only the beginning.

Thanks to the recently adopted tighter security at the entrance to the Museum, it was only a matter of hours before Lisa and Julian had been identified and the first call had come through to the Blunt's house on Long Island from Fine Arts Magazine, followed by Art News; and because it was a slow news day, it was only a matter for hours before the story of 'how the model of one of New York's Art Museum's most famous paintings had come to life' was on NBC Television news.

Louisa - the name Lisa now found herself stuck with, was persuaded to let herself be photographed wearing copies of the clothes worn by the original model and to let her hair down to resemble the portrait even more closely.

The fees, hurriedly negotiated to begin with by Julian's father on her behalf, were as nothing to those offered if she would only sign up with one of the major model agencies.

Finding himself becoming increasingly out of his depth, Paul Blunt telephoned Christine and explained the situation to her, and after a lengthy conversation, and unable to just drop her other responsibilities, she rang Alan Marsh, who was staying with his Mother in Greenwich Village

Of course, he realised why Christine had turned to him, but he wondered how many of those he had dealt with during the few idyllic years he and his equally beautiful wife had spent together before the accident, would remember him. One of New York's top models, after whom Christine had named her daughter, his wife had been the face of the most famous fashion magazine of the day. He had been driving them on their way to Paris when the accident had happened. No one had blamed him at the time - the car was driven off the road by a large truck coming in the opposite direction, well over on their side. He had taken the split second decision to drive over the verge into the adjoining field and down a steep slope, where the car had overturned.

Perhaps he could have squeezed past somehow?

There was nothing he could do for her now. But perhaps for her young name sake? She would have wanted him to do that

CHAPTER SIXTEEN

Les Deux Demoiselles is a small town where everybody knew everyone else's business.

The Estate of Pousin le Bas was an even smaller community. Before Christine left to join Alan and her daughter in New York, she asked Mel if she minded if Billy came to stay at Rousanne while she was away, which of course she agreed to at once, and Mayer willingly took on the additional responsibility of feeding him and getting him off to school - which in fact she positively welcomed as it helped to take her mind off worrying about her own son.

Billy would have preferred to have gone to New York too, but he agreed Rousanne would be interesting for a while. He had always loved the animals that visited the Vets' Surgery, and Tom had started to take him out on his visits to their farming Clients on Wednesday afternoons when there was no school. At other times there was always four year old Lotte and her younger brother Finn to amuse. For a boy of his age he was remarkably good with them, and they in turn adored him

Nichole had already got into the habit of meeting Mayer for mid-morning coffee during the summer, which the latter brought over in a flask to where they then sat in the sun down by the river for half an hour; and when Autumn arrived and it was often too cold to sit outside, they took it in turns to meet, either at Rousanne or in the Estate Office. Once in a while, Eva would join them, and as a result, she got to know Nichole as well and they started to call themselves the 'Three Musketeers!'.

Andre was pleased and amused to hear this. It was not always easy for outsiders to make friends in a small provincial town, and he had no worries about his wife being indiscrete

Alim was also happy to see Mayer starting to look less stressed. The only one who had reason for concern was Phillipe. As far as he was concerned, they were the ingredients of an explosion which if inadvertently mixed, could blow his plans apart. But for the time being, he did not see what he could do about bit.

Such was his concern, he never gave Billy a thought.

Neither did anyone else.

In contrast, with the proceeds of the first five thousand bottles safely delivered to the Bush Organisation and the prospect of similar sums assured, Stephane and Dale agreed that the way was now open to do something they had talked about for years and that was to extend the Winery. Plans had been drawn up over two years ago, and with just a few modifications as a result of further ideas, it only remained now to seek firm quotations, and they agreed that in addition to inviting local builders to tender, it would worth while putting an invitation in the Midi-Libre.

In deciding to fly to New York, Christine had had no doubt Alan was perfectly capable of dealing with the financial inducements being offered by a number of modelling agencies to sign up her daughter, but she remembered how the first Lisa, her Mother's friend and Alan's wife, had struggled to lead a normal life after she had been sucked into the world of High Fashion from which it had seemed there was no escape. She arrived soon after the first offers started to come in.

In the event, she need not have worried. It did not take Lisa long to make up her mind, and within a day of her mother's arrival told her that spending her life as a clothes horse was not how she saw her future at all. This came tumbling out when they were having supper with Alan and his mother and she was surprised that both of them, far from being disappointed, seemed very relieved.

She did not tell them that a main part of that hoped for future was the possibility, no matter how remote it seemed now, that one day Dale would come to love her as much as she loved him, and she was content to let them assume she was thinking of her career as a star athlete.

Christine deliberately avoided the subject for the rest of their stay, leaving Alan Marsh to fend off the Agencies, but it became obvious they were not going to give up, and they decided, reluctantly, to cut short the sightseeing Alan had arranged for them, and on their return to New York from Boston, took an early flight back to Paris

With the energy of youth, Lisa was up early their first day back and went for a swim in the river which was warmer than the air temperature at that time of day as the snow on the Massive had not yet begun to melt - and would not do so for at least three more months.

Feeling quite human afterwards, she got dressed in her track suit and trainers, and decided to take a jog round the Estate which would give her the opportunity to see what if anything had happened while they were away without appearing nosey - and who knew whom she might run into!

She knew work had started on the extension to the Winery and made that her first port of call.

Scaffolding was already in place and she stopped to call out' bon jour' to a young man who was already high up on it screwing some more steel tubes into place.

He paused, holding a short length of tube in his hands to look down at her smiling up at him. 'Hi!'

Lisa frowned slightly. She did not know him, although there was something familiar about him.

'Are you Lisa? He said in English.

Lisa nodded. She had to shade her eyes with her hand to look up at him as the sun emerged from a low cloud.

'I just got back'.

'I know they were expecting you'

'Do I know you?'

The young man shook his head.

'No. But you know my Dad. I'm Vincent Withers'

Light dawned.

'From Australia?.'

'Yeah'

'I thought you sounded different'

Vincent pulled a face.

'You sound pretty different yourself' he said stoutly, and Lisa looked contrite.

'Sorry. I didn't mean to be rude!' She smiled, then added. 'It's interesting!'

'Well, that's OK. I don't mind that!'.

Lisa paused for a mo0ment, then she said 'Does my mother know you are here?.'

'I don't know. we got taken on by Mr Meuse and his son. Dad saw their ad in the paper

Lisa nodded thoughtfully, then she said 'She's going to have quite a surprise!'

'Does it matter?.

'I don't know'

Vincent paused, then smiled.

'You're as pretty as they said'.

Lisa shrugged, hesitating for a moment, and feeling suddenly and uncharacteristically awkward, she said 'I have to go now, or I'll stiffen up'

Vincent nodded. 'OK. Nice to meet you. I have to join some more pipes'

He watched as she resumed her jogging until she rounded the building and out of sight.

In another world, the brief fame - or notoriety, of Henri and his two friends, Marcel, the son of the owner of the bar where they usually met, and Jules, a junior mechanic at the Renault Agents on the edge of the town, faded into obscurity, but they were aware that the least infringement of the terms of their release on bail and they would find themselves serving the rest of their sentences in the far less pleasant surroundings of the jail at Clermont. And when they did suddenly hit the headlines again, it was for the very different reason - that when they got back into the Renault Megane which Jules had borrowed for the week-end without his Employer's permission, and which they had left outside a night club on the outskirts of St Fleur, it blew up as soon as he turned on the ignition killing all three of them and seriously injuring two young women who were still standing beside the vehicle having yet to allow them elves be persuaded to get in.

Emily Withers, Vincent's twenty year old sister, phoned Holly at the Clinic as soon as they had settled in, and after telling her who she was, asked if they could use any more help. She still had two more years before she could qualify as a staff nurse, but Holly saw her later the same day, and after reading the report from the hospital in Sydney which Emily was able to produce, had no hesitation it taking her on, on the spot

CHAPTER SEVENTEEN

The sudden demise of Henri and his friends caused little distress locally except to their families and the families of the two young women who had been badly injured. The owner of the car which had been destroyed was the only one besides at all upset, but only when the insurance company drew his attention to the clause in their Policy which specifically excluded liability for 'Acts of Terrorism', and despite his efforts to argue that the explosion must have been caused by a leaking fuel pipe, they refused to pay up.

Inspector Farbre and his team established beyond doubt, despite the condition of what was left of the vehicle, that a stick of explosive had been wired to the ignition and that probably meant it had been done when the three were inside the club, but they left open the alternative, in view of the intricacies involved, that the actual wiring had been done while the car was still in the garage and the explosive added at the last minute.

Any involvement with the injured girls was dismissed as there were several witnesses who had been at the club that night to testify that they had been picked up by the deceased earlier in the evening and that they had obviously never met them before.

Detailed searches were made of where the three had lived - two still with their parents - Henri, in a small apartment over a barbers in the centre of town, and it was here that a diary was found - mostly recording its owner's sexual exploits - but also referring to his time in Jail and the bitterness he felt about the misinformation which had led to their targeting the girl friend of one of the local police. The vitriol was equally divided between whoever their contact had been and the girl herself.

Having brought the diary back to his office, Fabre studied it carefully and it was not long before an idea began to form in his mind: was it possible that the girl Fiona had been mistakenly killed by one or other of the three instead of Eva? Also, had someone else come to the same conclusion and taken revenge accordingly?

If that were the case, it opened a whole new range of possibilit9ies, the most obvious being Dale Meuse.

Lisa decided she should tell her mother of her encounter with Henry Withers' son, but by the time she had an opportunity, her Grandmother Holly had already phoned from the Clinic to tell Christine about Emily, touching only briefly on the girl's father and brother, on the assumption that her daughter would already know all about them

When she had put down the phone, It did not take Christine more than a few seconds to realise that unless she was prepared for a huge family row with Stephane and Dale on the subject, there was not much she could do, and looked forward to coming face to face with Henry unsure just how she would feel seeing him again. Eventually, she decided to grasp the nettle, and as soon as she could, walked across to the Winery.

Henry smiled warmly as soon as he saw her and came down from the scaffolding where he had been working with Vinvent. and put his arms around her for a warm hug before she had time to think whether she wanted to or not.

'Chrissie, It's wonderful to see you again!' He released her but continued to hold her at arm's length beaming.' I wondered whether we should apply for the job and would have understood if you had not wanted us anywhere near the place!' He continued to smile as Christine disengaged herself, frowning slightly.

'I'm glad to see you looking so well Henry. Have you moved back permanently?'

Henry shrugged. 'Well, this is going to take more than a year. Then we'll see'

Christine said 'I had no idea you had applied for the job. I was in New York with my daughter when it all happened.'

Henry looked serious. 'I see. Does that mean you don't want us here then?.'

'Not necessarily. Stephane and Dale had every right to offer you the job without consulting me'.

'I see' Henry pulled a face and Christine could not help smiling.

'Why don't you show me what you are doing?'

Henry looked relieved, then smiled.

'Why don't I? That would be a good start'. He turned to Vincent who had now come down to join them. 'This is my son Vincent'

'Hi!'

'Bon jour Vincent!.' Christine held out her hand which Vincent took and shook warmly.

'This is the boss lady' his father added.

'Bon jour Madame.' After a moment's pause he added 'I have seen your daughter'.

Christine smiled. 'Lisa. So I gather'

'She is very beautiful!'

Christine chuckled and glanced at the man now standing beside her.' I see you take after your father!'. She paused for a moment then she said 'why don't you show me how you are getting on, then perhaps we can go into the office for some coffee?'

As the Bible says... 'and that was the morning of the first day'

It remained to be seen how the rest of it would pan out!

CHAPTER EIGHTEEN

Most of the work on the Winery involved doubling the capacity for storage - not only to accommodate the harvest from Les Hirondelles, now coming into full production, but provide the facility to hold the Vin Superior longer in accordance with the decision that now cash flow was assured, income from more mature wine would be considerably greater.

It was an exciting time - particularly for Dale. He would never forget Fiona, but he was young enough to hope that in time the grief would lessen.

He was scarcely aware of the transition when his first thoughts in the morning were not of her but of all the things that needed his attention. The development of the Winery was an additional boost, but above all was his love of the vineyard; of walking along between the sunlit rows early in the morning before breakfast smelling the unmistakable aroma of the vines as the overnight dew slowly evaporated, and the way the sun shone through the leaves in the spring. seeming to turn the green to red. He knew he was so lucky in the love with which his family surrounded him, although the obvious adoration of Lisa, flattering in itself, was a concern, despite the assurance of Mel, when he confided this worry to her, that it was just a crush that would surely be transferred soon to a boy her own age.

Perversely, although this was of some comfort in one sense, he knew that when the inevitable happened, he would miss the warmth and beauty she offered him so unconditionally and without a thought for the future. He persuaded himself that his own feelings were totally paternalistic and that his affection for Billy was the same, but snide remarks by his brother did not make it any easier, and as Lisa herself had once pointed out to her own brother, he was a boy and she was a girl.

The goading by Phillipe got worse as time went on, then suddenly it stopped when the other announced one morning that he had decided to return to New York to take up the offer of a Partnership in Lloyd's Firm. He had never discussed his need to raise the considerable sum needed as a premium to be able to do this, and no one but Sara Cevant, Eva and her husband had any idea how he had thought to do this. But Sara had been uncomfortable about this the more she thought about it, and eventually, and without telling anyone, contacted Lloyd and asked if there was anyway Phillipe might be admitted without the premium. Lloyd had told her that, as far as he was concerned, it was not a problem, but all the other partners in the Firm had paid and would not see why Phillipe should be made an exception. He did suggest however, that if she wanted to help him, there was no reason why she could not lend him the money - She had ample funds, and it could be made conditional on his repaying the loan with an appropriate rate of interest over -say, ten years which he would easily be able to afford from his share as a partner of the Firm's profits.

Needless to say, Phillipe leapt at the chance when offered and agreed to her request that he said nothing of this to the family - merely that, as his father was now almost fully recovered, his duties called him back to New York, and in contrast to whatever turmoil his original plan might have caused, he left with everyone's blessing. Only Nichole was upset by this having hoped that he would ask her to go with him - but he never gave her a thought and she left herself without giving notice.

With both Phillipe and Nichole gone, there was an urgent need for help in the office if Christine was not to lose touch completely with Mel at Rousanne. After consulting with Christine and Dale Stephane offered Lisa the job on a temporary basis until someone could be found to take it on permanently, on the understanding that she could take whatever time off she needed for training, and certainly only until she had to leave anyway to start at the Physical Training College in Clermont.

She was more than happy to accept this. Like most of her contemporaries, she had grown up with computers and the Internet and picked up the office routine easily.

Although he foresaw no an immediate problem, without making it too obvious, Dale had avoided contact with Lisa as much as possible, but he could not avoid going into the office frequently. In the event, he was impressed by the speed with which she picked up the routine, and within a few weeks was doing the job as if she had been doing it all her life. He was also grateful that although she always seemed delighted to see him, her attitude towards him in the office was businesslike and respectful.

He would have been surprised if he had known that Andre Fabre had cross checked his movements on the day and evening Henri and his two companions had been killed and had thankfully eliminated him as a suspect. He also did a similar exercise regarding his brother Phillipe before he left and was happy to do likewise.

Billy was not sorry to see the back of 'Uncle' Phillipe. He had never shared the rest of the Family's admiration and sensed that his professed affection for them was a sham disguising a potential threat - the exact nature of which he did not know - but felt to be real. Nevertheless, he was aware, more than anyone, of the love his sister had for 'Uncle' Dale, and was unhappy when she took the job in the Estate Office. Unbeknown to him, his Mother was equally concerned for the same reason, although it had enabled her to resume her work with Mel, and for that she also felt guilty at allowing it to happen.

Sitting in his office with is chair tipped back, Lieutenant Fabre stared at the ceiling.
If neither of the Meuse brothers, then who? Who else had a motive?

*** *** ***

There is a hill overlooking Les deux Demoiselles. It was favourite place of Jeannine Berger, Sara Cevant's assistant, who used to take her lunch up there when the weather was fine. It was crowned by a small stone walled plot with just a few trees - too small for any agricultural use, and had lain dormant for so long, the original owners themselves were long forgotten until some bright spark in the planning department of the local Council recommended it be adopted as 'terrain libre' and offered on the market as a building plot.

As soon as she saw the notice which was erected on the site, Jeaninne had begged her father to lend her enough money for the deposit, and with the aid of a local Notaire obtained a mortgage for the balance.

All this was soon forgotten by everyone except Jeannine herself, who wondered if perhaps one day she would meet someone who would love the place as much as she did herself and want to share a small house they would build on the top of the hill there with her. But not long after the for sale notice was removed, she disappeared. Her mother eventually inherited the land but wanted nothing to do with it until Eva, who took over Jeaninne's job came across the Title Deeds in the desk used by her predecessor.

At the first opportunity, Eva herself had climbed the hill and sat with her back to the South facing wall looking out over the town towards the mountains of the Massive Central some twenty miles distant. The wind was blowing lazily from the South and broken clouds drifted towards her casting shadows which moved towards her before passing over her shoulder and out of sight behind the trees. Wild orchids lined the wall, their perfume dissipated by the wind, but now and then, when there was a lull, the scent was almost overpowering.

When she got to her feet Eva had been surprised to be questioned by a young policeman who had climbed the hill from another direction -Andre Fabre- the man she was to marry, but of course, neither knew that at the time.

Jeaninne's body was found buried just inside one of the stone walls and any idea of building a house up there was abandoned, but Sara helped the dead girl's mother to commission a bronze memorial in the figure of a young girl sitting on the rock where her daughter used to sit to admire the view, and this was placed in exactly that spot'

There had been a small ceremony attended by Jeannine's family and a few others who had known her, but then the top of the hill fell silent. Only one person came regularly to bring flowers - Alim, who had once hoped that one day all the obstacles between them might be overcome, but who had stopped seeing her for fear of those who resented their relationship and might do her harm.

Mayer knew he did this, but never objected, being wise enough to leave the past in peace.

It was on such a day, just after he had placed the flowers at the foot of the wall where there was less risk of them being blown away that he was surprised to see Asmara walking towards him smiling,. After greeting each other, they stood in silence for a while until Alim, who felt uneasy at Asmara's presence for no particular reason he could think of said 'I did not now you came up here'.

After a moment, the other turned to him and nodded.

'I don't. I came to see you. I knew you came up here and I thought it was a good place where we could talk'

Alim frowned and shook his head slightly before saying 'we could talk anytime '.

Asmara remained silent for a few moments more, then he said quietly' I'm sorry to be the one who has to tell you Alim, but Saaed is dead'.

Alim stared at him, eyes wide with shock before he managed.' How?'

'He was killed' Asmara said quietly, 'fighting for what he believed in'.

Alim looked away, then took a shuddering breath.

'How do you know?'

'We eventually managed to trace him'

Alim remained in silence for a long time shaking his head occasionally. Then he turned back to the man beside him and said 'Are you police?.

Asmara's shook his head.

'No. But we are on the same side'

Alim stared at him again but it was Asmara who spoke first.

'We think you are the one who killed those three'.

There was another pause before Alim said 'As long as they were alive, Eva was in danger'.

Asmara nodded again before he said 'We thought it must be you'

'They were the same people who threatened Jeannine'

Asmara paused again before he said' you had no right to take the law into your own hands'.

'The law did nothing to help us. Now I have lost my son'.

'I'm sorry'

Alim looked at him wearily and said 'Are you going to hand me over to the police?.

After a moment Asmara shrugged. 'I cannot see what is to be gained by such a thing'.

Alim continued to stare at him in silence.

'What about Mayer?' he said eventually

'I think you should both leave as soon as possible'

'Leave?Why?

Asmara stood looking down at him before he said softly 'We are not the only ones who might guess the truth!

That evening Alim did tell Mayer what Asmara had told him about Saeed, judging that she had a right to know, but he did not tell her anything else about their meeting. Mayer refused to believe him at first and went round to the Winery to confront Asmara for herself, only to find that he had left having told Stephane that he was urgently needed elsewhere.

This was not too much of an inconvenience as far as Stephane was concerned as normal work in the Winery was on a purely sales and mainenance basis while the building work was progressing. But Mayer, having no choice but to accept what she had been told by her husband, turned on hjm bitterly for not having kept better control of the boy, then went to their room and wept.

After nearly an hour, there was a knock on the door and Eva came in, and after sitting beside her on the bed took her into her arms.

After she left, Alim went upstairs, and finding his wife calmer told her the rest of what Asmara had said. He also sat on the bed beside her and looked so miserable she put her arms around him and they wept together.

Sometime before dawn Alim and Mayer agreed that there was no way they were going to run away from somewhere and people they loved and who loved them. They would do their best to carry on as before, as never before had there been such a need for them to do so

CHAPTER NINETEEN

Emily Withers struggled for a while settling into the Clinic owing to the inadequacy of her school girl French, but Holly was bilingual -as was her father Henry - and both of them did what they could to be helpful; and at the end of the day, she was an attractive young woman, who laughed easily, and when all was said and done, delivering babies and setting broken limbs was the same the world over - as were the various infectious diseases that warranted more than home care.

Although she stayed at her grand-parents with her father and brother while they were making up their minds whether or not Les deux Demoiselles was for them all on a long term basis, she did not see as much of them as they did of each other to begin with, and it was more than a month before Holly told her the following week-end was a national holiday and the Clinic would be closed except for emergencies, so she decided to visit where her father and brother were working and see what they were up to as they had decided to work on through the holiday.

They had just finished showing her round when Dale appeared, and after being introduced he invited them to take a break and walk over to the office with him for coffee.

Lisa busied herself getting extra cups for everyone then sat and chatted with Emily while the men discussed the next stage of the development, which would involve removing part of the roof.

The two young women got on easily, and before the others went back to work, Lisa invited both Emily and her brother to a dance to be held at her old school on the Monday, which was part of the holiday.

When they arrived where the dance was to take place, Emily was immediately aware that Lisa became a centre of attention, with young men vying each other to invite her to dance. She herself had done her best to make the most of herself, with a light blue summer dress she had brought with her from home in the hope that she would have some reason to wear it, but she knew there was no way she could compete with her new young friend. But Lisa went out of her way to make it clear that she was with Vincent and unavailable and all but one accepted her refusal with good grace and turned to Emily instead.

Some women might have resented this, but as a result, she was rarely without a partner, several of whom came back a second time, and one particularly charming young son of a client of Tom Field made it clear he would very much like to take her out the following week-end.

The evening came to a sudden end for all three of them however when the police arrived looking for them to request that Emily report at once to the Clinic where an employee of the Estate had been taken with serious stab wounds.

The police car took all three of them, and after first dropping Emily off, took the other two to the Estate where Stephane, Dale and Henry Withers were already being interviewed by Inspector Farbre while a crime team went to work, but he broke off and turned to Lisa and Vincent as soon as they arrived.

'Thank you for coming so quickly' he said.' I take it Miss Withers has gone to the Clinic.?

Both nodded, and Lisa turned to Stephane.

What's happened?'

'It looks like someone tried to set fire to the place' he told her.

'You can probably smell petrol 'Fabre put in.' We found an empty can over there.' He pointed across to the other side of the building'.

Dale said 'Alim must have interrupted them and got knifed for his trouble'

Lisa opened her mouth to say something, but shook her head instead.

'Is he going to be alright? Vincent said, as Fabre turned back to him.

'Who are **you**?.What are you doing here?'.

Before he could speak Henry answered for him.'This is my son' he explained.' We are working here together'.

'I see.' Farbre nodded 'And you were at the dance with Lisa?'

'And my sister.'

The Inspector nodded again, then he said 'The wounds that young man suffered were serious, but we have already heard, not life threatening. So at least we are not dealing with a murder'.

'No thanks to the cowardly bastards who attacked him' Moulin said joining them, and Farbre nodded again.

'That's true. When they realised what one of them had done, they ran away without doing what they had come for'.

'But If it had not been for that phone call, he would have bled to death before anyone found him' Dale said.

'What phone call? 'Vincent demanded.

'Farbe said 'we don't know who from. Probably, one of the intruders who did not want a murder rap on top of everything else if we caught up with them.' He turned to Moulin and said 'Have we finished here?'

The other nodded.

'We've done what we can until the morning. They must be local. There's no sign of any vehicle tracks'.

It was only then that Dale said suddenly 'has anyone

CHAPTER TWENTY

As soon as Holy said he was well enough, Farbre visited the Clinic to speak to Alim, but he was only able to add that there had been three of them, but they were wearing balaclavas and there was no way he would be able to identify them. It was pure luck that realising he had left his phone, he went back into the Winery to get it.

'I don't know whether 'luck' is the word I would use if I were lying there' Farbre said sympathetically.

Alim nodded, then he said 'I owe the Solomons everything. There is nothing I would not do for them.

Farbe nodded himself, then stood up. 'Thank you for seeing me' he said quietly.' You are a very brave man. Don' t get up!'

He grinned, and seeing Alim frowning added hurriedly. 'Sorry... just my silly sense of humour!' He rested his hand gently on Alim's shoulder.

'Just get better. In the meantime we'll do everything we can to find the people who did this to you.

He went out, closing the door behind him and started to walk back down the corridor to say goodbye to Holly.

That done, he went outside and got into the car where Sergeant Moukl in was waiting for him.

'Well?' Moulin demanded, without preamble.

Farbre adjusted his seat belt, then turned to him.

'Nothing!'

The two men stared at each other, then Moulin moved to start the car, but before he did Farbre said' The strange thing is, the way he looked at me when I said we would do everything we could to catch the people who had put him there'. He paused before adding 'almost as if he didn't want us to!'.

Thy following day, a report came through from the police at St Flour who, like all others within a fifty mile radius had been notified of the attempted arson attack on the Estate Winery and the wounding of the person who had disturbed them: a man had been admitted to the nearby hospital with serious wounds having evidently tripped and fallen on the knife he had been using to open some parcels. It probably had nothing to do with the report they had been sent, but the hospital had told them they were surprised at the extent of the wounds from such a cause.

Farbre and Moulin drove over to St Fleur immediately, but were too late. The duty nurse informed them that the injured man had already been collected by the two friends who had brought him in.

To no one's surprise, the record of the name and address given at the time of his admission proved to be false.

It was decided to install an intruder alarm in the Winery, and as an additional precaution Tom gave them a big black dog called Bessie who needed a home.

She was cross between a black labrador and a full sized poodle with whom everybody immediately fell in love. She would not have hurt a fly, but she was large and barked at strangers so it was agreed she would live with Christine, close to the winery but far enough away from the Vet's Surgery on the other side of the river so as not to alarm visitors.

Billy and Lisa willingly shared looking after her, and she willingly looked after them - particularly Billy, whom she decided almost immediately needed her special attention. Her basket was put in the kitchen, the outside door of which was fitted with a dog flap so she could wander in and out whenever she chose. But despite Christine's discouragement, she often padded upstairs and lay beside Billy's bed so that he reach down to fondle her ears until he fell asleep, when she would then go back downstairs again and out into the yard to sniff the night air until satisfied that all was well until finally curling up in her basket until dawn, or a fox, or some other night wanderer sent her shooting outside again to give them a good barking at - which woke up everyone up except Billy, who was often dreaming about their adventures together. But, as Stephane pointed out, she was only doing her job.

Alim took quite a while to recover - not just from his wounds, but the trauma of what had happened. Mayer visited him at the Clinic every day, and so did Dale, who often stopped to talk to Emily before leaving, and she began to look forward to his visits more than she cared to admit to herself to begin with. She often walked over to where her father and brother were working and was disappointed not to see him at the same time if he was tied up in the office. But more often than not, he would stop whatever he was doing, and after he had run out of things to show her on the Estate would walk back with her up into the town to where she lived.

As promised, a week later, Laurin Girard, the young farmer's son who had met Emily at the dance, invited her to come and see where he lived. She debated with herself whether or not to accept his offer, but she had seen very little of the countryside since arriving from Australia, and decided there could be no harm in it.

She was made very welcome by Laurin's parents and was fascinated to see all the animals and the modern automated milking parlour, but it became apparent during the course of the day that Laurin himself was attaching a greater significance to the day, and when he stopped the car at a lonely place on the drive home, had not only kissed her, which she had expected as only fair, but then tried to undress her - which she didn't. A row ensued and the journey then continued in silence until he came to drop her off where she lived.

Having pulled himself together by then, Laurin apologised, which Emily accepted with a smile and a light kiss on the cheek, but after thanking him for the day, she got out of the car and closed the door quickly before he could say anything else.

Whether they were aware of the moment when their friendship became altogether deeper, if there ever was such a definable moment, one day, when Dale was making his early morning inspection of the vines, the sun came up, filling him, as it always did in the Spring with an extra sense of well being, only now he stopped and was suddenly flooded with happiness at the thought of seeing Emily again, only to ask himself, how could he feel like this after what had happened to Fiona!

He heard a bark and turned to see Billy in the distance walking towards him with Bessie at his heels, except for when some particular scent required a short diversion. Billy saw him and waived. quickening his step, which the big dog took as some sort of game, barking and jumping up happily. Then, just as suddenly, Dale felt at peace. Fiona would always be part of him and he was sure she would not have wanted the memory of the love they had shared to stop him loving Emily. That was what was so wonderful about love - it had no limits. A new baby never diminished the love of its parents for their existing children, which just expanded to take the newcomer on board.

He bent down smiling to accept the enthusiastic greetings of Bessie, who just loved everybody - although Billy, best of all, of course.

One person who was not happy at what she could see of the developing friendship between Dale and Emily was Lisa. But the diving competition school pool, to which she had been given unrestricted access. Billy, of course, was aware of his sister's unhappiness and did what he could to be extra thoughtful, but he knew that in the end, she would have to accept what he had always guessed would be inevitable. He made friends with Vincent and often looked in after school to see how they were getting on.

Alim was discharged from the Clinic and was anxious to get back to work for Stephane and Dale, but he tired easily and Billy was allowed to take over the tractor after school, as Lisa was now tied up in the office, to help with hoeing between the vines to keep the ever threatening weeds at bay, and on Wednesday, when there was no school, he and Vincent ate their lunch together after Christine brought it over to the winery, where she was sure to find them - and not forgetting some dog biscuits knowing for sure Bessie would otherwise be given half the boys sandwiches.

Although he brought his own lunch, Henry also looked forward these visits which helped, finally, to overcome the initial awkwardness when they had first met again, and he was delighted when she invited he and Vincent round for dinner. She invited Emily too but it was her week on night duty at the Clinic.

Lisa was not sorry. She did not dislike Vincent's sister, but found it hard to put her relationship with Dale out of her mind whenever she thought about her, and she determined to concentrate on Vincent for the evening, although she had no real feelings for him, one way or the other. He was a nice looking, strong young man who took after his father in his open and pleasant manner.

Billy had told her he asked about her a good deal and she suspected her brother was hoping she and the young Australian would be drawn to each other - even if that meant her going back with him when the Winery was finished, unless he decided to stay. Billy knew no one would ever replace Dale, but if his sister was going to be unhappy for the rest of her life he imagined she could do far worse!.

The evening was a success. Henry and Christine reminisced about Les Hirrondelles, the much smaller Estate downstream on the other side of the river where they had first met when the Englishman, Richard Chambers, to whom Christine was married briefly, had decided to greatly enlarge the house attached and had employed Henry to do the work.

Billy drew Lisa to tell about her trip to New York and how it had ended with their mother having to go over and rescue her from the Metropolitan Museum of Art. And when Christine had laughingly put the story straight, Vincent said to Lisa 'But don't you regret that? Turning your back on fame and fortune?'

Lisa shook her head, but before she could say anything else her mother went on brightly 'She's a country girl at heart - aren't you, darling.?' She looked round the table 'We still get rung up by different Agencies wanting her to become a clothes horse like my mother's best friend, whom she's named after'.

Lisa frowned 'When was that?'

Her mother smiled at her and said 'Oh, I don't know...last week I think was the last time. I'm sorry. I didn't say anything, but you did make it clear you weren't interested"

'You should still have told me'.

Christine's smile faded.' I've said I'm sorry. If it happens again, I'll let you know...or you can speak to them yourself'.

There was a moments' silence then Vincent said seriously 'I've always thought you were quite special. I'm not surprised!'

Further conversation was suspended by Christine insisting that Billy stopped feeding Bessie under the table and that the dog be put outside, and when that had been done, they all agreed it was time for ice-cream and everyone else got up again to help carry the dishes out into the kitchen.

So the moment of tension passed - if not forgotten.

*** *** ***

The sun grew hot by late April. The water in the river was still cold but the keenest swimmers, or determined sun bathers started to reappear at the riverside bathing place which Andrew Solomon had made fifty years ago before opening it to everyone, and these included Lisa and Vincent. When she saw him in the water and diving from the small platform on the river bank, she determined that the next time she went to the school for training she would ask if he would like to come with her, but It still came as a surprise to discover then that his diving from the highest board was as fearless and at least as good as her own. But she had to drag out of him that he had competed in the Sydney Gala, and although he had never come first, had a silver and two bronze medals hanging on the wall of his bedroom back home.

187

Despite his protests, Lisa lost no time in letting everyone know about Vincent's previously unmentioned talent, and Henry raised no objection to his taking time off to go with her to the various competitions. She managed to persuade him to enter for some of the events, and although he never won anything - did not disgrace himself either.

For Billy, this was an entirely satisfactory development, but one day, in early July, when work on most vineyards, by tradition, paused before the Vendage and when summer holidays were taken, Bessie disappeared. She was eventually found half dead by a neighbour, trying to crawl out of a ditch by the river where she had evidently been thrown after being savagely hit on the head.

Dale carried her very gently to Mel where for several days her life hung by a thread, an X ray having established that she had suffered a fractured skull

Billy said some men had shouted at the pair of them the previous day during one of their explorations of the land on the other side of the river leading up to the woods. He told Dale that one of them had been carrying a shot-gun and he guessed they were poachers. Anyway, the pair of them had run away, although he had to drag Bessie by the collar, and It seemed not unlikely that she had gone back to confront them. Billy was then forbidden to go back over the river, but that was scarcely necessary as he spent most of his time after school sitting beside Bessie's basket reading to her until she started to show signs of improvement, and even then he had to be persuaded to go back home to sleep and have proper meals

In the course of taking the X rays, Mel discovered some cloth between the dog's teeth.

In the normal way, the injury of a guard dog would not have involved the local police, but in the light of the recent attempt to set fire to the winery, when he heard what had happened, Andre Farbre sent Sergeant Moulin to get Billy's full story, and when he returned to report, he brought with him the fragments of cloth Mel had found in Bessie's teeth and which she had kept, having anticipated that they might give some clue as to who she had tried to see off.

As, according to Billy, one of those who had shouted at them earlier had been carrying a shot gun, Farbre again had the recent movements of everyone local with a licence but once more, all concerned had waterproof alibis for the time when Billy had been shouted at, and an additional check showed that none had clothes that matched the fragments torn away by Bessie before she was knocked unconscious. But the more the Inspector thought about it, the more it started to seem compellingly familiar.

In a discussion with Moulin soon after wards, Farbre observed that after the murder of the daughter of the Chef of the Bridge hotel they had followed exactly the same procedure without success.

Moulin thought for a moment. then he said 'Do think there is a connection, then?'

Fabre shrugged. 'At this stage, we obviously have no idea. But in both cases we are looking for the owners of unregistered shot-guns. Is it stretching the imagination too far to consider if they are one and the same?'.

His subordinate paused for a moment before saying 'that's quite a thought!'

Farbre smiled grimly, then added 'But just say we *are* looking for the same lot ...does what happened to the dog help us at all?'.

Moulin said 'Would they expect us to try and establish a connection?'

'Not unless we gave some cause'.

Moulin said 'Like show more than a passing interest in an injured dog.'

'Exactly!'. Farbre nodded, then both men stared at each other before Moulin said 'So where do we go from here?.

The other paused for a moment, staring at his assistant before saying softly 'We wait!'

CHAPTER TWENTY-ONE

On the surface, life appeared to return to normal. Bessie seemed to recover physically, and was allowed to go home. Billy was allowed to have her basket in his bedroom as a temporary concession after she showed no wish to resume her night patrols. From a guard dog point of view, her new fear of strangers, which sent her running for shelter as soon as she saw one, meant her usefulness as a guard dog was virtually nonexistent. But she was much loved, and no one blamed her, although the possibility of getting a second dog was raised by the Insurance Company.

Two Cuckoos arrived in April. No one had ever heard of such a thing and Vincent said it must be a good omen. They called to one another across the vineyard most of the afternoon. Their voices were slightly different - one a little lower than the other, but they were hard to spot flying quickly from one tree to another and most assumed they were husband and wife They fell silent when the sun went down, their place being taken by the nightingale singing from its customary branch of the tree outside Billy's window.

Billy did not have many close friends at School. He was not disliked, but he was not really interested in Soccer, preferring to get home and drive the tractor, or participate in whatever else was going on as soon as possible. The parents of some in his class mates still retained 'opinions' concerning the Solomon Family, but for the most part these were of no interest to their off spring one way or the other, and they certainly did not want to do anything to jeopardise their use of the swimming place by the river on the Estate.

Angelo Vogel, a boy the same age as Billy, was his only close friend. He was a bit of a loaner himself, having even less interest in Soccer and had managed to persuade the school that he needed all his spare time for lessons and to practice the piano at which he was outstanding and brought it no little kudos in local competitions and recitals. Son of Italian immigrants, his father was a musician himself and travelled regularly to schools in nearby towns as well as locally to give lessons, but in his son, he recognised a potential that could take him far beyond such modest, if much appreciated, activities.

Billy admired his friend and sometimes went home with him to listen to him practice, while Angelo earned some envy from his intimacy with a member of the Solomon family - in many peoples' eyes, the nearest thing they had locally to celebrities. Even if they were foreign, the family had raised the reputation of Poussin le Bas almost to the equal of the Grande Cru Estates of Bordeaux.

Angelo enjoyed Billy's standing invitation to go home with him after school and at week-ends when practising allowed, but his real interest when he did so, apart from exploring the Estate with him, was in the Vet Practice next door run by Billy's Mother and Aunt, and he usually ended up there while Billy himself was helping out in the Winery or driving the tractor - which was how he came to know Bessie, taking especial interest in her recovery. Being a stranger - although a small one - Bessie was slow to accept Angelo's proffered affection at first, but he was both sensitive and patient, and by the time she was allowed home, she was happy to go out for walks with him - firstly with Billy as well, but then, when the other was busy, with just the two of them. Christine wondered if her son might not become unhappy by this development, but whatever the other two got up to during the day, Bessie was always overjoyed to see Billy when Angelo brought her home, and to settle down in her basket beside his bed at the end of the day. She mentioned it to Mel, who laughed and said perhaps it was like Bessie had acquired a favourite uncle to play with but who would never take her father's place. Christine accepted this, smiling, but remained doubtful. She knew Billy would be heartbroken if he felt she had really transferred her affections, but there was nothing she could do about it, and to bring up the situation with Billy himself might only ruin the friendship between the two boys - the last thing she wanted.

As the summer progressed and Bessie's confidence in her new 'uncle' deepened, Angelo took her on the exploration of the river bank up-stream. It reminded him of the river near where his grandparents still lived on a small farm in the Veneto in Italy - even to the similarity of the distant view of mountains. They sat together and shared the sandwich Angelo's mother had given him and they watched the kingfishers Billy had told him to look out for. To begin with he tried tossing a few sticks into the water to see if Bessie would jump in to retrieve them, and although she watched interestedly as they floated slowly past downstream, showed no inclination to do so.

Although the piano was Angelo's main musical instrument, he also played the guitar and a small harmonica, the latter of which he usually carried with him and often pulled out of his pocket on a whim to play - usually when by himself. No one had ever taught him this, but compared to the piano in particular, it was uncomplicated and relaxing, and so, as he sat with Bessie by the river after their sandwich had gone, he often played softly to her and she sat listening - quietly most of the time, only occasionally joining in with a low growl. But the sound made their presence known.

One day Angelo decided that the time had come to explore the other side of the river where there was a forest just beyond a stretch of open ground. He knew there must be footpaths there as he had seen men carrying shot guns disappearing into the trees - probably looking for game, and he had heard the occasional shot. Billy had told him once that his mother had made him promise never to go over there, but that did not apply to him, and one day, putting the harmonica away in his pocket he started to walk further upstream until he came to a small cascade that had been reinforced at some time with concrete and where it was easy to paddle across.

Having reached the other side he turned, and was surprised to see that for once Bessie had not followed him and backed away from the edge nervously despite his encouragement. After a few minutes he shrugged and pulled out the harmonica again and set off towards the trees. She heard the sound of him playing fading into the distance and whined worriedly, but for the life of her could not summon up the courage to enter the water to follow him.

Eventually, the sound faded to nothing - probably when he reached the trees, and Bessie swung round and started back the way they had come to tell Billy.

When she came back by herself, no one attached any importance to it to begin with - guessing that she had taken fright at something and turned tail, as she had done on several occasions with Billy himself since recovering- the last being when they had gone with Uncle Tom to visit a cow which had decided to give birth prematurely out in the field, and as soon as Bessie had seen where they were going had high tailed it back to the car.

'She never used to be like this' Billy had assured the farmer, feeling compelled to explain - not that the farmer was interested, and Billy had then flushed with embarrassment, kicking himself inwardly for feeling he had to justify her evident cowardice. After an hour, Dale went looking with Billy holding Bessie on a lead.

They eventually came to the spot where they had sat eating the sandwich and Bessie started to sniff round to see if by any chance a morsel had been overlooked. But she did find the paper wrapping that must have fallen out of Angelo's pocket as he was always careful not to leave such things behind. She then started to pull Billy further along the river bank untll thy came to the cascade where she stopped, wagging her tail and barking.

A full scale search of the land between the river and the trees was eventually organised including everyone from the Estate, Angelo's parents and their friends and a team from the police including a blood hound. This last led them unwaveringly towards the forest. but there, just a few yards into the trees, it seemed the trail went cold, the dog pushing randomly here and there into the bushes beside the track in mounting frustration.

The dog's handler said he had rarely experienced such a thing. It was almost as if the boy had disappeared into thin air.

'Why would anyone want to kidnap Angelo Vogel anyway?' Sergeant Moulin said after they finally rested from their efforts and sat in Inspector Farbre's office looking at each other across his desk.

Farbre shook his head and took a sip of coffee from one of the cups they had drawn from the machine out in the corridor before collapsing wearily by the Inspector's desk. Then he said 'You never knew Christine Solomon's brother Andrew, did you?'.

'Only by repute - the soccer star?'

'That's right. Anyway, a long time before that, he was kidnapped.'

'Kidnapped!' Moulin looked at him in astonishment.

'It was before your time - mine too, come to that .... but my Boss, Chief Inspector Goudon was involved.'

'Who would want to kidnap a footballer?!'

'Andre smiled a little impatiently. 'He was only a schoolboy then...but the point is' he continued before the other could say anything 'it was a mistake.They picked up the wrong boy'

'Who's 'they?'

'They never found out for sure. But the Boss told me they became sure they were after Gus, the son of Lisa McPherson, the Super Model who was left a big interest in the Estate by Billy, Holly's brother.'

Moulin paused, then he said 'I remember now- Christine Solomon married Gus, didn't she?'

Andre nodded. 'Years later. And when he was killed in a plane accident in America, she became the virtual owner of the Estate'. He paused again for a moment then went on 'anyway... whoever, and why... the wrong boy was kidnapped, and I've just got this feeling with Angelo we've been here before.'

Moulin looked at him for several seconds then he said 'they were after Billy!?'

Andre said 'They are the same age, and Angelo was out with Billy's dog.'

'But why would 'he shrugged ...'whoever, want to take Billy?'.

'The virtual son and heir to the Estate! How better to harm the Solomon Family?!'

Moulln said 'Do you think the same people are involved? But Andre shook his head'

'Not after all this time.But what about whoever tried to torch the Winery?'

CHAPTER TWENTY-TWO

Dale and Emily announced to the family that they were engaged to be married.

'So which was worse - to stay and watch the person you loved the most in all the world finally turn his back on you forever, or accept the alternative of becoming someone you really did not want to be?!'

At least she did have the alternative, and maybe one day she would meet someone who would love her. But she could not just run away - she owed Billy and her mother more than that.'

What she had to say did not come as a surprise to either. But the fact that she was able to tell Christine that she had asked Alan Marsh if she could stay with his mother in Greenwich Village until she had settled, both in a job and somewhere to live came as a considerable relief, and when Christine called to thank him and he told her that it was probably time he visited his mother again and would be happy to go with Lisa and help her find a reliable agent to steer her in her proposed new career, she felt a weight lift from her shoulders, some of which she realised she had been carrying ever since she realised her daughter's hopeless infatuation with Dale.

Even so, it did present problems. At the first opportunity, she asked Madeline if she knew where Nichole had gone and if there was any possibility of her coming back, but it did not take long to find out from her family that she had gone to live in Bordeaux where she was settled with a good job in a managerial position and was highly unlikely to want to come back.

Christine had not run the Estate Office for several years and had no wish to give up her partnership with Mel, but she agreed to catch the ball for as long as it would take to advertise for someone else.

And in what seemed a bewilderingly short space of time, she found herself saying goodbye to her daughter accompanied by Alan at Toulouse International and sitting once more back at her old desk in the Estate Office, answering the telephone and dealing with orders.

One result of this was to bring her into daily contact with Henry Withers but, surprisingly, although she still liked him, the spark had gone as far as she was concerned and the moment inevitably arrivede when she had to tell him in as many words.

Jean Franz Associates who had offices on Madison Avenue was the first firm Alan Marsh introduced Lisa to. Mrs Franz, who used to represent his wife Lisa, had since taken a back seat, but she still held the purse strings and it was she' who at their first meeting, introduced them to her daughter Kim who looked as if she should be a client herself but who, her mother assured them, had only just joined the Company after cutting her teeth with one of their main competitors who had been most reluctant to let her go, not only because of her ability but because she now had an inside knowledge of the opposition.

Kim had laughed when her mother said this, but when they went with her to her own office, both Lisa and Alan were soon impressed with the younger woman's ideas. 'Not too much and not too soon' she told Lisa at the beginning of their discussion. 'You have a lot to learn, and where so many young girls go wrong is to allow themselves to be swamped with seemingly glamorous invitations before they know how to handle them' She glanced momentarily from one to the other before concentrating on Lisa: 'If you will trust me, I will help you build a career at a pace you can handle. I can see you have the looks and figure, but that's only the start.' She glanced at Marsh. 'I'm sure your wife would have agreed. She trusted my mother and became outstanding. If it hadn't been from your tragic accident, she would have become a legend!'

The acceptance of Lisa by the Agency was a formality, and when she had signed all the papers, which, as she was still under age in New York, needed to be counter signed by Alan Marsh acting as her temporary guardian. Alan had foreseen the need for this before they left, and at his suggestion Christine had instructed her Notaire to draw up a document which she in turn had signed to cover the situation.

An early celebratory dinner at a small Italian restaurant just around the corner from where they were staying in the Village followed. Alan's mother was invited to join them but asked to be excused as it was her 'Poker' night'

'Poker!' Lisa had laughed, delighted now to be able to relax.

'And why not?' the old lady said with a grin.

'Well, I thought you'd be playing Bridge or something!'

'Pah!'

And that was why there were just two of them sitting at a small table on the edge of the side walk outside Monte's Tratoria, having just finished their first course of calamari when a man stopped in front of them smiling.

'Well, I'm dammed. Lisa!....and Alan Marsh, if I'm not mistaken!'

For a heart stopping moment Lisa looked up to see Dale looking down at them. He had followed her! But as Alan got to his feet to shake hands, she realised it was Phillipe, and by the time he explained that he had no idea they were in New York and that he just happened to be on his way to the home of one of the Clients of the Firm he now worked for, she had recovered enough to smile in return.

Alan invited him to join them, and although Phillipe sat for a moment, he said he really could not stop. 'She isn't the sort of Client you keep waiting' he admitted with a grin -' but now I know you are in town, I'll certainly catch up with you'.

As Phillipe got up to leave, Alan gave him the number of the Agency and the other dutifully noted it in his phone before slipping it back in his pocket. Then, after shaking hands with Alan, and bending down to give Lisa a brief peck on the cheek, he waved and set off, soon to disappear round the first corner.

They watched him go, both giving an answering wave just before this, then turned back to face each other smiling. But before either could say anything the waiter arrived with their second course of Chicken Piccata.

When he had gone, Alan raised his glass of the 'house' Montepuiciano they had ordered to touch hers.

'Here's to your success then!'

'Thank you! 'Lisa paused then added a touch whistfully' Even if it does seem a long way to have to come!.'

Alan nodded.'I guess it must seem like that! 'he said, nodding sympathetically 'But I'm sure it won't be long before this place starts to feel like home'.

They both took a sip then put down their glasses and picked up their forks.

Lisa said 'This smells delicious!'

Alan grinned. 'This place is famous for it. It's just chicken. It's what they do to it!.'

They started to eat, and after only a few seconds Lisa murmured in appreciation

'Mmm! This really is fantastic! What <u>do</u> they do to make it taste like this!?'

'It would be more than the Chef's life was worth to tell you!' Alan said laughing.

'I can imagine!'

Lisa put down her fork and took another sip of the wine before she said 'they have our wine over here don't they?'

Alan nodded. 'Oh yes. But not in a place like this, obviously'

He picked up his own glass before continuing. 'New York seems like a big place, but it's really a lot of villages, each with its own character -and food. He paused, then went on 'I'm not talking about Broadway and Times Square - places like that - although I guess even they have their own flavour. I'm sure it won't be long before you come to love it...and have more friends than you know what to do with!'

Lisa looked doubtful. 'I don't know about that' she began, but Alan interrupted.' Well you've already found one... or rather, he's just found you'

Lisa resumed eating for a while before she said 'I've never felt very comfortable with Phillipe, Alan.'

'Oh?'

'Billy doesn't like him at all!'

Alan shrugged. 'Billy doesn't know every thing. He's still a child'.

Lisa paused before she said 'He knows a lot of things other people miss. Mother says he takes after our father'.

* * *

Angelo was very frightened. He could hear them arguing, but he was blind folded and had no idea who they were and where they had brought him. Then everything seemed to happen at once.

He heard a woman' s voice, raised in anger, then a shot, followed by a whimper. He was lifted to his feet, and still blind folded, led out of where ever his kidnappers had held him and pushed into a car, which drove off almost immediately

'You can take that thing off round your face he heard the woman say, but after he had done so and looked around, the car suddenly came to an abrupt halt and the woman, who had caught sight of him in the driver's mirror, twisted round to look at him properly.

'Who are you?' she demanded. 'What have you done with Billy?'

Angelo started to cry. 'I haven't done anything with him; he sobbed. 'From what those men were saying, I don't think they wanted me'.

The woman stared at him for a few more seconds, then she said' Well don't snivel. Consider yourself lucky!' And without another word turned back and drove on until they were on the edge of Saint Fleur then stopped to let him out.

'If you keep walking up this road, you'll come to the Gendarmarie' she told him. 'Tell them who you are, and I expect they will look after you'.

Angelo did as he was told, and as he watched the car drive away he thought perhaps he should have thanked her, whoever she was.

CHAPTER TWENTY-THREE

Kim assured Alan that they would accept full responsibility for their new client and his mother was delighted to have a lively young lodger. Only then, and when he was satisfied she was happy for him to do so, did he say goodbye and took the flight back to Paris.

Despite her assurances, and the exciting new life that now opened before her, Lisa felt very lonely after he had gone and had to make an effort not to let her mind keep getting drawn back home ...and Dale.

It was several weeks after the chance meeting with Phillipe - when she thought he had forgotten all about her -he suddenly turned up at a shoot for a range of shoes where she and two other young models had been sent by Kim for a magazine running a promotion for Easter vacations in the country. It was not the most exciting for any of them 'we don't even get to show much leg!' one complained'. But the fees would pay the rent and Lisa enjoyed making two new friends.

She saw Phillipe talking to one of the photographer's assistants behind the camera before he saw her, then he turned, and seeing her staring at him, waved and grinned.

Her two young colleagues looked at him rather enviously when they broke and Lisa was able to speak to him - he really was very good looking - but she barely had time to beckon them over to be introduced when the assistant called them back for another set up.

'Look, I can see you're busy'. Phillipe said quickly.' Why don't I come back when you've finished and we can go out and get something to eat somewhere?'

Lisa nodded. 'Yes, I'd like that' she said. 'I'm sorry you've wasted your time'

'Never mind about that.' he assured her smiling, then glanced across to where they were repositioning the camera. 'I'll have a word with the Boss man and get some idea when they expect to wrap.' He turned back to her. 'In the meantime, perhaps you'd like to be thinking where you might like to go?'.

'Oh, I know that already' Lisa said laughing. 'Grandma Holly told me when I was little about going to a restaurant at the top of the Rockefeller Center. I've wanted to go there ever since!' Then she hesitated doubtfully. 'But I'm not dressed for anywhere smart' she added, pulling face.

Phillipe smiled confidently.' Don't worry about that' he assured her. 'You look gorgeous! Rockefeller it is then. It's just as well you said, they get pretty booked up so I'll make sure to reserve a table.' He kissed her on the cheek briefly, then walked over to speak to the Director of the shoot.

'Who <u>was</u> that demanded one of the two girls, as they were getting into position and Lisa shrugged casually.

'Oh, just one of my uncles from back home' she told her.

'Some uncle!' The other one protested. 'doesn't look much like an uncle to me!'.

'And what is that supposed mean?'Lisa demanded.

'Well, he doesn't look at you like one then' the other said with a grin, and before either could say anything else the assistant came across and said the Director had decided he wanted them to go to the dressing room and change before the next shot.

Phillipe arrived a good hour before he was finally satisfied. By which time all three of them were tired and Lisa would have preferred to have just caught a snack at MacDonalds with them and gone s home, but she did not feel she could say so, and by the time she had changed and he had taken her up-town to Rockefeller in a cab, she had her second wind as was beginning to look forward to their date - she supposed she would have to call it!

The cab dropped them in 49th Street and they walked round the corner past the skating rink to the main entrance. There was a restaurant on the ground floor with window tables from which it was possible to watch the skaters, but Lisa said she would much rather go up to the one with the views over the whole city Holly had described.

When she was finally tucked up in her own bed back in the Village, which she was already starting to think of as home, having been escorted back there in a cab by Phillipe, Lisa reviewed the evening. She felt guilty she still regarded him with some reservation. He had gone out of his way to give her a good time. The meal had been really enjoyable, and the view looking down town all the way past the Empire State, now multi-coloured flood lit, to the Battery at the end of Manhattan Island and the Statue of Liberty out in the middle of the harbour, was every bit as thrilling as her Grandmother had said. Phillipe had been attentive and kept her amused with stories of some of the stranger cases he had been inviolved with. He had made no attempt to kiss her when he dropped her off and had simply given her his business card and asked her to contact him if she would like to go out with him again.

Lisa had put the card away safely in the top draw of the small dressing table before getting into bed, but she really felt no particular wish to see him again and guessed that, duty done, he would not feel any such need either.

Phillipe had an apartment in a building on the Upper East Side; not as luxurious as the one once occupied by Lisa's famous name sake and where Holly had stayed; there was no view of Central Park being on the opposite side of the building, but it was comfortable and spacious enough to have impressed a number of young women who had been happy enough to spend a night there.

After going into the living room and pouring himself a Jack Daniels before settling down to watch the late night news, Phillipe thought about the evening he had just spent with his niece - although she wasn't really his niece - she was no blood relation at all. She was certainly a beauty and it would be doubly satisfying to possess someone he knew thought, at the moment, only of his brother. He knew, If he were to achieve this, he would have to be patient. She would have to want him - whether for love, or in loneliness, he did not really care. It would be an amusing game, but he had plenty of time to play, and the prize would not just be her willing body, surrendered to whatever novelty he chose to introduce to her, but Dale's feelings when he realised the stupidity of his loss and to whom she had transferred her affections.

CHAPTER TWENTY-FOUR

Angelo's parents drove over to the Gendarnerie at St Fleur to collectt him as soon as Sergeant Moulin telephoned them to report their son was safe. He said that his superior, Lieutenant Farbre, would like to see them back at Les deux Demoiselles as soon as they felt it would not upset the boy to tell them exactly what had happened.

In fact, Angelo recovered quickly but asked if his friend Billy could also come, and far from objecting, Farbre was delighted, providing, as it did, a perfectly natural way of exploring the possibility that the Solomon boy had been the real target without, seemingly, making much of it.

Even so, he was astounded when the meeting was finally arranged when Billy interrupted what his friend had been saying to interject with total conviction 'It must have been Martha'.

The two policeman looked at him, then at each other at each other before Farbre said tentatively 'What makes you say that, Billy?.

The boy turned to look at him then said simply 'It's the sort of thing she would do. She's very fond of me, and if she thought it was me.....' He paused for a few seconds then added worriedly' She won't get into trouble will she?'

'For rescuing you?!' Farbre shook his head. 'Of course not!'

'Well, there is the question of her shooting someone.' Moiuin put in mildly

'Serve them right!' Angelo's Mother said fiercely.

'Well, French law does not generally approve of its citizens shooting each other' Farbre observed. 'But I don't think, in this case, we shall be pressing any charges! He allowed himself a faint smile before turning to Moulin.' I think you might pay the lady a discrete visit, however. It would save wasting time and she might have some information pointing to who kidnapped Angelo here - and who knows what else!'.

'She was supposed to have handed over all her late husband's armory' the Sergeant pointed out'.

Just as well she didn't!' Angelo's father put in, and Farbre nodded before glancing back at Moulin.

'You'd better check on that, though' he agreed, then turned back to take in the rest of the them.

'One thing I must ask all of you 'though...especially you two' he said looking at the two boys 'is that no mention is ever made outside this room that Martha Germain may have been the one who rescued Angelo and shot one of the kidnappers in the process, or her life will be in considerable danger until we manage to round them all up'

When the others had gone, Moulin said' In the light of what you just said, are we justified in disarming her completely?'

Farbre nodded before he said 'I was thinking about that. He took a deep breath, then he said 'we really cannot allow her to go round shooting people no matter how well intentioned. But until further notice, I want a twenty-four hour watch kept on her cottage.'

Moulin nodded, then he said 'Can I tell her that?'

'I don't see why not. It might make her a bit more co-operative!'

* * *

Phillipe was too busy to give much thought to Lisa for a while until he opened the week - end edition of the New York Times, and while he was picking up the pile of supplements which he managed to drop on the floor, there she was on the first page of the fashion section wearing a one piece bathing suit in dark blue - his favourite colour - and which showed off her long legs and incredible figure to perfection On the first page inside there was a write up about her and how she was a niece of the famous Lisa MacPherson who had dominated the fashion magazines until the tragic accident which had cut her life short.

He went back into the small kitchen holding the magazine to pour himself another coffee then settled at one end of the sofa to read the rest of it.

When he had finished, he allowed the magazine to slide onto the cushion beside him and sat for a while thinking. Then, he glanced at his watch. It was Saturday. He had said he might give one of the young women on the staff of the Firm a call, but on second thought, this might be just the time to contact his 'niece'.

Lisa was genuinely surprised when she saw who was calling, and hesitated for a moment, deciding whether or not to pick up, but she guessed he would only persist until he reached her, and she might as well tell him now that, nice as it was to have seen him, she really did not feel comfortable making a habit of it.

When she put down the phone ten minutes later, she glanced at her watch. Of all the things he could have suggested, the chance to go riding the following day from a stud owned by one of his wealthier clients not far from Bridgeport, Connecticut was irresistible, and in the circumstances she could hardly refuse to spend today with him. Perhaps he was as lonely as she felt herself sometimes, and which her sudden fame had done little to alleviate.

It was a brilliant sunny day, and by the time he called she had changed into a sequined skirt, cut just above the knee and a light pink, arms length blouse given her after a recent shoot that she thought Phillipe might appreciate. As soon as she opened the door to him and caught the look on his face she knew she had not been mistaken.

'Wow is all I can say!' he said grinning.

'Thank you'. Lisa smiled modestly. 'Just a little thing I ran up on the machine when I knew you were coming!'.

'In a pig's ass you did!' Phillipe retorted

'Do you want to come in?'

Not if you are ready to go'

'I'll just get my bag then. It's right here'

She turned and picked up a small bag which matched the colour of her blouse from the table just inside the door, then came out onto the step, turning to close the door behind her. 'Mrs Marsh has already gone out' she explained.

'Great -then let's go' He held out his hand to take hers as they walked down the steps

'I thought we'd have City day today as we're out in the country tomorrow. Maybe walk along to Washington Square Park and sit in the sun for a bit with a hotdog... then stroll up Sixth Avenue as far as Times Square?'

Lisa smiled as they reached the side walk and started in the direction he had suggested and with him still holding her hand. 'That sounds wonderful. I'm usually shooting past all the places I'd really like to see in a cab!' she said happily, then he stopped suddenly to face her.

'But what about shoes? I forgot to ask'.

Lisa smiled again. 'Don't worry, I must be psychic. I changed into flats at the last minute!' She turned and they resumed while he started to tell her his plans for the following day

It was early Autumn, a time when the New York weather tries to fool everyone that the summer is going on for ever. The Newspapers had reported that the trees in New England were past their peak, but in Washington Square, the plane trees still clung possessively to their leaves.

Many of the Park benches were occupied by students from the nearby New York University. laughing amongst themselves between classes, and here and there some older people were doing Chinese exercises in slow motion. One young man was practicing juggling, and a pretty girl rode around on a mono-cycle distributing leaflets advertising a drama 'happening' in a nearby loft theatre in which she also happened to be the star.

There were no benches free, but Lisa spread out her skirt and sat on the grass while Phillipe went to get their 'dogs' from a vendor on the opposite side of the Square. She watched him go, then sighed, suddenly feeling more at peace than since she had left home.

She smiled when he came back and handed her one of the paper wrapped sausages before sitting down on the grass beside her.

'I hope you like onions and mustard' he said, unwrapping his own.

'I adore onions' Lisa assured him.

'Good. I ordered plenty, so watch you don't drop them on your skirt!'

'I won't'

It did not seem that long since breakfast, but Lisa suddenly felt hungry and bit into the hot dog, gratefully accepting a paper napkin just in time to wipe mustard from the corner of her mouth before some of it fell on her lap.

They ate in contented silence for a while, then Phillipe said 'Do people recognise you? I mean from your pictures?'.

Lisa thought for a moment. 'It's happened a couple of times' she admitted. 'But I don't go out much by myself'.

Phillipe nodded. 'I guess it's early days' he said, and Lisa pulled a face.

'Don't say that' she begged. 'I'd hate it if I didn't have the freedom to just wander around by myself if I felt like it.'

'You'll just have to go home if you don't like it' Phillipe said after a few seconds.' But I thought it was something models just got used to'.

Lisa shrugged, then she looked around. 'I love it here' she said. 'Thank you so much for suggesting it'

Phillipe nodded. 'I thought you might like to have a quiet day for a change' he said with a smile.

Lisa chuckled. 'I would never have associated you with a quiet day Phillipe 'she teased, and he returned her smile.

'You'd be surprised!' I've got an apartment by Central Park that most people think is positively monastic! As a matter of fact, I thought we might order something from the deli round the corner and have a nice quiet supper in tonight instead of eating out for change.'

'That's a great idea' Lisa said quickly. 'I'd love to see where you live. - as long as we're not too late. If we're going out to see that friend of yours tomorrow, I've got to dig out something suitable to go riding in before I go to bed'.

Phillipe smiled.' Don't worry. I'll make sure to get you back no later than ten'.

CHAPTER TWENTY-FIVE

After a visit to Macy's on 34th street where Phillipe was surprised to find Lisa's main interest was in the pets department on the top floor, but she explained that she had quite enough to do with clothes during the week, but even so, she allowed him to buy her some 'naked straps' in the shoe department which matched her skirt and which she insisted on wearing immediately, accepting his offer to carry the bag with her flats in the mean time

The rest was window shopping on Fifth Avenue, except for a visit to the Museum of Modern Art on 53rd street which Lisa loved and Phillipe felt confident in assuring her they were unlikely to find a picture to which her resemblance might trigger an incident.

They finally reached the apartment a little early to place an order for supper, but Phillipe opened a bottle of Poussin le Bas Superior, which he told her he always kept in stock, and by the time they had drunk several glasses on relatively empty stomachs, Phillipe was emboldened to kiss Lisa with considerably more passion than the last time and she was of a mind to let him. They finished the bottle then rang the Deli to place an order for six o clock and he opened another bottle to be going in with in the mean time.

'Shall we go into the bedroom?' Phillipe suggested, re filling her glass. I think we'll be more comfortable'

After a moment's hesitation, Lisa nodded, then she stood up and put her glass on the nearby coffee table. 'Just a minute. I don't want to crease these'

He watched facinated as she cooly removed the skirt and blouse and laid them on the back of the sofa before turned to face him.

'I take it this is what you have in mind?' she said, staring at him, wide eyed.

She was so beautiful, and seemingly hungry for what they were going to do together. He had never felt so aroused in his life and moved quickly to take her into his arms. Her breasts were naked, and before he reached her, she put out a hand to stop him for a second to step out of her thong, then stood facing him, breathing quickly as she awaited his embrace.

They came together, and while her tongue sought his, she felt his hands press hard against her naked shoulders pulling her closer until, suddenly, s he heard him gasp and a moment later he collapsed onto the floor

Lenox Hill hospital was only a few blocks away and Lisa only just had time to dress before the ambulance arrived. The crew did a number of procedures to restart his heart before taking him down to the waiting vehicle on a stretcher. She was allowed to go in the ambulance with him

Lisa waited in Reception until a young doctor came out of the emergency room where they had taken him to tell her they had been able to stabilise his condition.

'It was a close thing, he told her. 'Are you his girl friend?'

Lisa shook her head but she said 'we were just having dinner together. We come from the same small town in France'

The other nodded.' Then you know all about him' he said.

'I know quite a lot about him'

'Does he live by himself. Here, I mean?'

'Yes'

'That's a pity. It could have happened any time. He's lucky you were with him'.

Lisa thought for a moment, before she said 'can I see him?'

The doctor nodded. 'Of course. Just give us a few more minutes'

'How long will he have to stay here?'

'Not more than a few days. But it won't be safe for him to go back to living alone for quite a while'

Lisa said 'All his family are back in France'

The other paused for a moment before he said 'What about you?'

Seeing her expression he went on 'well... maybe that's something you can talk about.'

*** *** ***

Fortunately, one of the conditions of Phillipe joining the Partnership had been to sign up the firm's medical insurance scheme. This had added not a little to the cost, and the monthly premiums for all the partners were considerable, although graded, fortunately, for the junior partners, proportionately to their profit share. Lloyd himself visited Phillipe in hospital and assured him that his position was in no danger and that the scheme would not only cover his hospital expenses but the cost of home care for as long as he needed it once it had been decided he could return to his apartment. Two women were taken on for this purpose - a house keeper who did the shopping, cooked his meals and generally looked after him during the day, and a semi-retired nurse who arrived when it was time for the other to go home; slept overnight in the spare room, then left when the housekeeper took over again - simply to be on hand should Phillipe have another attack.

This was all right as far as his medical condition was concerned, but he knew he would have gone out of his mind with frustration had it not been for the few friends he had made at the office who visited him, and above all Lisa, who came to see him as often as she could - sometimes several times a week, and as his condition continued to improve he was allowed to go for walks with her in Central Park just the other side of 5th Avenue. He came to love her, his original feelings towards her long forgotten. Lisa herself could not help become aware of the change in his attitude, not only towards she herself but the world at large. He seemed a so much nicer person now and assumed his brush with death was responsible. To some extent she was right, but it was different - in ways that might have disturbed her if she had known the truth.

Eventually, it was it was thought that before going back to work it would do him the world of good to go home for an extended vacation, and he asked Lisa if she would go with him.

Kim was not thrilled but agreed to a break of a few weeks and so, when she had honoured the bookings Kim had already made for her, they were on their way, and although Lisa was eagerly looking forward to seeing her mother, Billy, and the rest of them. she was wondering how she would feel now towards Dale. She was not the only one.

CHAPTER TWENTY-SIX

Lisa found her old room waiting for her, and Phillipe was welcomed back to Rousanne. even by Dale, although he wondered if his brother's return was only until he was completely recovered or if he would want to take part again in running the Estate. Dale had always looked up to his brother, but things had moved on while he was away and he wondered what part Phillipe could usefully play now. He was not hostile to the possibility but comforted himself most of the time with the thought that once he was feeling better, it was more likely he would want to go back to New York. In the mean time, he and Lisa had obviously grown close, and apart from not having to worry about her infatuation with him anymore, it was another reason they would probably agree that each had far more future back there.

Mel suggested he allowed Holly to check him over after the journey - particularly if he wanted to be able to drive, and although he said he had never felt better, agreed to make an appointment at the Clinic, after which Holly said she was of the opinion there was no reason why he should not get himself a car, but advised against any long journeys until she ran the rule over him again in a month's time.

A small Mazda was duly purchased from the local garage, which enabled him first to pay a courtesy call on Immobliers Cevante, where he was made wecome by both Sara and Eva, but surprised to find they were already aware of what had happened to him.

Despite Dale's worries that his brother might upset the apple cart in some way, although he expressed interest in all the recent developments- particularly the extension to the Winery- Phillipe showed no sign of wanting to interfere.

Vincent was the first of the newcomers he met, apart from Emily, who was on duty at the Clinic when he went to see Holly, and he met her again when she came looking for Dale when Phillipe was still in the Winery. He already knew their father Henry and listened frowning and shaking his head occasionally when told by him of the attack on the Winery and how it would have been so much worse but for the bravery of Alim.

It was over a welcome home supper given for both Lisa and Phillipe by Christine on their second night back that Phillipe met Billy again, who introduced him to Bessie, and the whole story of the kidnapping of his friend Angelo and the near fatal injury of Bessie occupied much of the rest of the evening until it was time for boy and dog to retire.

When it was agreed time for all of them to turn in, Lisa walked with Phillipe down to the river through the vines as far as Macus' punt, which he had used to come across earlier. They put an arm around each other and were content to enjoy the silence of the night except for the murmuring from the river, and the occasional hoot from a barn owl further downstream. There was no moon but the clear sky was crowded with stars and soon their eyes became accustomed to what light there was.

It was the first time they had been completely alone together since their return, but when he turned on reaching the boat, instead of taking her into his arms to kiss her as she expected, he let her go of her altogether and stood, looking at her for a moment in silence.

'Phillipe...Is something the matted? she said after a brief pause, and she saw him nod slightly.

'What?' Lisa demanded. 'For heaven's sake tell me!'

'It's not you' he said eventually.

'Then what is wrong? Are you not feeling well again? 'She looked at him anxiously

'You know I love you? 'he said after a few seconds

Lisa nodded before she said gently 'I'm not blind. but...'

'I owe my life to you'

'All I did was phone for an ambulance. Besides, it was all my fault for getting you all hot and bothered' she added with a mischievous grin, then reached forward to hold him again.

'You were so beautiful! Then I went and spoilt it all!'

'It really doesn't matter now' she assured him. 'Besides, we've got our whole lives....'

'No"!' He held her away.' I love you too much for that. There are things about me....'

'What things?'

Before he could answer, they heard Bessie bark, and a moment later she was all over them. Billy arrived a few seconds later grinning and slipped his hand through the dog's collar to restrain her.

'I thought you must have got lost!' he told them, 'so I thought I would come and look for you!'

Phillipe forced a smile. 'No, not yet!' he said. 'But you can take her back now. I'm just going'

He reached forward to give Lisa a quick peck on the cheek.

'Good night then!'

They watched as he turned to launch the boat back into the water, then got in and started to push himself to the opposite bank using the single oar as a punt pole.

'Good night Phillipe' Billy called out, then glancing up at his sister's face for a moment, took one of her hands.

'Come on then'

She turned and allowed herself to be led back in the direction of the house.

CHAPTER TWENTY-SEVEN

Lisa did not see him again for three days until a car pulled into the yard and she heard a knock on the side door which led out into the terrace. Christine had already gone over to the Surgery and Billy was out somewhere with Bessie. She was already dressed in her favourite old overalls so she went to open the door expecting to find someone looking for the office, only to find Phillipe smiling at her. She could see his new car over his shoulder.

'Hi!' he lent forward to give her a peck on the cheek.

She did not know why it should be such a surprise, but as he had made no effort to see her, she had wondered whether he was either embarrassed or angry after their last meeting. But swallowing her surprise, she smiled in return and invited him in for a coffee, opening the door wide to let him in.

He sat as invited at the kitchen table before saying 'I'm sorry I haven't been over, but I've been busy'

'Oh?' Lisa put two mugs on the table. 'I haven't seen you around' She reached for the jug on the hob then turned back to fill the mugs. 'I wondered if you were cross with me!' she added casually

'Not at all!'. He looked at her with a shake of the head and picked up the nearest mug.' Why should you think that anyway?' Then continued without waiting for an answer: 'I've got something to show you'. He smiled mysteriously and took a sip of the coffee.

Relieved not to have a continuation of the other evening, Lisa asked 'What sort of thing?'

'It's over at Rousanne. It'll be quicker to go in the car'.

She guessed Dale was in the office. She had been helping him part time since she got back but there was nothing to do that could not wait, so after admiring it, Lisa climbed into the Mazda and he drove at speed up the lane, over the bridge then back alongside the river before pulling into the yard outside the Vet's Surgery. She had to grit her teeth a bit not to ask him to slow down, but then it was all over and he was opening the car door for her.

''Couldn't wait! he admitted grinning, then took her arm to guide her down to the paddock where there were two ponies grazing on the opposite side of the field. These came trotting across as soon as Phillipe called them.

Lisa gasped. One of them was Colleen!

At first, she could only fondle her ears, trying to hold back her tears, while Phillipe encouraged the other one to follow him down to the stable. As soon as she got a grip on herself Lisa followed with Coleen.

The two ponies followed Phillipe through the half door into the stable and set upon the pony nuts which he then poured into the manger. Lisa watched in silence from the doorway until this was done and stood back as he emerged without closing the door behind him.

'They can come out when they have finished' he explained, and was then over whelmed by Lisa as she threw herself into his arms.

'What have you done?' she managed eventually, pulling her head back so she could at look at him.

'Well, I thought, as I had done you out of the visit to that Client of mine in Connecticut, I would try and make it up to you.!' he said, grinning

'But you can't ride!' Lisa said wildly.

'No, but there is a young fourteen year old staying here with her parents bored out of her skull '.

Lisa paused for a moment, then she said more seriously 'That's wonderful Phillipe. But when they go home... or when we do, come to that?'

He let his arms drop, but stood facing her smiling before saying 'Don't worry. I've thought of all that. We now own both of them, but I've done a deal with the livery stables that they will look after them when we're away in return for us allowing them to be used for when they take pupils out. Not complete beginners, I made that clear, just those advanced enough to be trusted.'

Seeing her still doubtful expression, he added 'There is an alternative...we can take them with us when we go back, and my Client will look after them'.

After a few seconds, Lisa shook her head, smiling in spite of herself.

'You really are amazing Phillipe Meuse. I'm putty in your hands!'.

*** *** ***

When Christine heard what Phillipe had done, she advised Lisa not to worry about it now, but just to enjoy taking out Jennifer Lane, the young visitor to Rousanne - and this she did.

Despite the difference in their ages, 'Jenny' as she asked to be called was a bright attractive girl with a sunny nature and quick sense of humour, and the two young women bonded quickly.

Christine asked only that they stuck to the lanes and bridle paths on the Estate's side of the river, and one of the first outings Lisa took led past the town and up to the hill where she showed the young American girl the memorial to Jeannine Berger and was young enough to enjoy chilling her young companion's blood with the gruesome tale of her murder.

A few days later, Stephane asked Lisa if she would mind giving them a hand in the office with some new orders, and when told, Jenny asked if she could take Colleen, the more experienced and reliable of the two ponies out by herself.

On being given permission by both her parents and Lisa, she asked Billy, who was two years younger but with whom she had quickly become friends, if he would like to come with her, and although kicking himself for having to admit he had never learned to ride, he offered to walk beside her as long as she didn't go too fast!

With Billy having to walk, Christine did not expect them to go very far. They took the lane towards the bridge, passing Les Hirrondelles on the other side of the river, but when they reached the bridge, instead of turning right up into the town, they agreed to go on down the lane with the cottages where Billy knew Matha Grahame lived on the opposite side until they were out of the town altogether. Here there seemed to be no traffic and Jenny suggested Billy might like to climb up and sit in front of her - which he was more than happy to do, and so, quickening to a trot they reached the spot where vineyards gave way to wood land closely bordering the road.

Jenny brought Colleen to a halt, and was about to turn back when Billy pointed to the entrance of a broad track leading into the trees.

'Let's see what's up there' he suggested

Jenny frowned. 'Just a lot more trees I should think' she observed.

'Oh, go on' Billy pleaded.' It must lead somewhere'.

Jenny hesitated, then she sighed and encouraged the pony forwards. But when they were only a few yards along the track, Coleen came to a halt and no amount of encouragement could persuade her to go any further. In fact, she swung round and made to go back.

'Bad girl!' Jenny protested hauling on the reins, but Billy slipped off onto the ground and took hold of the pony's bridle.

'Leave her to me' he said confidently and guided the animal back the way they wanted to go. But after only another twenty yards she suddenly dragged the bridle out of his hand and set off up the track at a gallop and leaving Jenny no choice but just to try and stay in the saddle.

Billy watched in alarm as they disappeared up the track. For a few seconds he heard the sound of the pony's hooves, the crashing of breaking branches and the yells of the helpless rider. Then. all was silent.

Billy stood still listening but there was no sound to indicate Jenny had managed to regain control and was on her way back, and without the previous din, the wood made sounds of its own: the drip from the canopy of trees of moisture from the overnight rain onto the carpet of fallen leaves, and the fait rustle of the remaining leaves in the treetops. Then there was the indefinable smell of the forest which was a combination of rotting vegetation and the fungus which clung to the tree trunks.

Billy set off determindely up the track, and for a few yards he heard nothing but the sound of his own progress up the track.

Then he heard a girl scream - it could only be Jenny, and started to run as fast as his legs would carry him. Then there was another scream, followed by a single gun shot. Billy came to a halt, but there were no further sounds and he broke into a run again without giving any thought to what he might be running into.

He reached a clearing and paused on the edge. The pony was standing motionless with its loose reins hanging down and he started forward again to discover Jenny lying on the ground, evidently dazed after having fallen off. He hurried forward and dropped onto his knees beside her. It was only then he saw she had a revolver in her right hand. She started to leaver herself up on one elbow and he reached forward to help her sit up.

'Are you alright? What's happened?

The girl promptly burst into tears and he hugged her comfortingly.

'It's all right' he murmured. 'You're alright now. What happened? Where did you get the gun?'

Whatever he was expecting, it wasn't what she gasped next through her tears.

'Oh, Billy. I think I've killed someone!'

It took some while before he was able to help- her to her feet. Then, while she stood hold ing onto the pony's bridle for support. he started to look around and almost immediately saw the body of a man half concealed in the bushes where he had evidently fallen backwards after being shot. A shot gun lay beside him

Nervously, he moved closer, ready to jump back at the first sign of movement. He had never seeen a dead person before, but he screws0d up enough courage to bend down and move the branches so he could see the man's face.

Despite being contorted in death, he recognised who it was at once. 'Uncle' Phillipe.

* * *

Both Jenny and Billy were taken for questioning by Andre Farbre while Phipippe Meuse's body was taken to the Clinic.

Billy was released almost immediately when the girl confirmed his story that when she was fell off the pony when she came to a sudden halt in the face of a man standing in their way pointing a shot gun at them, he had been left behind.

She heard the man cock the gun, but instead of pointing it at her, she saw him take a position looking back up the track and from the way he was holding the gun in readiness she just knew he was waiting for Billy. He was going to shoot him first.

She screamed, but the man barely glanced at her and she realised she had only made sure Billy would hurry all the more to find her.

She had struggled to her feet and fumbled in Colleen's saddle bag while she miraculously stood still until she had pulled out the revolver her Mother had insisted she took before agreeing on the two of them going out alone. She had pointed it at the one waiting for Billy, but before she could fire he saw what was happening and quickly moved to knock the revolver out of her hand, but at the last second the pony shied away and he hit her on her shoulder, knocking her to the ground instead, then spun round at the sound of Billy hurrying towards them, calling her name.

Although lying on the ground, Jenny managed to lift the gun to which she had clung and fired. She did not know at first if she had hit him, but then she heard a crash as he fell into the bushes, and a moment later, Billy was beside her.

Farbre accepted that the shooting of Phillippe Meuse had been done in self defence. At least, that's what the girl had presumed, although the deceased had not actually attacked her except to try and knock the gun she was pointing at him out of her hand.

The policeman had reason enough to believe that Phillipe Meuse's intention had been to kill Billy and that he would undoubtedly have eliminated the American girl as a witness afterwards. The problem was that although it undoubtedly saved the lives of both of them, Jenny's Mother, Alice Lane had no business to have given her daughter the gun which was used to kill Phillippe

Meuse, nor indeed to have had one in her possession, no matter that, as Joe Lane, her husband explained, it was purchased quite legally in Phoenix, Arizona, their home town, where such things were sold without restriction for self defence, and youngsters like their daughter were taught how to use them responsibly so that they were not a danger to themselves, or anyone else.

But in France, Farbre told them, to carry unlicenced fire arms was a serious offence and it was a mystery how it was not detected in their baggage when they arrived - and needed looking into

Joe Lane pulled a face. 'Well it certainly wasn't done with any wrong intent' he said.' Fact was, I guess we never gave it a thought. I see now we should have done, but we arrived in Portugal where we have friends from when I was working in Brazil. Then we hired a car and drove here. I think it was time for lunch when we arrived in Lisbon and after taking one look at us decided we couldn't say boo to a goose and passed all our bags without looking at them. Same on the land frontiers!'

Farbre asked them to wait while he made a call, and when he came back told them it had been decided not to pursue the matter of the gun. It would be confiscated, of course but they would be allowed to leave the Country and fly home after their daughter signed a written statement. It was possible, but unlikely they would need any more information, but in the unlikely event they did need to speak again, it could be arranged at the French Consulate in Phoenix

CHAPTER TWENTY-EIGHT

In April it would be Billy's fifteeth birthday. Lisa had promised to fly home from New York bringing her new husband Alan Marsh with her.

Alan was known to the family, of course, but the news that they had got married by specia;l licence came as a shock, bearing in mind the difference in their ages, but it seemed from a number of phone calls that they were very happy and had done it on the spur of the moment just after Alan's Mother had died leaving Alan her house in the Village. So as they would be arriving in time for the birthday party it would be a doubled celebration

Billy was looking forward to surprising his sister with the news that Tom had been giving him riding lessons, so they would be able to go out riding together.

Now he was fifteen, Billy be be going to a Lycee at St Flour where he would become a weekly border and stay until he took his Baccalaureat qualifying him for further education. All his contemporaries who wanted to go any further had already applied to a number of univdersities but he had his own ideas.

'Do you think I could go to the Agricultural College in Montpellier and do Viticulture – like Dad' he suddenly sprang on Dale after coming home from school and going into the Estate office when he guessed the other would have more or less finished for the day.

Dale swallowed, then pulled himself together. 'You'd better come and sit down' he said smiling – 'but close the door'.

Dale pulled the chair visitors normally sat on round to face his own, then waited for Billy to sit down.

'What's brought this on?' he asked as soon as he had done so and watched as the boy screw up his face for a moment in concentration. 'Have you talked to your Mother? 'Dale went on without waiting for an answer.

'Not yet', Billy admitted, relaxing his features. 'I'm sure she will agree, but I thought it more important I found out how you felt about it first. With uncle Stephane retiring I 'm sure you will need more help, but I wasn't sure if you could wait for me to grow up'. He smiled then and Dale chuckled.

'Well ...to cut to the chase, as they say, there is nothing I would like more than have you as a partner. And I'm sure your mother will feel the same.'

Billy's smile broadened.

'After all, your Mother owns half the Estate' Dale went on, 'so one day you and I will be the bosses, and I'd far rather we ran the Estate together than find myself working with a stranger!'

214

'The Collage has long holidays' Billy said happily 'so you won't have to wait for me to graduate before I can start to help'.

Dale nodded, then he said suddenly 'What about Bessie?'

Billy looked thoughtful. 'I've thought about her of course. I've already asked Mum if she would have her basket in her bedroom during the week while I'm at St Flour'.

'What did she say?'

'She said she thought it was a good idea if Bessie was agreeable'.

Dale kept a straight face.' And what did *she* say?' he enquired innocently.

Billy looked at him, then burst out laughing. 'I'm sure she thought it a good idea too!'

Dale nodded, smiling.'Then that's settled' he said.

Christine was thrilled when they both came to tell her of Billy's decision. And when the time came for him to start at St Flour, as agreed, she moved Bessie's basket into her own room.And when it was time for bed, before she went to sleep, she reached down and fondled her ears so neither of them missed Billy quite so much.

In the Spring, Dale now had a regular companion for his pre-breakfast walks through the vineyard.

Every now and then Bessie paused and raised her head to sample the air as they walked between the rows, rather like a human cupping a hand to their ear the better to hear Dale thought. He knew her sense of smell was a hundred times more sensitive than his own and he wondered what she took for granted in addition to the combination of moist earth, the young leaves on the vines, still touched with dew, and the trees which lined the river behind them which he could smell himself.

As it was, he was reliant on what he could see, and the feel of the young vine leaves which were quite red when he held them so the sun shone through them, and as a final resort, the roses which were planted at the end of alternate rows and which would signal the onset of any infection long before the vines themselves.

He loved these early morning inspections. Before he had gone off to the Lycee, Billy had always come with him. And the knowledge that the boy would be his partner one day had added to the joy he felt as he looked forward to his wedding to Emily in a few weeks time. Even so, he often thought about Phillipe, the brother he had looked up to for most of his life. The Vineyard had not been enough for him except, as had slowly emerged, an asset to be sold to further his own career. To some extent, Dale could understand that, but still found it almost impossible to accept what Lieutenant Farbre had told him one day when the other had finally called him into his office and laid before him the evidence of his brother's determination to let nothing stand in his way. He only hoped that, in time, the memory of that meeting would fade and he could finally put it behind him.

These thoughts were broken by Bessie barking and romping away – probably in pursuit of a rabbit or hare. Dale smiled - her nose may have lost none of its sharpness, but it had been a long time since her legs had been up to catching either. He whistled her back.

The sun climbed into the cloudless blue that was expected before the spring rains interrupted their work for a few days – necessary as they were. Then, hopefully, the final spraying before the long summer took over when nature took control and dictated whether or not the Vendange would be what they all hoped for.

At this time of year, the atmosphere was unaffevcted by either mist or heat haze and the mountains of the Massive, twenty miles to the South and crowned by the Pic de Midi stood out like a painting by Constable.

He came to the end of the row to find Bessie waiting for him. Here the heap of cuttings from the final weeks pruning still smouldered. Without a breath of wind, the smoke rose into the sky in a single, thin column, locally believed to denote devine benediction. Dale knew that was just superstition, but the Vineyard had been a blessing to the Solomon family and it was up to him and Billy to make sure it never ceased to be so.

Bessie barked, wagging her tale as she looked up at him.

'Yes, alright. You too'.

The dog barked again.

'But breakfast first. I know!'

Dale turned and together they made their way back to the house. He expected Bessie could already smell it!

THE END

Printed in the United States
By Bookmasters